MW01144431

CAUSEWAY

Harry Stone

Grosvenor House
Publishing Limited

This book is published by
Grosvenor House Publishing Ltd
Link House
140 The Broadway, Tolworth, Surrey, KT6 7HT.
www.grosvenorhousepublishing.co.uk

A CIP record for this book
is available from the British Library

ISBN 978-1-83975-760-0

'Life can be whatever you want it to be once you've found the key'

Kt1984 2001

Causeway:

- an artificial link between otherwise isolated islands
- allowing communication which would otherwise be difficult
- a vital element in the communication structure of an archipelago
- easily becoming impassable and dangerous in violent weather
- a lifesaving link but quite capable of being a threat to life itself

Contents

Prologue

The Far Isles are almost imaginary, but not quite. Rather think of them as an amalgam of real island communities which offer individual, but largely similar experiences of life in isolation. The Far Islands archipelago lies somewhere off the Atlantic coast of Europe and is a distillation of all the Atlantic islands you have ever known. Their spirit is fiercely independent and their peoples are proud of their heritage. They are 'Islanders'.

The islands were occupied from the sea soon after the ice retreated 10,000 years ago. The larger islands, with acres of flat farmland, were settled first, and remain the most populous. Some of the rocky islets have never attracted permanent settlement and a few marginal ones were once settled and then abandoned as their people found surviving there too challenging.

Population numbers have always been dynamic, and the cultural and ethnic mix of the island peoples has fluctuated too. They have suffered triumphs and disasters over the centuries, and there is no doubt that the Far Isles have developed a magic all of their own, largely thanks to the spirit of their people.

This magic is also based partly upon natural forces, which most of humankind neither understands nor accepts, and partly upon the undeniably supernatural powers which, for unknown reasons, permeate the fabric of the place.

The Far Isles are no strangers to violence, and their very isolation has exposed them equally to malevolent marauders and to the threats of the wildest weather. The impact of violence, and the uncertainty of life, forms an important part of the background to almost everything which happens there.

Rich in history and blessed with magnificent landscapes, the Far Isles present the perfect backdrop to the microcosm of human existence which they so perfectly support: safe but challenging; beautiful but dangerous; caring but risky; life-giving but potentially life-taking.

People who visit the Far Isles will quickly make up their own mind about the place. Haters will leave on the next boat. Lovers will stay as long as they can, certainly return, and may well settle there as soon as they can throw off the shackles of their life on the mainland. If you do ever go, and you do enjoy it more than anywhere else you have ever been in your life, be very careful – you may end up writing a book about it.

Chapter 1

You English?

He was exhausted after the return trip, which had taken far longer than he expected, but Simeon Gibbons had something important to do before he finally dropped onto his bed and crashed out. He had thought about it as soon as he went onto the highest section of the observation deck, to watch the shoreline receding into the mist, when his homeward journey began over 15 hours before. It was something he always did, watching the shoreline recede. One of those rituals of travelling he had developed over many journeys. The farewell moments; a time for reflection and sometimes a time for sadness.

There is, inevitably, a degree of regret about leaving good places, and it seems all the more poignant if you watch a place that you very much enjoyed visiting, diminishing behind the broad white wake of a ferry's stern. It is surprising how soon the land you had recently been part of, grows smaller as the distance extends. Even slow ferries have the power to reduce the size of the scene quite quickly as they gather pace across the water, eventually putting the land out of sight.

Simeon decided then and there, as he watched the pier finally disappear into the mist, that whatever time it was when he got back, he would spend time putting the figurine into its rightful place.

A long journey lay ahead before he reached home, but his adventure was officially over as soon as the ropes were slipped off the stone bollards of the ancient dockyard. He was now in the hands of the crew, and his control over his own destiny suddenly diminished.

He watched the carefully maintained, but well-worn loop ends of the heaviest mooring ropes splash into the water, as the two forward crewmen tugged on the much lighter guide lines to pull the bigger ropes on board. As he watched this final act of separation, thoughts of his return home began to form in a mind that had been overwhelmed by the Far Isles for almost three weeks.

He picked up the familiar sound of the powerful electric motors driving the huge pulleys which hauled-in the heavy mooring ropes and watched the familiar sight of the crewmen guiding the ropes onto the deck, skilfully arranging them so they formed a secure figure-of-eight pattern around a pair of adjacent bollards. The pressure of winding them in so tightly, squeezed seawater out of the thick ropes and they gradually took on a lighter hue as they became drier. Just like a traveller wringing out his socks over the sink.

The ferry moved off, almost imperceptibly at first, as the captain carefully disengaged from safe contact with the land, and put to sea. Once clear of the harbour wall the ferry gathered speed, the wake developed, and

Sim's moments of reflection began against the backdrop of departure.

The sailing went to plan but the drive home was one of the worst he could remember, with motorway hold-ups and long queues at the services adding several hours to his journey. He was glad not to be queuing for a charging point; the electric car owners were facing a three-hour wait to fill-up, and even then, they would probably be limited to 200 miles before the next stop. Saving the planet had its challenges for the EV brigade. These were sharp reminders that he had returned to the reality of real-world chaos, after being immersed for so long in the deep calmness of the islands.

Reminding himself that most accidents occur in the final three miles of a journey he sharpened his concentration as he came off the M25 and headed towards the river. Chiswick was quiet at this time of night and his parking space was empty, right outside the steps to his front door. The usually busy suburban area was quiet enough, but his side street was silent. No lights in anyone's windows, no movement anywhere in the cul-de-sac, not even a fox.

Simeon closed the car door quietly onto its first click and let the power-close do the rest. Lights flashed twice as the locks slipped into place, the power-fold mirrors nestled against the door panels and the alarms were set with a quiet beep. He walked carefully up the flight of stone steps and smiled as the familiar white panels of the Rock Door faced him. He was glad he had chosen the one with the small coloured glass panel.

The random security timer had put the hall light on just as he arrived, and the mock stained-glass pattern cast a rainbow of light onto the top step. He smiled and wondered if that was just coincidence, or whether the island's magic had travelled home with him. He turned around to look along the street. An essential security precaution in this part of London before you reached for your key.

A resident had been murdered on her own doorstep soon after Simeon moved in. She failed to notice the mugger who had stalked her to her own front door. The cosh he used to make stealing her bag more straightforward had ended her life. The felon was never caught.

The street remained empty, but a light suddenly went on in a dormer window at the far end of the opposite row of Edwardian terraces. Someone on an early shift perhaps, or maybe a sleeper startled by a bad dream. He was amused by his own speculation and reached for the fob.

Relieved to be turning the key in his front door at last, he suddenly panicked. He couldn't remember the alarm code. He had 20 seconds to recall it before the embarrassment of a loud siren call waking up the whole neighbourhood. With five seconds to go he remembered it and punched the keyboard – 121212.

He laughed at himself, and as the sudden adrenalin rush subsided, he felt the tiredness flow back. He had an even greater need for sleep now, even a fully-clothed sleep on top of his bed would do nicely; the classic post-adventure instant crash out appealed to him. It was a powerful call but he knew he had a final act to complete, effectively drawing a line under his latest expedition.

He rolled the Himalayan carpet back and lifted two small sections of floor board. Reaching down into the dark space, he opened the small strongbox and retrieved the carefully wrapped packet from under the floor. Unwrapping the small bundle very gently, he removed the charm bracelet and held it up so that he could see all the pieces dangling from it. He hadn't handled it for over a year and he enjoyed holding it in the light from the Anglepoise, slowly turning it round as he looked for familiar charms. Most of them brought back memories.

The bracelet was so loaded that it would have been quite impossible for it to be worn comfortably, but that wasn't the point. It wasn't really a bracelet any more, it was more of a memory bank. A unique record of times gone by.

Attaching the figure was a fiddly job but he was happy to spend time doing it properly. He had to get it right so the long-haired man didn't fall off at some later date. After all he had been through, losing the figure would have been unbearable. He looked at it carefully and admired the craftsmanship which had carved out the features of the man's torso and head, and particularly the characteristic hair, which was beautifully done. It took a few minutes to attach it properly to the chain, but that was fine because it gave him time to think, and time to remember.

Sim was a traveller. He had always been one for as long as he could remember. In his head, at first, when he was too young to do anything about his yearning, but as he had grown older he had steadily converted his wistful dreams into practice and by his late twenties he was a professional. He was an expert in what he called 'the remote'.

He soon learned that while travelling to remote places was challenging enough in itself, the challenge didn't end when the journey was complete. Even after a perfect journey, the next challenge presented itself – finding a good place to stay, which was best done in advance, of course, whenever it was possible to do so.

There was never much choice of accommodation in remote places, and the challenge increased in direct proportion to the remoteness of the place you headed for. Finishing the adventure of travelling, by staying in a bad place always contaminated the experience; all that work and planning, all that journeying, all those risks, spoiled by the eventual discomfort and disappointment of poor accommodation. Sometimes getting the accommodation right could be harder than planning the journey itself.

Great accommodation is essential to fully appreciating remoteness, and Simeon was fortunate in that respect. Whenever he visited the Far Isles, he knew that he could apply all his attention to the magic of the place because his creature comforts would be more than adequately catered for, which would cause him no stress at all, in fact, quite the opposite. Thanks to his hosts, his level of comfort would add to the pleasure of the trip rather than detract from it.

Journeys are usually an adventure in themselves, especially long ones which are undertaken rarely; perhaps for a one and only time. Everyone knows that there is always an element of luck involved, so fingers are crossed, lucky charms touched. The best wishes of friends and loved ones are received with embarrassed thanks and phrases like: 'Safe journey'; 'Let us know when you get there' and 'Stay safe'.

However good the journey is, first-time stays are always a bit of a gamble, and one-time stays even more so. Sim's friend and fellow travel-writer, Darcy Blue, likened first stays to Russian roulette.

'You spin the cylinder and pull the trigger, hoping to God the chamber is empty!'

The risk is exacerbated when the place is so remote that most people have never even heard of it, let alone actually been there. Internet evidence might exist but that is most likely to be factual rather than subjective. It would be historical, geological, archaeological, or cultural evidence rather than a personal view. Facts are important but it's feelings that really count.

There may be some reviews on Tripadvisor and a few photographs on a personal website perhaps, but Google Earth doesn't reveal much more than the best local maps, and Street View never makes it to remote places at all. In fact, the very proximity of a Google camera car would simply say: 'This place isn't remote anymore.' Real remoteness and streaming video evidence simply don't compute. Finding great accommodation in a remote place is like finding treasure, and Sim knew it. It turned out not to be the only treasure that the islands gave up to him.

Simeon Gibbons, the professional traveller, did remote all the time, and he made a living out of writing about it. He was a travel junkie, and he was hooked on places that most people would never even think of visiting. He collected remote visits like his grandmother collected little silver trinkets for her charm bracelet. Simeon was entranced by her bracelet as a youngster and had added quite a few to her collection over the years.

The bracelet made Grandma easy to satisfy, present-wise, and he made a tradition out of adding to it from an early age. Giving her a charm every birthday and Christmas made him feel happy, and he always believed it made her happy too.

He still missed her, even though she had been gone for some years, and he still collected charms, just as if she were still there to receive them. He began the tradition, as a child, by collecting very simple things from Christmas crackers and bits and pieces from fairgrounds. She was always thrilled to receive them and she made a fuss of him, which made him feel happy.

When he was a young teenager, he found things on school trips to historic houses, museums and battlefields.

He often bought a suitable item for the bracelet with his pocket money when the school party visited the inevitable gift shop. The other kids bought sweets or maybe a fridge magnet for their mum.

Simeon was able to be much more adventurous in his choice of charms when he began to travel for himself. Predictable tourist trinkets at first: Big Ben, the Eiffel Tower, the Sagrada Familia. Then evidence of more adventurous journeys: Sydney Opera House, the Petronas Towers, the Ring of Brodgar, an Easter Island Moai. Some of them were genuine silver, but most were bronze or brass or some sort of cheap metal. Grandma didn't mind what the trinkets were made of. For her the fact that Simeon remembered her so fondly meant everything.

When Simeon went truly remote, the charms went up another gear: a pyramid from Tenochtitlan, much rarer than the similar one from Machu Picchu he had bought the previous year; a silver penguin from the NATO Base Sierra Pappa, a rather predictable code name for its location at the South Pole, a pewter polar bear from Spitzbergen, given in gratitude when he paid the woman in the remote fishing community handsomely for a dozen bars of locally-made soap.

The little metal alien from Area 61 was a real prize. The owner of the store swore it was a real extraterrestrial artefact found around the neck of a humanoid creature, a grey, who died on the dissection table in the 1950s. The man also said that he had been abducted by aliens in the 1950s, a claim which rather reduced the chances of his artefact story being true. Simeon laughed at the idea but it was the one charm that was never hung on his grandma's wrist – just in case it carried an alien curse.

He wore it round his own neck for two years, dreaming that it might ward off evil by emitting some invisible alien power, until he discovered by accident, that it was slightly radioactive. He consigned it to a metal box in his desk draw and often wondered if the radiation had been enough to cause him harm. Sim was always glad he hadn't exposed Grandma to that risk.

She wanted him to have the bracelet when she required it no more, knowing that he would treasure it. There was no dissent after she passed. The family were more interested in her savings and property being distributed fairly. Sim was welcome to the bracelet. He was content. It was all he wanted from her.

He treasured it, and it lay safely, carefully wrapped in soft non-acidic tissue paper, in the small strong box he kept under the floorboards at his terraced house in Chiswick. His frequent absences increased the likelihood of burglary. The strongbox held sufficient cash to tide him over if he did suffer a break-in, along with some important legal documents and the bracelet. The alien stayed in its box in his desk drawer. Simeon thought that if a thief took it, they would deserve the radiation it would douse them with. He carefully rewrapped the charm bracelet and placed it back in the box, replaced the floorboards and rolled the carpet back to cover the hatch. Job done, Simeon Gibbons fell onto his bed and crashed out, expedition style.

Despite his worldwide experiences of remoteness, Simeon counted the Far Isles as his favourite location and he returned there for at least a few days every year. His journey to the isles was adapted to the time he had available. Flying when he was in a rush, driving all the way and using the long ferry crossing when he had a couple of weeks to spare.

He loved the ferries. Boarding them was always exciting – they swallowed you up into another world. Humming engine vibrations, the unique mixture of smells, the movement of the boat over the water, the announcements over the Tannoy. On the Far Isles ferries the safety announcements were always given in English and Gaelic. Sim had fun trying to invent the most amusing, alternative-comedy versions of the safety warnings.

'Panic immediately and let the crew escape first.'

'Don't bother with the lifebelts, they don't actually stop you drowning, and the last time we tried the lifeboats two of them sank.'

If he thought of a really good line, he would laugh out loud and people probably thought that he was suffering from an anxiety attack, nervous about the sailing. But nothing could be further from the truth; he loved ferry sailing anywhere, but especially to the Far Isles.

Movement on board could be rough and uncomfortable if the weather was bad, but most of Simeon's experiences of the long crossings had been fine, sometimes almost flat calm; quite remarkable given the average weather in those exposed stretches of sea.

However he travelled to the Far Isles, the accommodation was always the same, and staying in the small guesthouse at Solas was one of the island's gifts to Simeon. He had discovered it by accident when he met a young artist in a London gallery, near his Chiswick terrace, during a rather elitist viewing which he had stumbled into.

Simeon was heading to the local coffee shop he often used when he had some free time. It was privately run and it beat all the local chains by a mile. The chains littered every high street and provided a consistent, predictable and decent-enough service, but individual shops like this one could be very special. Simeon's favourite was excellent because the owners, a young Turkish couple, really loved what they did and took a pride in every cup they served.

They had never been on a corporate team-building training day in their lives, nor did they even know what 'brand identity' and 'employee engagement' meant. Their coffee shop was the best simply because their care shone through in the rich honesty of their drinks and in the elaborate ritual of service, they always insisted on providing. It was a pleasure to be a customer there, and with comfortable seating and excellent Wi-Fi, it was a perfect place for Sim to be.

The Gallery, for that is what it said on the board above the large front window, was in the same row of upmarket shops as the Coffee Place, sharing frontage with a letting agency, a picture framer, a wine shop, a kid's boutique and a second-hand bookshop straight out of a trendy film. He paused as he passed the Gallery, intrigued by the activity which was clearly taking place inside. He put the coffee shop on hold and sized up the action behind the large window.

He would not normally gate-crash such a place, and even less such an event. The artwork would be overpriced and the people who were likely to be attending would almost certainly be insufferable. It turned out that he was almost right on both counts.

Something made him swing towards the entrance which was being monitored by two large men in smart suits. When he was challenged at the door by one of the Venezuelan security guards Simeon picked up the accent immediately and responded in Wayuu, guessing that the tough guy spoke it in preference to Spanish. The man smiled in surprise and let him in with a gesture of welcome Simeon had not seen since Merida. He responded appropriately with a smile and a slight bow of a tilted head, the classic greeting of friendship for Wayuu speakers.

The guard raised an appreciative eyebrow and his smile turned into a grin. Nobody in England had ever spoken to the brothers in Wayuu before, not even the embassy staff. They would talk about the encounter with the Englishman for years to come, never knowing who he was or why he knew their language.

Inside the gallery things were as awful as he had expected, but there was free champagne and decent sushi, so he made the most of it. He didn't need to avoid conversation; nobody wanted to speak to him anyway, and he was rudely ignored.

He imagined that the gallery was owned by someone's posh son who had never done a day's work in his life, and that most of the stuff on display was probably done by someone else's titled, talentless relative who couldn't get a proper job. It certainly looked like it. They probably read History of Art at university and scraped a pass. The highly polished but appalling show was there simply to give the West London social elite something to do on a wet Chiswick afternoon.

He gave the exhibits a cursory glance, amused by the poor quality and amazed by the prices but then something caught his eye. Seven pictures of standing stones and one wonderful perspective view along a causeway with an intriguing escape tower rising from one of the side rails. The causeway seemed to lead to some unknown place just beyond an almost flat horizon; somewhere the narrow roadway invited you to discover and explore.

The paintings of the stone circles and monoliths were the only artwork of merit in the whole place and the causeway picture was showing something Simeon had never seen before. It seemed to be a bridge to a mysterious place which could perhaps have been either the past or the future. He decided that the causeway was like a time machine. A magical bridge with more than three dimensions. The collection of paintings pushed Simeon's childish cynicism aside.

He walked up for a closer look. Nobody else was paying them any attention so there was room to move around and view the work properly. He was able to look carefully and he drank in every detail. He looked at them from a distance and from close up. He moved from one to another, and then back to the first as he made comparisons between them. They seemed to move their perspective as he moved his eyeline. They were more than just excellent paintings, there was something magical about them. He sought out the artist, hoping they were there. She was easy enough to spot.

Like him, she was being left alone by the glitterati, who preferred their own company rather than spending time talking to a 26-year-old punky-looking woman with paint under her broken nails and a tattoo on the side of her neck. Simeon liked her on sight and introduced himself.

She knew he was OK right from the start, and she was relieved to meet a normal person at the show. She allowed her natural smile to greet him. Less teeth than the professional smile but softer lips; altogether a more welcoming face. He asked her about her striking acrylics of the standing stones and she said they were local to her home and that she knew every inch of them.

'Magical place,' she said.

Simeon smiled, but he didn't say that he knew that already. The magic was evident in her pictures and he knew that it was the capturing of that magic which made the works so special.

'They were the first things I ever painted; been doing them since I was a child.'

He told her how much he liked them. He marvelled at the detail and the clever use of perspective, the colours of the sky and the stones themselves, and said he felt almost as though he could have walked into the picture and touched them. Then he asked about the causeway.

'Our islands are linked by causeways,' she said. 'We depend upon them for getting around, for linking up. That one is the oldest of all and if the tide comes in quickly you have to use the tower to escape if you get caught out!'

She seemed to listen carefully to his expression of his feelings for her work, and he thought that she felt the warmth that praise and recognition always bring. She began to lean towards him. He described how he could imagine feeling the weathered faces of the stones, gently exploring with his fingertips the exposed mineral crystals protruding from the lichen-bearing surfaces of the tall monoliths. He said that he wanted to walk across that ancient causeway.

He said that he kept thinking that they were doctored digital images; Photoshopped art. She enjoyed convincing him of their originality, uncertain whether comparison with digitised photography was a compliment or an insult. He finally asked the question which was to lead, him, eventually, to find what would become a favourite place: 'Where are they exactly?'

'They are exactly in my back garden on the Far Isles,' she laughed. 'Well not really my back garden but just over the fence. I can see them from my bedroom.' He had no idea where she meant, but he intended to find out and to go there.

They left the gallery together. He took her three doors away to the Turkish coffee shop and bought her a decaf latté; he settled for an Americano. They talked for two hours, and he offered to buy as many of her pieces as he could afford after the show was over. The Chiswick elite bought none; Sim bought all seven for £6,000. It was all the savings he had until his next commission fee from Channel 4, but that would more than put his finances back on an even keel.

During their conversation she gave him full instructions on how to find the stones and, most importantly, where to stay when he got there, for it was Mairead, the artist, who put Simeon, her new client, in touch with the McKinnon's. He called the warm, welcoming, interesting, decent people who ran his accommodation the Mac's. He called them that to their faces and they always smiled at the gentle leg-pull. 'Everyone's a Mac, but we're 'the Macs' Simeon,' they used to say with mock pride.

Not too much gentle leg-pulling in that part of the Hebrides, more of an English thing maybe, perhaps that's why they seemed to enjoy it. Their welcome was genuine, and if he had to write them a reference, he would have said: 'Their attention is perfect, their company enriching, their food wonderful and their malts to die for.'

They warmed to Simeon because they knew that he connected with their land and their history. He was learning to understand it, and they liked that. They enjoyed helping him with his learning, just as he had helped their granddaughter, Mairead, that day in the London gallery. She had told them about him and promised that they would like him, because she did. She was right; she usually was.

They talked a lot. He telling them of his travels, they sharing the island's secrets with him. He always had a carefully planned itinerary but he was sensible in his flexibility and paid attention to the latest wildlife sightings, the weather and current gossip about interesting locations and events.

On that day his first idea was to walk out onto the machair in Traigh Bay and explore the promontory. It was a plan which was both weather and tide critical, but on that particular morning the portents were perfect. He had tried and failed before, but today the prospects looked good. Mrs Mac told him to make the best of it claiming, 'It's easier to get a good crossing to St Kilda than it is to walk the far dunes in good weather.'

The Macs had told him of the remains of a Bronze Age village to be found in the high dunes right at the far end of the peninsular, which would be all the more intriguing because hardly anyone knew they were there. They had been exposed in the Great Storm, two years before. The storm, which killed some local people and destroyed a lot of property, also revealed the remains of the ancient settlement, probably itself destroyed by a tempest, centuries before. It would probably be destroyed again by the next one, so the temporary exposure made a trip along Traigh even more urgent that year. In 12 months' time, it could all be gone.

People who spend their lives in isolated places keep a lot of secrets; it's their way of having some control over things; their way of helping themselves to feel better than the richer and pushier incomers who invade their space from time to time with their sense of humour, their motor launches and expensive 4x4's, and sometimes even their helicopters.

A popstar had flown in to Solas some years before. He came in a helicopter off the yacht he had borrowed from a Middle Eastern oil billionaire. Everyone was thrilled. They were happy to meet him, have pictures taken, and to ask him for an autograph. The Mac's five-year-old grandson Cal, had asked Paul if he wanted his autograph as he'd just learned to write his name. Paul said he would be delighted and Cal carefully executed his signature on a piece of faded Basildon Bond from the stationery rack in the Co-op shop. Paul was really appreciative of the boy's gift and the Macs hoped he hung on to the precious piece of work. They still talk about the day Paul flew in, but they never told him about the Bronze Age village. They rarely shared that secret with incomers; Simeon was lucky.

It was a short drive from Solas to the end of the causeway where the Range Rover could easily find a place to park, out of the way, by a small rock outcrop which just pushed through the sandy soil. It was the last trace of solid geology before the shifting bottomless mass of Traigh sands. A family of mink were exploring the rocks. They disappeared under a ledge when the car door slammed shut. Simeon saw them flash out of sight and stood quietly for a few minutes to see if they would appear again, but they were watching him carefully from their dark hiding place, and would wait until he left before resuming their exploration game.

Mink were a menace on the islands and ruthlessly hunted by council pest control officers who drove around in vans with 'Report mink sightings to us' stencilled on the sides. Wild animals are always wary of humans, but the Far Isle mink were especially so, probably sensing that the islanders were ganging up against them.

Far beyond the rocky parking place stretched the shore. Nine miles of wide, flat, clean, golden sand. Anywhere else it would have been packed with tourists but, in the Far Isles, such beaches are almost always deserted. The walk along the sand was almost timeless. After the first few paces Simeon Gibbons entered another world. He hardly seemed to be getting anywhere for ages. The thin line of small dunes edging the beach was just the same along its entire length. The low, lapping waves slopped against the sand with lazy regularity, hardly moving more than a couple of feet towards him before they paused and slipped back towards the waterline.

There were no reference points, nothing to tell him if he was making progress or running on the spot. That dynamic worked its own magic: time was standing still even though it was still passing at exactly 60 seconds to the minute; 60 minutes to the hour, same as it always did.

But far from being irritating, the timelessness of it, the apparent lack of progress, the impossibility of measuring how far you'd actually moved, was liberating. Here Simeon just became part of a beautiful landscape which might have looked exactly the same 8,000 years ago when the ice finally gave up its grip and the land began to readjust to the isostatic freedom allowed when only the air pressed down upon it.

He was no more or less important than the grains of sand, the light breeze, the small waves, the distant gulls or the seals lounging at the water's edge. He felt part of the place and walked as carefully and quietly as he could. Fitting into the place, avoiding small succulent, salt-tolerant plants trying to bind the shifting sand into an embryo dune, he avoided even stepping on any of the millions of empty razor shells cast up by the last gale.

After however long it was, and he really had no sense of time at all, the fringing dunes started to get bigger, higher, and altogether more physically present. After another mile the dunes were like cliffs and there needed to be a gap somewhere to access the interior of the promontory otherwise an enforced scramble up the front of a 100-foot sand dune would have to be contemplated. He didn't want to do that; dangerous for him, damaging for the dunes.

Timelessness slowly suspended itself, lifted by the appearance of a dark mark in the far distant dune face; it became a target and his brain switched to planning mode, shaking him out of his dreamy state. Slowly the mark became a gap in the dunes and from a closer view it became a valley through the sand hills which, he hoped, would eventually lead him to the village. He aimed for it. He had covered eight miles but he didn't know it.

He turned off the beach and ventured through the steep sided valley of sand. A remarkable feature in its own right, this unexpected gorge was loosely bound with pockets of marram grass scattered around its steep slopes and there were signs of recent sand slides with cones of newly fallen sand reaching out onto the valley floor. Simeon kept to the central path of shell debris carpeted with lichen and small wild flowers as it wound its way towards the other side of the dune belt. The interior of the promontory was a huge complex mass of machair and old dunes, small on the map but tiringly big in real life. It was like a vast new world; a scene from *The Land that Time Forgot*.

Simeon had a moment of panic. What if after all this effort the village couldn't be found, even though the secret had been shared with him by his trusting hosts. He dreaded being the pathetic incomer who talked the talk but couldn't walk the walk. Would the locals be offended when they knew he couldn't honour their trust and enjoy their ancestors' ancient settlement simply because he couldn't find it? Would they laugh at him when he left and make him a story to be told on the dark winter nights?

'Nice enough lad Simeon, but he couldn't find the village.'

Simeon was snapped out of his anxiety when the stranger appeared. Simeon didn't see the man until he was quite close; he no idea where he came from, certainly not from the direction of the beach. The beach was deserted, there were no other vehicles at the rocks and the peninsula was unpopulated, so there were no locals. Strangely it wasn't as much of a surprise to Simeon as it should have been. There was no 'you made me jump' moment. It was as though the stranger was supposed to be there, as though Simeon should have expected him to turn up.

He was younger and a bit taller than Simeon – strongly built and fit. He wore simple walking clothes, good quality cotton by the look of it, quiet colours, certainly not synthetic, breathable fabric. He wore simple leather sandals tied around the ankles with a leather thong, and he wore a small bronze pendant figurine around his neck. There were no brand marks on anything he wore. His skin was brown in a weather-beaten sort of way, and most remarkably he had a mass of long, tangled, dyed-blond dreadlocks. He spoke with a soft Hebridean accent but his voice was strong and confident, and his remarkable features reminded Simeon of the ancient people he had spent half his life studying.

For some reason of facial architecture, he reminded Simeon of something between classical Aztec and those Neanderthal reconstructions he had seen in the Max Planck Institute. Leipzig didn't count as a remote place but the world of the Neanderthals intrigued him enough to draw him there. They were truly our most important ancestors and we were only just beginning to realise it. They were no more extinct than the dinosaurs; you just had to look at a garden bird to see the T-Rex in it. You just had to look at strong men and women to see Neanderthal DNA.

He exhibited Aztec toughness and Neanderthal looks. Simeon immediately expected the stranger to appreciate good art and carefully crafted artefacts. He expected the man to appreciate standing stones like the ones the girl in the London gallery had painted.

'You English?' it seemed like a statement of fact rather than a question.

'Yes, are you Scottish?' A rather feeble attempt at disarming humour.

He smiled easily; they were going to get on together, it seemed.

'I'm not Scottish, I'm an Islander.'

Simeon had heard that before from the modern people of Solas, and from the peoples of the many Pacific islands he had travelled to over the years. Orcadians didn't want to be Scottish and Shetlanders even less so.

The islander asked Simeon a second question: 'Are you just walking about or are you looking for Udal?'

'I think I'm looking for Udal if that's what you call the village.'

He smiled again. 'Aye we called it Udal 6,000 years ago and we still call it Udal today.'

'Come on and I'll show you the way, it's easily missed.'

He ambled comfortably along at a pace chosen to keep Simeon close. When two men meet in such isolation anything could happen. Most likely would be a curt nod and a brief 'Hello', followed by them ignoring each other. Less likely in these parts would be 'Good morning', followed by polite conversation about the weather and the cricket. Most unlikely would be the easy, flowing conversation that developed over the next few minutes as though the men had known each other for a lifetime and had had many such conversations before.

They discussed facts about the land, the village, its people, the secrecy of its location, the direct line of descent from those Bronze Age folk to most of the people of Solas today. He asked Simeon a lot of questions about where he was staying, where he came from, what he did, what his friends were like, where he had been before, where he would be going to next. Everything was about Simeon; nothing about the stranger.

He was interested in the chance meeting in the Gallery which led Simeon eventually to Solas, and now to Udal. He asked the name of the young artist and smiled when Simeon revealed it.

'Mairead' he said, and then repeated it.

'A name from over the sea. I've known a few women with such a name.'

Simeon wanted to ask him about them but he resisted the temptation, not wishing to break any thoughts the stranger was enjoying.

After a long walk there was a short climb up to the top complex of a very big dune system on the Atlantic side of the promontory, and there it was – Udal. It was all low-walled enclosures, turf and stone, outlining buildings perhaps. They stood together on top of a series of high dunes and, slowly, Simeon surveyed the whole area with an experienced eye. It almost looked like a scene from a film set, carefully arranged to conform to the archaeology consultant's guidance.

He was experienced enough to pick out individual buildings and to differentiate between what were probably houses and what were probably storage rooms. He could identify the remains of small paddocks and guessed that they contained a few goats or even sheep to provide milk. There were small mounds of shell debris on the furthest dune tops and Simeon thought they were probably dumping grounds of some kind, or maybe even burial sites. He wanted to explore the place properly and work out how the remains fitted together; but knowing that time was limited, Simeon was lost in simply staring at it all, trying to memorise what he was seeing.

He cursed himself for forgetting his camera. He didn't even have his phone to record any images. It would all have to be down to memory.

The man left Simeon to his thoughts for a while, and then spoke, breaking the spell. He pointed to a large, flat stone on top of the highest dune and invited Simeon to sit on it. He guessed that Simeon needed a breather and was looking after his guest with a sensitivity which belied his tough appearance. Simeon looked doubtful about the suggestion and the stranger reinforced his invitation with a warm and disarming comment:

'Folk have sat on that for over 6,000 years he laughed, it'll cope with you for a few minutes.'

Simeon sat on the slab and felt the shape contain him. It wasn't as flat as it appeared; it had been shaped by many users over the centuries, slowly eroded by humans sitting on it, removing microscopic grains of hard rock each time they shifted. He noticed some words carved into the front of the stone; he thought they said 'Nareath Anathnid', but they were almost worn away.

'It's called the Main Seat.'

Simeon assumed that was what the words meant.

'People sat on it whenever they wanted to tell a story. We tell a lot of stories on the islands and a lot of stories have been told here from that place you now occupy.'

'If you tell me a story, I'll show you round the village. Does that sound like a deal to you?' Simeon was flustered and chose the safe escape route of modestly sticking to the obvious.

'I could tell you about all the places I have been, but I think this place deserves more respect than that, and it wouldn't really be a story.'

He then remembered Mairead and imagined her visiting this place.

How about I tell you the story of how I found this place, after I met the woman called Mairead at an art show?

'Try it.'

The stranger sat down on the sand and listened carefully to Sim's account of his meeting with Mairead and her pictures of the stones. How he took her for coffee and bought all her pictures. How she put him in touch with the Mac's and how his love for the Far Isles surpassed all his other experiences of travelling. The man seemed genuinely interested in Simeon's yarns.

Eventually he took the dialogue over and, with a wistful smile, said: 'I know the people you call the Mac's, and I know of the girl too,' and he added: 'think of a longer story about the girl Mairead for next year, and I'll look forward to it.'

Simeon had passed the test and the stranger knew it. It was time to move and look around Udal. The guided tour was detailed and wonderful. He made up names for people who lived in each house and told Simeon details of their lives in such a way that he felt that he briefly became part of their world. It was as if the stranger knew all those families personally.

This was a real story, told with imagination and impressive attention to detail. Simeon realised that this was probably the standard of Main Seat storytelling; a skill developed by members of this local clan thousands of years before. The simple, priceless, skills of speaking and listening.

Perhaps he was an official guide; someone employed by the tourist board for occasions such as this. Perhaps the Mac's had organised it. In order to test his theory, Simeon suggested that he should do guided tours. The stranger said that he would never do that.

'We don't want too many visitors', he said.

'If they find it by accident, fair enough but not many will do that, and if they get sent here by the Solas people, then I'll probably help out.' Simeon realised that, whoever this man was, he wasn't a tour guide.

After more than half the day had passed, it was over. The stranger looked at the sun in the sky, pondered, and then simply said: 'I must go now.'

After a firm, dry handshake and a swift 'Farewell', he made-off down the sand slope towards the Atlantic beach. Simeon didn't want to watch him go, but after a few seconds he stole a glance in the direction the man had walked – the stranger had just disappeared.

It took three hours to get back to the car. A mink was playing around the rear offside wheel but it scooted off into the rocks again as Simeon approached. He checked the tyres to see if they had been gnawed but they seemed to be OK. Back at the guesthouse the Macs waved naturally when they saw his car approaching.

Simeon let them drive it around the island when he stayed with them and they loved it. It had leather interior, Bowers and Wilkins sound system, ice-cold air-con, multi-adjustable seats, all the bells and whistles. Ninety-five thousand pounds worth of motorcar. A veritable supercar, they said.

Their Defender was 26 years old, worth £600, and hard to drive, but it was more truly a part of their lives than Simeon's expensive car was of his. His was a treat, a status symbol, theirs was a workhorse, and sometimes it was the difference between life and death. They didn't let Simeon drive it.

They sat together outside as the sun began to set over the Atlantic. A perfect Hebridean day, evolving into a perfect Hebridean evening. The soft breeze kept the midges away. The coffee was good and the whisky was perfect.

'So, what did you think of the village then?' asked Mrs Mac.

'Brilliant, astounding … what can I say?'

'We saw you walking all the way up the beach and it was obvious that you were the only one on the trail today, we thought you might miss it, it's easily done.'

'I probably would have missed it but for the guy I met.'

The atmosphere changed slightly and the Macs glanced at each other. Mr Mac took a deep breath and got up to fetch something to eat. Mrs Mac insisted again that Simeon was alone on the promontory but then asked a simple question.

'Did you talk to him?'

'Yes, for ages, he even asked me to tell a story from the Main Seat.'

'Did you?'

'Not really. I sat on the stone but I couldn't think of a proper story worthy of him, so I told him about meeting Mairead at the gallery and how I found this place.'

'Was he interested?'

'Yes, he was actually, and he asked me to tell him more about her next year.'

She shook slightly as she breathed in.

'You met him then. I've met him too. A few of us have but not everyone. We don't know why or how he chooses. You must have done some good work somewhere, he appreciates that.'

'You've been gifted.' she added.

After a pause she said: 'You must come back next year with a story. He'll be there, waiting for it. Make it a good story for his sake. He's the only one left, and I think it must get very lonely for him. The only one left.'

'You mean from Udal?' asked Simeon

Mrs Mac confirmed what Simeon was already starting to believe: 'Yes, from Udal.'

Simeon didn't question her assertion for one second; it made complete sense to him. They sat quietly with coffee and whisky and nobody touched the food for quite some time. It went dark around them and they eventually went their separate ways, leaving only crumbs on the plates.

A week later Simeon finally made it to the main ferry port to begin his journey south. With over an hour to kill before the ferry loaded, he wandered into the local museum. He didn't really like museums much, he usually already knew more than they could tell him. He would far rather be out in the field doing his own research. But there might be something here which reminded him of his stay. He looked at the gift shop but there was nothing he wanted or needed.

He wandered into the exhibition zone and then turned a corner into a small room: The Udal Collection. He was excited to see the village name and wondered what the room would contain. Only bits and pieces really, drawings, maps, photographs but nothing to accurately locate the village. Described as a Victorian archaeological mystery, the remains of the village of Udal were thought to have been completely destroyed leaving no trace in a violent and prolonged Atlantic storm which hit the islands a hundred and 50 years before.

The Museum didn't acknowledge the reappearance of the ancient village; Solas people are good at keeping secrets. Udal hadn't been washed away; that storm had simply buried it under the sand for 150 years and the recent storm had exposed it again.

In the corner of the small room was the one surviving major artefact from the Victorian exposure; the heavily carved stone lid of a man-sized sarcophagus. The warrior depicted in the carving, which covered the length of the stone slab, was life sized and arranged in the classic Celtic burial pose with his helmet, shield, sword, spear, dagger, smock, leggings and laced-up sandals. You couldn't see his face because of the nose guard but you could not fail to see the long curls of his dreadlocks hanging untidily below the rim of his helmet.

Simeon smiled as the pieces of the ancient jigsaw finally moved into place; not the sort of sense that most people recognise in their busy modern lives, but the kind of mystical sense that made life really worth living for Simeon, the traveller who believed in magic.

Leaning on the guard rail on the top deck of the big ferry as it began its two-hour crossing, he watched the coastline of the Far Isles receding into the mist. Simeon knew he had 12 months to work on a story worthy of his new friend's ear. A story about the girl in the gallery.

He would have to find out more about Mairead. He wanted to meet her again anyway and this gave him the perfect reason to do so. He would ask her about Udal and whether she knew of the stranger. Simeon smiled at the thought of all the stories the stranger, Warlord of the Isles, Protector of Udal, must have heard over the past 6,000 years.

It was going to be a challenge. The man with the dreadlocks, part Aztec and part Neanderthal, didn't invent any of those names, or the details of his people's lives, and Simeon knew that his story had to be both long and true, for the stranger would be able to tell the truth of it.

All the way home he kept checking his pocket for the small bronze figure Mrs Mac had pressed into his hand as she shook it when she said goodbye to him on the pier. It was a perfect replica of the Dreadlocks Man. She had found it in the sand near Udal, a few days after the storm. It was a small bronze figure of the Bronze Age warrior, just small enough to hang from a charm bracelet.

Chapter 2

The Gallery by the Sea

William Shutt seemed normal enough on the face of it, but his calm and rather ordinary exterior hid a desperate need. He needed his own beach so that he could scream at the sky.

He chose his beach carefully and he visited it often to perform his essential ritual. He had been sky-screaming for quite some time and had chosen an isolated place so that his secret need would never be discovered. He wasn't sure if he was ashamed of it, or just wanted to avoid the embarrassment of having to explain his strange behaviour to others, who wouldn't understand, and, as a result, probably would doubt his sanity. Life was challenging enough without having to struggle with the stigma of being judged as a mad man. But he needed to do it, and he wisely decided to keep it to himself.

The fact was that William teetered on the verge of some sort of mental illness; his bitterness was eating him up and his anger was damaging his health, increasing his blood pressure, raising his levels of anxiety, destroying almost all his wellbeing strategies. He was a landmine, primed and lethal, just waiting for someone to tread on him. William was aware of all this.

He was disarmingly honest about his self-realisation. He knew his strengths, although there weren't many of them, and he knew his vulnerabilities, but worst of all, he knew his failings, and they haunted him.

He woke up thinking of them and they emerged from the shadows whenever he had nothing to do. Even a few seconds of inactivity were enough to let them in, and when he had hours to spare, they ran riot. His coping strategy was simply to plan some sort of activity to take up the time. He aimed at something for the morning and something for the afternoon. It was hard work and he often failed, and the resulting gap-time was difficult, to say the least.

It was then that he needed to scream at the sky.

William was known to pupils, parents and colleagues as 'Shutty'. He taught secondary science for almost 20 years but he finally gave up when the target-driven culture, which had been sapping his job satisfaction for 10 years, eventually snuffed out the final vestiges of enjoyment he found in explaining the wonders of physics and astronomy to generations of unbelievers. It was a process which had brought him immense satisfaction for years, but things had changed, and certainly not for the better.

The process of teaching and learning steadily became irrelevant to the bosses; results were all that mattered. As the outcomes overtook the experience in the tiny minds of the shakers and movers, the real educationalists gradually lost heart. Worn out by the target-chasing, they slowly lost their voice and eventually lost their vocation. The smart-arsed gurus weren't bothered in the least, every time a good teacher gave up they could be replaced with a National College clone who would always be on message.

Shutty wasn't just a good teacher, he was a great teacher. Teaching was his life.

He used to love it when understanding dawned and a youngster's eyes widened suddenly and they said: 'Oh I get it!' He proudly remembered the priceless moment when a surly, deliberately inarticulate unbeliever, with a 14-year-old's distain for school, saw lunar craters close up, for the first time through Shutty's reflector telescope. As he adjusted the eyepiece and the silver surface came into sharp focus, the boy gasped in disbelief. He was speechless for a few seconds, uncertain how to react as he desperately searched his limited lexicon for the right words to express his delight, and he finally just said: 'Fucking Hell!' in a very loud voice. There was a moment of shocked silence then everyone, including Shutty, just laughed.

He was proud of the numbers who had gone on to A-level and Highers, and beyond that to university. More than 20 pupils to his knowledge had gone on to post-doctoral research posts, three were already professors, one in Canada and two in England, and one had become a knighted senior civil servant in the Ministry of Defence, after a glittering young career in radar research at Malvern.

He was equally proud of the hundreds of pupils who left, not for a life of science, but for other lives, with at least a broader appreciation of physics and astronomy. Kids who chose literature or geography, modern languages or nursing, were persuaded not to be science-phobic. His teaching showed the relevance of science and humanised it. Non-believers became believers. They understood science well enough to know that investing in expensive projects like Hubble, CERN and the Large Hadron Collider was worthwhile, even if you didn't understand the detail.

His students would never object to science or stand in the way of sensible investment. He thought of them as the silent majority, who were science fans without being scientists, and they were as important to him as the professors. All that achievement in 20 years, marginalised by the educational establishment who couldn't teach, couldn't organise, couldn't appreciate and most importantly, couldn't care less.

Shutty loathed the professional politicians and jobsworth local officials who simply focused on their own careers without any real understanding of teaching and learning, and had no real love for young human beings. To them, schools were part of the problem, not part of the solution. When William screamed at the sky he usually shouted, 'They couldn't organise a fucking piss-up in a fucking brewery.' Then he cried.

He was very angry, very frustrated, and he felt very denied.

Effectively excluded from his vocation by the political dickheads, the chancers who wrote stupid books about how to teach the perfect lesson, and 'super-heads' who were 'parachuted-in' and 'turned schools around'. He despised local civil servants who skilfully increased their salaries and pension entitlements while steadily cutting school budgets to pay for it all, oblivious to the human impact of their selfishness. He hated all of it, all of them; he just wanted to teach kids science.

Marriage had been just one casualty of his condition. His family gave up on him when the move to the islands didn't make any difference to the educational nonsense. They retreated to Manchester and he was losing touch with them. That really hurt him, much more than he could have imagined. His family used to be everything; now it seemed that they were almost nothing. He imagined that the already reduced contact would shrink further: birthdays forgotten, Christmas presents for the kids reduced to cheques in the post, a new partner for his wife. It was only a matter of time before she became his ex-wife. He screamed at the sky because he had nobody else to take it out on.

He was far too young to draw his pension and he needed to work to maintain his modest lifestyle. He considered the MOD base at Vanich but it was on another island, across three causeways, and there may have been no opportunities there anyway; the place was shedding technical staff, not recruiting them. The fast jets still boomed around the hills on training exercises but they never landed now and even the big Cold War radar stations were only on standby in case the all-seeing satellite surveillance systems went down.

Shutty had a theory that the next big war would be fought by men with smart-phones programmed with the latest Armageddon apps. He put the idea to a hill farming shepherd who laughed and said we should buy them all an Xbox and let them fight it out in private so the rest of us could just get on with surviving.

'They don't have to launch missiles to make life difficult for us, it's hard enough as it is.' Shutty loved the wise words of ordinary people. They were worth a million soundbites. But even wise shepherds couldn't halt Shutty's decline.

He knew that he was drifting dangerously, he simply didn't know what to do about it. It was like flying blind in a rising storm. He didn't realise how close he was to hitting the ground but he suspected that the inevitable impact wasn't far away.

He drove into the gallery car park more to use the facilities in the main building than anything else but he needed a coffee fix too. He imagined sitting quietly in the café section spending some quiet thinking time alone. The setting would be pleasing enough and most importantly, it wouldn't be busy going by the empty parking area, even though it was mid-summer. He had been to the gallery a couple of times over the years but it was usually very busy and he found fussy crowds in confined spaces a bit difficult. It was a pleasing place though and the series of rooms were well developed. It would be especially pleasing it if was as empty as the car park seemed to indicate.

The Gallery sat in splendid isolation close to the shore, accessible only by a long, hard gravel, gated driveway. Viewed from the road it seemed to be a collection of farm buildings by a large farmhouse. They were all painted white, and it looked impressive on a sunny day. It was worth a picture from the road, if you had a telephoto lens.

Inside the old farm buildings, it was different. It consisted of clean, minimalistic, beautifully designed interiors, and the combination of the traditional and the ultra-modern worked well together. Clean smooth-plastered walls contrasted with bare stone sections and the thin, grey, aluminium window frames mimicked the shapes and patterns of the long-rotted wooden sashes of the original buildings. The flagstone floors were beautifully laid with a deceptively smooth surface to avoid trip hazards, and a clever finish highlighted the structures in the neatly sliced rock; structures which had formed in desert lakes half a billion years ago.

Short sections of polished pine complimented the flagstone perfectly. New, compared with the ancient Caithness flags, the timber was nevertheless old by human standards. Five-hundred-year-old Monterey Pine brought over from Canada by the returning emigrant ships two hundred years before. The outward journey carried terrified, destitute family groups into the unknown. The return trip covered its costs by importing timber, just about the only commodity the new world had to offer at the time.

The elegant modern furniture and very cool lighting gave an overall feeling of fashionable modernity, and the style of the very modern sat happily with the rather more ancient aspects of the old farmstead.

Shutty liked the Gallery very much and relished the opportunity it gave him to enjoy good design and reflect upon a million thoughts, provoked by the setting. It was so much better than dwelling on those thoughts which haunted him, alone at home. The Gallery by the Sea provoked better thinking: thoughts about design and creativity; thoughts about the island's culture and history; thoughts about the possibility of a better sort of life altogether.

The small coffee shop served very good pastries which came from somewhere on the island; somewhere near the old MOD place he thought. Three girls he used to teach had opened a business there and they were making a name for themselves as bakers. He would think of them if the Gallery had some of their stuff. He smiled at the thought of remembering better times by eating a croissant and silently hoped those kids wouldn't make the same mistakes he had.

If the café was quiet, it would be the ideal place for him to sit and think, have a coffee and a bite to eat, stare at the artwork, look at the sea through the long windows, and begin to sort his head out for the day, and maybe even for the days, ahead. Even great coffee wouldn't solve the rest of his life but he was a scientist and he believed in small steps.

He smiled at the thought: 'One small step for man.'

He parked carefully and pointed the car forwards to make for an easy escape if the car park filled up while he was inside. There was only one other vehicle, a well-used Defender with off-road tyres and a snorkel, which he assumed was the owner's daily drive.

The place was empty apart from the woman who ran it. He'd only met her once and didn't relish a long conversation with her; he was a bit scared of socialising at the best of times but powerful women like her, presented a real challenge now. He thought that they could see right through to his failure with a glance, and immediately write him off with contemptuous ease. He preferred his own company, it was safer. No other customers would be a good thing, but being alone with her probably not so good. Swings and roundabouts, the story of everyone's life.

She wasn't a local, she wasn't even British, Scandinavian maybe. She was tall and good-looking with eyes that fixed you when she spoke. Gave you the impression that she was completely in control; she could switch people on and off. Reyja, she was called. She had founded the gallery with her husband, 10 years before, but he left her for some reason and disappeared from the islands. Nobody seemed to know the full story, perhaps she didn't know it herself.

It was a mystery rather than a scandal and people soon took it for granted that he had simply gone. People often moved off the islands, it had happened for centuries. Reyja had remained alone since the disappearance; there had never been another relationship although there had been plenty of attempts. When efforts were made, they were simply brushed away. She would have been quite a catch: one night stand or long-term relationship; either way, well worth the effort. But all efforts failed and soon the local men referred to her as 'the fridge'.

Shutty walked in through the open double doors and wandered past the desk where Reyja usually sat and suddenly stopped when he saw the computer. The set up was well-ordered, everything was neat and tidy but it was the Mac screen that arrested him. The screen saver showed the beach where he screamed at the sky. It took him completely by surprise.

Was it just a disconcerting coincidence or was it telling him something; inviting him to scream at the ceiling maybe, the thought made him laugh nervously? She heard him and came out of the back room, all tall and confident.

He was six foot one, she was six foot one and a half. He drew himself up and she relaxed down to match his eye level exactly. Steely blue eyes, clear as anything, no real spark though as they locked on to him. He was still smiling about the screen saver so his face was benign, relaxed and the creases round his eyes were happy lines. They made his eyes smile.

She was confused by his accidental pleasantness. Men usually froze when she stared at them, sensing her contemptuous disinterest. They either looked away or returned the look of hostility. But this was different. Shutty's pleasant smile disarmed her. It was as if they were old friends sharing knowledge and understanding in the shorthand code that real friends always use when they are in company but just have eyes for each other.

Momentarily disarmed she softened visibly and smiled back at him. She could have said 'Good morning' in a strong and controlling sort of way but she didn't. She just said, 'Hello' and she said it softly as though she had been expecting him to come for ages. She placed one hand on the desk to steady herself, without realising why she suddenly needed the reassurance of something solid.

Shutty didn't really notice the change in her that he had managed to achieve in a split second when other men's efforts to soften her had failed so miserably for years. He just felt relieved that she was being nice to him. He just said, 'Hello' back to her and kept smiling.

Reyja stood, staring at him, saying nothing for three or four seconds, her mouth slightly open. He found himself in control of a social situation for the first time since he'd walked out of the classroom. Old skills kicked in. He needed to give her the confidence that he could be trusted, that they could hold a conversation, that he was ready to listen to what she might have to say, that she was not on trial, and, most importantly, that he was not judging her. He was never going to judge her. He would be the only man in her life who would never judge her.

He remembered why he came into the Gallery in the first place, and more than anything he needed the toilet and a coffee, but he would put those needs on the back burner for a few seconds and help her out. He suddenly felt useful. From useless to useful in five seconds, not bad going for him.

He noticed her hand gripping the edge of the desk and realised that she was really struggling for some reason. She reminded him of countless youngsters he had helped when they were lost in the challenging world of high school. He was good at handling situations like this; moments of serious doubt; he knew what to do. He knew how to include people and rebuild their self-belief; great teachers always did.

He maintained the smile and the eye contact and decided to continue the conversation in a way that would let her back in by giving her power over a decision; he simply said: 'Gosh I'm so glad you're open, any chance of a coffee before I buy all your pictures?'

She laughed and touched his arm with her free hand. She had absolutely no idea why she did that. She wasn't a toucher and since the disappearance she never did hugs either. She took the chance to engage. The unexpected, gentle humour of his answer prompted an emotional response; she felt relieved by his smile, his unwavering gaze and his simple, self-deprecating approach. He was even setting himself up by saying 'gosh', almost inviting her to respond.

'Nobody says gosh on these islands, you must be English!'

'Goodness gracious, what a perceptive young lady you are,' he said in a music hall posh English accent. It was clumsy but it worked.

They both laughed.

'Thanks for the young,' she said, 'for that you get the coffee for free.'

'Why thank you kind lady.'

'On condition that you let me join you.'

He was within an inch of snapping back with a Groucho Marx impersonation, tapping off the ash from an imaginary cigar and saying, 'Hey lady you can join me anytime.'

But he didn't, and for years to come he thought that his decision, not to do the Groucho, was the most important decision of his life. It would have set completely the wrong tone. Pointed their conversation away from natural towards scripted. Away from mindful towards mindless.

Away from exciting towards predictable. 'Why thank you kind lady,' was probably going too far, but the full Groucho would have definitely been a deal breaker.

Avoiding Groucho kept open the possibility of something excitingly worthwhile developing.

He sat on a bar stool while she made them both an Americano with cold milk on the side, and they sat together at a small window table. He poured her milk in for her; she liked that. She was feeling cared for and she hadn't felt the warmth of that sensation for a long time. She had defences but they were more than just down, they were mothballed, just like the old gun emplacements which were dotted around the island coast. Important at the time but no longer relevant. She didn't need defences because she wasn't being attacked. She was being helped and something told her to welcome the aid and bask in the opportunity it provided for her to emerge from the darkness.

There was no awkwardness and for over an hour a most remarkable conversation took place.

They explored each other's histories and established common ground. They gradually built a trust and began to share things they had never talked about with anyone else before. They were both conscious of something special happening. Nothing interrupted their meeting; there were no cars arriving, no other customers, there weren't even any sheep outside the window to distract them. It was as if the islands ancient gods had gifted them this one chance to move on in their lives and to somehow help each other to do so. Shutty imagined a shimmering translucence passing the window at one stage but assumed it was a product of his migraine. He was used to that vision.

Time passed and their exchanges knew almost no bounds; nothing was sacrosanct, everything was gradually being put on the table. He told her about his teaching, his marriage, and shouting at the sky. She laughed at the sky shouting and said she understood more than he could know. He asked why and she said to wait and see.

'Wait and see.' She was inviting an extension of their time together.

His heart lifted at the prospect. Could she be his salvation, and he somehow lift her from her loneliness? She asked him what he shouted about and he told her everything.

She said she'd never heard of Ofsted. He said that made her the perfect woman. She blushed slightly and glanced away momentarily then stared right into his eyes, reached out and covered his hand with hers and just said, 'Why thank you kind Sir.'

He looked down at their hands and said, 'Gosh!'

They both laughed and the grip was squeezed so that her fingers turned white and his hand carried indentations well into the afternoon.

As time went by, they both had fleeting concerns about their honesty, about the risks they were taking, and they had moments of fear that it wouldn't last or that their secrets would be blurted out on social media before the end of the week, turning this unexpected, completely unscripted meeting from triumph to disaster. They continued to talk nevertheless, and some sort of mysterious trust overcame their fleeting doubts so the sharing went on. They both became teachers and learners; great teachers and great learners.

The island magic was working on them as surely as it had on chosen people for more than mere centuries, for the spirits were well into their eighth millennium and they were still as good at their work as they had been when man first blundered onto the Far Isles.

They both wanted it to continue forever, but practicality loomed large, and after an hour it was Reyja who took the first step in the next direction. She took a deep breath, drew upon a deep reserve of emotional courage and asked if he could help her for the rest of the day. She knew what a risk it was, she had no idea what the consequences might be, but something was sweeping her along. She was tough, intelligent and independent and she always controlled people and situations easily. Now within an hour of stumbling across this man, who she had never even met before, she was giving it all away.

Capitulating, she was barely holding her head above water as the current took her along. Now she was inviting him to journey a little further with her. She was inviting him into her inner sanctum, the place which had kept her sane since the disappearance; her refuge, her place of safety. She knew it was a risk. If it went wrong, she would have contaminated the one place she still loved, but she knew that she was going to take that risk anyway.

She explained that both her staff were off and she was expecting two coach loads of tourists so his help would be a lifesaver for the business. Being understaffed meant disgruntled customers who gave up on purchases, tired of waiting to be served, often giving up on even ordering a coffee and a cake. She convinced him that his help would be genuinely appreciated.

He agreed, and that was the second most important decision of his life. Firstly, he ditched the Marx Brothers stunt, now he agreed to stay and work with her. Lifesaving for the gallery maybe, life changing for both of them as it turned out.

Reyja showed Shutty how to use the card machine and the till and he picked it up easily. Then she explained how to use the Gaggia and made him do a medium cappuccino for them both. They were perfect, she was impressed. She showed him the price tickets and the code book which translated the letters on the tickets into a range of cash prices. He memorised them in a flash. He was ready to go. Just as they both heard the coaches crunching the gravel on the drive, she stood directly in front of him, put her hands on his shoulders and said, 'You are a very lucky man.' And kissed his forehead.

They spent the next hour and a half in a whirl of activity. They worked independently but when their paths crossed, they smiled and if they were close enough, she touched him. Hand on shoulder with a quiet, 'Excuse me' or both hands on hips to gently move him with a 'Could I just squeeze through there.' It was part of a wonderful game which Reyja enjoyed right from the start, and after about an hour he cottoned on and felt amused and excited by it. He didn't dare do it to her but he loved it when she did it to him. It was a wonderfully secret game being played before a packed house, who hadn't got a clue what was going on.

Shutty was mainly selling artwork and Reyja was mainly running the café. Shutty gradually upped the prices to the top end of the coded ranges as the tourists scrambled to buy pieces before their buses left. After the first half hour he was adding a one in front of some of the guide prices. A small silver-framed photograph of his screaming beach went for £175 instead of £75 and a locally produced pure wool scarf went for £135 rather than £50.

Shutty was in his element; he was the performing teacher, pleasing his class, keeping interesting conversations alive, allowing the productive classroom buzz to develop to exactly the right pitch, identifying the quiet one's who needed to be given the confidence to contribute and including them in the action while gently sidelining the garrulous, overconfident bombasts who were seeking to dominate.

A genuine Victorian steamer trunk, with its original destination labels carefully varnished onto its battered surface to preserve them, was bought by a woman from Boston, who agreed to pay carriage on top of the £500 asking price. Reyja was close by as he sealed the deal. She loved the way he handled the transaction, the way he treated the aging American woman with care and respect while cementing her interest in the trunk. He was so clever at including her in his conversation, making her feel as though she was in control of her decision to buy it, which she was of course, but only after his subtle influence had predetermined the outcome. He was a natural, she wished he had been her teacher.

She asked him to help her in the back room for a second. He followed her in and she turned and kissed him full on the mouth. She grinned and walked back into the Gallery and took the final drinks orders. They had sold out of pastries but they could still manage coffee. Shutty returned to the desk feeling bashful; he remembered stolen kisses at teenage birthday parties; it felt just like that.

When the coach finally trundled up the drive onto the main road Reyja and Shutty closed the double doors together, slid the bolt, turned the sign to closed and pulled down the blind. They had asked the coach driver to turn the roadside sign to closed too, which he did as he paused at the end of the drive to close the gate. They were alone, isolated and safe. They were elated and exhausted by the frantic trade they had just completed. It had all happened so quickly, it was all a bit of a blur, almost an unreal experience for them both. A veritable dream.

In truth, they were more elated by the relationship which they both knew they had developed by sheer chance, in a completely unexpected way, in just a few hours. It had taken their breath away.

When Reyja totted up the takings by totalling the till transactions she found that her income record had been broken. She had suspected as much even before she pressed the button, but it was good to see the digital confirmation of their success. She could just tell how successful the day had been by her overall feelings about it, and, for once, she didn't worry about the takings at all.

It had been a perfect experience; every single customer happy; lots of business done; a profit margin which would please the creditors, and all of it a result of perfect teamwork against a discrete backdrop of delicious intrigue. But it was more than intrigue, much more important than a tantalising collusion, much better than a furtive conspiracy to engage in something secretive. This was serious, life-changing stuff.

Reyja kept thinking of the word love and it wouldn't go away. She felt the power of the word pushing anger and disappointment aside. The word made her think of things which she hadn't thought about for a long time; she suddenly found herself wondering what he smelled like. She sniggered at herself wondering where the thought had come from. She had no idea.

Why had all this happened so suddenly? She didn't have a clue.

Her mind raced and she remembered her first boyfriend and their meeting on a local fairground in her small village home near Malmo. She thought of the helter-skelter and imagined that she was sitting on a well-worn coconut mat. She gripped the sides of the slide and held herself steady on the last inches of the flat platform before the sloping shiny surface which would send her on the exciting journey down the slide. She thought of how 'down' didn't do justice to the helter-skelter ride she was about to experience. It was only down because that was the trajectory that gravity demanded. In every other sense it was up.

In every important sense it was a journey forward, a sort of everlasting toboggan run through the next stage in her life. She moved the final inch towards the bright, well-polished metal surface of the slide, ready to let go.

They stood behind the blind, neither sure what to do next, but excitement and anticipation wove through their senses in equal measure. They savoured the moment in silence. It wasn't an embarrassed silence, it was more of an exciting pause, a prelude to the next event which they knew would be experimental for them both; not exactly a first, but the first for a long time.

Reyja let go of the slide and quickly gathered speed as the helter-skelter worked its magic.

They could never remember who spoke first.

'I think I need a shower and a gin and tonic.'

'Me too.'

So that's what they did, together.

It was as simple as that.

As they relaxed hours later, lying on the beach staring at the stars, so clearly visible in their thousands against the perfect darkness, he asked Reyja about shouting at the sky. He asked how she chose the screen saver and told her that it was his shouting beach too. She laughed and told him she went to that beach to curse her husband in secret after he had walked out. It didn't bring him back or explain his disappearance but it made her feel better. She didn't go there very often now, but the screen reminded her of the bad times she had fought through, whenever she turned the Mac on. She told him that from now on it would remind her of him instead of her husband. He knew then that he was stepping into someone else's shoes.

They compared angers and feelings about being hurt and laughed at each other's hang-ups and reactions. They didn't scream at the sky though; they didn't need to. They eventually exhausted their interest in the past and watched silently for shooting stars. There were plenty that night. The cosmos laid on an unexpected meteor shower for the scientist and the gallery owner and they watched in wonder as the silver streaks criss-crossed the sky, burning-out in brief instants of glorious brightness.

He could have given her chapter and verse on the astrophysics of small solid objects burning up as they entered the atmosphere, but he didn't. He just shared, with her, the fleeting glimpses of final brilliance as the meteors burned-out. A distant jet on a night nav-ex echoed through the hills and the sound rolled around like very distant thunder. The young crew had no idea that the unlikely couple were listening to them from their beach.

They were playing at mock radar avoidance by skimming the hills at zero feet, praying that their electronic systems kept them from hitting the ground. Steering it was the job of pilot officer William Cruachan, who was known to everyone as Ben. Navigation and weapons were in the hands of Sally Bowles, one of six female fighter crew in the squadron. Ben was pleased to be crewing with Sally, but the thought of killing her, if he flew into a hill, troubled him. He liked her a lot and she knew it. When they landed in East Anglia two hours later Shutty and Reyja would still be on their beach, gazing at the night sky, and both couples would be relaxing after a safe landing.

Like the Tornado crew, Reyja and Shutty had avoided the crashes they had been at risk of heading for. For Shutty and Reyja, it was their inner senses which had guided them wisely, more by good luck than anything else. For Ben and Sally's survival depended more upon the delicate and ultrasensitive terrain-following radar developed by one of Shutty's former pupils at TRE Malvern.

Calmness and satisfaction bathed both couples with a sense of mission complete. Shutty and Reyja had saved each other; Ben and Sally had been saved by physics.

The rumbling thunder had been manmade and there were no storms on the horizon; everything was fine, finer than it had been for a long time. When the shooting stars eventually moved on to streak across the skies of another world, Reyja and Shutty simply closed their eyes. They gave in to the night, rolled themselves into the blanket and began all over again.

They lay on the beach until dawn. Their beach had known the feet of islanders for thousands of years and it was certainly no stranger to emotion. It had been wind-blown and wave-dashed for centuries to its present position and when it moved further in, or further out, it would still be the same beach with the same powers.

When it eventually shifted with sea level change or storm surge it would still be their beach and it would carry their spirits along with those of the early Neolithic settlers, the Viking raiders, the Medieval crofters who had also once called it home, and the tearful memories of the miserable migrants for whom it was a final point of departure.

Reyja and Shutty joined a special group of beach people whom even archaeology would never fully appreciate, for some very important things in life are beyond detection. When the footprints disappear, there may be no physical trace left, but the magic remains for ever. The teacher and the artist both slept, calm in the knowledge that the magic had woven dreams for them and provided a way forward which only dreaming could create.

Chapter 3

A Long Time Coming

He was the biggest man on the big ferry that day, and he was heading towards his Vettriano moment without knowing what one was. He certainly didn't know that he would soon be providing serious competition for the anonymous couple, meeting up against the drab industrial background of the Methyl Power Station. He had never even seen the picture. His reunion with Henrietta would be the culmination of this two-hour crossing; it was a reunion that had been a long time coming.

Some things are worth waiting for even though the wait can be more than painful. He knew that the reunion would be special, and he was quietly excited by the prospect. Nobody would have noticed his feelings, he was well trained in the art of keeping calm, revealing nothing, not even under the unimaginable pressures of capture and interrogation. Poker face wasn't in it. Poker life more like.

The big man had been away too long. It wasn't his fault, except that he had chosen his career, and once chosen it had the capacity to drag him away at a moment's notice. The only way to avoid the wrenching departures, and the long separations, would be to resign his commission, and he wasn't going to do that.

Jack Vettriano should always be in people's minds when they travel; he provides a way of looking at life which is useful when moments of reflection present themselves; when someone else's view of life helps to put things in perspective. A Vettriano lens is particularly rewarding in the island settings of the remote North West, but most people don't have it. They don't have it because they simply don't understand the richness it could bring to their view of life.

For people without the lens, life, just as it is, provides a sufficient set of challenges; they don't need to look at it through an artist's eyes. But, if you do look for it, Jack's imagery can loom unexpectedly out of the sober, beautiful background of landscape and architecture on the Far Isles, as surely as it can from the austere industrial backdrop of a coal-fired power station.

When it occurs, the Vettriano view of life can enhance existing beauty as surely as it can enliven a sometimes rather dour and sober impression of human existence. For the experienced JV-moment spotter, there will always be a potential for colourful and stylised interpretation. There will always be a chance to read emotion and intrigue into a scene which would otherwise seem, at best, normal. Those stylised snapshots do exist out there, but for the most part they go unnoticed.

A rare and immaculately restored bright red Ferrari passing a ruined fish factory, unnoticed by two local parents intent on their argument about a bathroom conversion, but drawing a head-turning reaction from their twelve-year-old son, who stares in open-mouthed disbelief as a car, he thought he would never see, drives right by him.

A bright white cruise ship passing impossibly close to a beautiful, rocky coastline, ignored by the passengers who are dancing faultless Samba on the open deck, to the music of a Bossa Nova band. The passage of the huge vessel is quietly cursed by a local man, sea fishing from a lonely beach, resenting the intrusion and totally missing the animated artwork floating by.

A stylish couple sitting side by side on a pair of seaside chairs, watching the Hebridean sun setting into distant storm clouds, his controlling arm around her compliant shoulders, both of them wondering about tomorrow and coming to different conclusions, irritating the attendant who wants to take the chairs in.

A beautiful, red-lipped and purple-haired young shop assistant, brave enough to be a genuine hardcore Punk in the sombre setting of the local one-stop-shop, her facial piercings and neck tattoo failing to hide the stunning young woman behind the disfiguring disguise, but still drawing the distain of the conservative clientele.

A couple heading towards the only Airstream on the busy camp site, after stumbling back from the restaurant across the causeway, she with a red military jacket, a long, tight, black pencil skirt and red-soled Louboutin's. He in a smart black suit and an open-necked white shirt, bow tie unfastened and hanging lop-sided around his neck, his hand gripping hers rather too tightly, drawing tutting jealousy from the people in the other vans, secretly following the couple's slow progress towards their aluminium condominium through slightly parted net curtains.

Pure Vettriano, all of it. When the Vettriano scene suddenly appears, the aficionado's attention is drawn to the occasion with a fascination as powerful as any face-to-face experience with his original work in a Glasgow gallery.

In a place where things move slowly as a matter of course, the JV moment can freeze everything for a few seconds, allowing the seasoned interpreter to sit back and appreciate the magic of contrast. Vettriano seems to understand one of the many dilemma's women face as relationships develop, the inevitable conflict between attraction and exploitation, and he resolves it best when true lovers meet.

Exploitation was never on the agenda when the JV moment came on this occasion. Rather, it was to be an all too brief celebration of perfection; the confirmation of one of life's great gifts; a perfect relationship. The big man was in for a treat; whoever was meeting him was likely to be just as pleased with the moment too.

The sea route provides the first step on the journey to the Far Isles and it is long enough to demand some activity to prevent travellers from becoming too bored. Most passengers occupy themselves with a combination of reading, eating and occasionally gazing, in an absent-minded sort of way, at the sea.

Half of the passage is within reasonable distance of a coast and the hills provide a picture worth painting, whatever the light. Sea-watching can be rewarding at any stage of the journey. Careful scrutiny reveals a proliferation of land and sea birds and regular sightings of dolphins, but the occasional whale is always only ever seen by chance. No amount of careful watching guarantees a whale sighting. If someone cries 'Orca' they've just been lucky, and however quickly the others look, they will already have missed it.

A gannet or two will track the boat once it leaves the shore a mile or so behind and the deep water begins. Watchers will notice, and look for, the yellow patch of identity confirmation gannets conveniently provide for the amateur; experts tell by the 'jizz'. For watchers, the sight of the gannets gliding across the water below mast-top height would be comforting evidence that things were normal. A common sight but a welcome one; sometimes confirmation of normality is important, especially on the uncertain seascape inhabited by the ferry.

If suddenly there were no gannets the spotters would be immediately concerned; something would be going wrong. The amateurs wouldn't notice and would remain blissfully unaware of a disturbance in the system. If calamity portends, amateurs are always the last to know. Not everyone even notices the birds, but everyone notices the other people, and they all pay at least passing attention to their fellow travellers.

It is natural for people to indulge in people watching and sharing a busy summer crossing with a few hundred other people on a calm day, provides plenty of opportunity. Competition between temporary travelling companions starts as soon as boarding begins. Seasoned travellers who commute regularly know exactly what to do. Quickly bag the best seats, nearest to windows, nearest to the widescreen TVs, furthest from toilets; whatever suits their needs best. The most thick-skinned use bags and coats to cover the next seat too, ensuring some personal space.

The less experienced passengers just drift around, uncertain at first where to settle, but gradually the decisions are made and many will stay outside if its fine, feeling that exposure adds something to their adventure, putting them closer to nature, somehow making the experience more authentic. If the weather is wild everyone but the watchers will be inside.

On that particular day conditions were misleading and most of those who went outside at first, filtered back indoors as the steady breeze chilled them off and they grew tired of the constant buffeting. The coastlines were distant smudges and inside the lounges and the self-service café, well over two hundred souls settled down with their distractions. The watchers outside were rewarded with the sight of a pair of White-Tailed Eagles, and for one lucky observer, there was a brief glimpse of a whale's back as it broke surface before rolling forward and diving into one of the deep trenches occasionally shared with Russian submarines.

It was a relatively calm sea on that day, despite the breeze which had cleared the decks. Breezes bother humans, but they don't bother the sea. A stiff breeze blows hats off and screws up eye lids but it can only create low waves which don't disturb the big ferry. It's the swell created by distant storms in the deep ocean which cause discomfort for passengers and, on that day, there was just the slightest swell and no real wave height. The comforting vibrating throb of the engines reassured everyone that the large vessel was more than capable of powering its way across the sea which isolated the Far Isles from the mainland.

Calm enough on that day, but there were clues that the passage might not always be so benign. The chairs and tables were screwed to the deck and the table tops had a small fence round their rims to contain sliding cups and plates. Sick-bag dispensers were screwed to the walls near the toilets and every corridor had stout metal handrails for stumbling passengers to grab. None of that stuff would be needed on this crossing though, and the fortunate crowds of passengers needed to have no concerns about the sea's behaviour.

There were families, backpackers, fiddle players, a school party, off-duty crew, a Cambridge University geology field trip, lorry drivers and, of course, the big man: the Royal Marine Commando.

If Royal Marine Commandos are in the family, you can spot them a mile off. If not, they will be less easy to identify, unless, like this man, they are wearing the uniform. He wore his outfit well, and the quiet lovat green service dress, which was designed to be low-key but classy, succeeded on both counts. There were five medal ribbons on his lapel and one of them was the Victoria Cross.

He wore the beret in the way that all Commandos manage to achieve; the gravity-defying angle and small area of grip it seemed to have on his closely cropped head, almost inviting it to fall off, but it never would. It was the simplest of head dresses but the hardest won, and the owners always wore it with pride; the Green Beret.

Special Forces people come in all shapes and sizes, and they are not all huge. Sometimes they can be short, sometimes wiry rather than muscular, but they always look fit, and they always are fit, both physically fit and fit for purpose. Honed by the mental as well as the physical preparation they go through to enable them to take on tasks no human should ever be asked to complete. This guy was the huge version, he was six five when he slouched and he would have looked 10-feet tall charging at you with his war paint on, firing from the hip.

Like all intelligent big men, he was very comfortable in his own skin, confident of his capabilities, poised in his stance, balanced in his movements, considered and considerate in his actions. In this company he had nothing to prove and nothing to fear. He had arranged his kit carefully around him so he could quickly grab it, and, while it rested, it formed a clear barrier between him and anyone who sat remotely close by. He didn't look around but he had already taken everything in. He was content. He was in a very safe place, at sea, on quite a big ship, no obvious threats anywhere near him.

He was on leave from action, probably in the Afghan or Syrian Theatre, or possibly in one of the remote sub-Sahara trouble spots, or even in the Horn of Africa. He could have been advising defence forces in Latvia or even working on the current, and highly controversial mission, to support rebel forces in Burma, where his illustrious predecessors had fought the Japanese during the Arakan campaign in World War Two.

If he had been in action somewhere, he would almost certainly have seen men die and he would have probably killed people, possibly in events which would never be reported. He was leaving horror behind for now and returning, whole and uninjured, to someone on the islands. The only reason for coming here would be that he belonged here, and that he belonged to someone here who was desperate to see him.

In times of quiet reflection alternative outcomes are always worth thinking of, and considering them helps to put everything in perspective. He would have known people who had been killed in conflict; in Northern Ireland, in the Falklands, in the Gulf, in Afghanistan. He would know that any one of their deaths could have been his own. He would remember sitting with a father whose son had been blown up at the age of 18, not long entitled to wear the beret; he would remember comforting a young wife and mother bereaved by a sniper's bullet in the harsh desert where a secret campaign was being won, acutely conscious of the fact that there would be no victory celebration for this young woman whose husband became a legitimate target for terrorists as soon as he enlisted. He would remember helping to carry the closed coffin of a dear friend when they returned him to his family and the whole town stopped for the funeral.

This particular Commando was still in one piece though, and he looked good. Whoever was waiting for him would already know that he was safe, but they too would know what the alternative outcome might have been, or might yet be in times to come. They would relish the homecoming moment but, despite their delight, enjoyment would be short-lived, for they would soon begin to dread the next departure and what it might lead to.

The unspoken terrors haunted the thinking of everyone concerned with such work. However well they were suppressed, they were always there, lurking in the background, likely to present themselves without invitation, during moments of reflection.

IED, blown to raw meat pieces, closed coffin.

Headshot by sniper, no head left: closed coffin.

Helicopter accident, no remains left after the fireball subsided: empty token coffin.

Worse even than those horrific outcomes: captured, tortured and executed on the internet for the world to see.

But as the moment of contact approached, his waiting folk were only interested in killing time in the terminal as the big ferry made its final approach to the islands. Whoever they were, they would find their man whole and healthy, fit and well, all his limbs intact, only his memories in need of treatment. Over one hundred people stood and sat in the same busy lounges for two hours. They barely exchanged glances, preoccupied with their own mental preparations for their meetings. Some regulars would have known each other well, others at least by sight. They all belonged to small communities and paths often crossed. Others would have been complete strangers, one-time tourist travellers fulfilling a long-held desire to visit the Far Islands. Whoever they were, they would all have noticed the man in uniform.

Strangers might have thought his presence unusual, but regulars knew that it was not unusual to see servicemen in this place. Service life was a normal career choice for island folk, and passengers familiar with the Far Isles would have done no more than notice him. He was a major, whom even his men called Lachy. He was serving in the recently re-formed 46 Commando. Originally a crack wartime unit, they fought the 12th SS Hitlerjugend in Normandy, just one year after they had been first formed, and they were fighting against the odds for the rest of the war too. They lost half their men in action during two brief World War Two campaigns.

The 12th SS were crack troops; more than the Taliban of their day; more like ISIS perhaps. They fought well and literally took no prisoners. Some said they were mainly brainwashed psychos, and they probably were.

Brainwashed as kids and growing into young adults who saw nothing wrong with slaughter. By adopting that one essential principle, 'take no prisoners', the SS transformed themselves from elite troops into murderers. They were excellent role models for today's terrorist groups.

New 46 had been tackling terrorist murderers for 10 years, but RMCs did take prisoners and they treated them well. The original unit even took the young soldiers of the 12th SS into custody after capture and kept them safe. The 46ers always believed that it was the mark of difference between Allied troops and the SS Panzer Grenadiers, perhaps the difference between their two respective cultures, which determined their behaviour towards captured enemy troops. We took prisoners, the SS Germans didn't, and to be honest, most terrorist groups didn't either.

The 46 were disbanded after the war, as cost-cutting became the first imperative on day one of the peace. The new 46 were re-formed as a specialist, anti-terrorist unit, when the threat of Muslim extremism grew around the world and every nation needed to take it seriously. They espoused the moral principles of their forefathers; even terrorists would be taken alive if possible. Live capture pleased the Intelligence Service by providing much-needed information, but, more importantly, it satisfied their own beliefs and reflected their key values about human life.

This guy was no murderer, he would take prisoners, but he would also take a life without hesitation if his own life, or the lives of others, were being threatened. It sometimes seemed like a mystery why anyone from these beautiful islands should put themselves in harm's way, fighting a politician's war, but, whatever the reason, the fact is that they do; they do and they have always done so, and that's all there is to it: a fact of Far Island life. An old shepherd once told some drunk, loud, angry, loutish, wild-camping tourists to be very careful whom they offended: 'This place is full of ex-special forces,' he said, and he wasn't wrong.

Young men from remote farms and tiny villages had lost their lives in almost all the conflicts we have ever been party to, inspired to answer the call of duty by the opportunities a serviceman's life provided as much as by a genuine belief that it was somehow their personal responsibility to answer the call. In one of the most isolated village halls in the whole archipelago the traveller may stumble across a small metal plaque commemorating the sacrifice of a 28-year-old local lad who gave his life flying a Tornado in the Second Gulf War. He would have developed the ambition to fly fast jets by watching them regularly exercising over his island. He would have watched from his primary school playground and been thrilled when they roared overhead.

One governor wanted to complain to the MOD, but the headteacher convinced the Governing Board that the passage of the low-flying fast jets thrilled the children and provided them with a valuable insight into a world they would otherwise only experience on TV. The children were always excited when the sounds first echoed around the school and they were experts at predicting the direction of flight, spotting the jet when it was a smaller dot than a distant gull. The fast jets were a wonderful, gravity-defying sight. At 400mph at 200ft between the hills against a blue and cloudy-white sky. Flat at first and then climbing and twisting, banking away into the blue, leaving only the echoing roar of its engines behind, long after the dot disappeared.

In secondary school he would have known all the aircraft he ever saw by make and name, he would have known their capabilities and limitations, and he would have begun to make plans to join the RAF. He would have kept himself fit, made sure he was good at maths and science, gained his place at a good university, joined the Air Squadron and soloed quickly. Eventually he would have realised his dream: fast-jet pilot, the cream of the cream, a 'Top Gun'.

Not consigned to multiengine, not destined to fly Hercules or tankers, but selected to fly the very best aircraft his country flew. He had dreamed of flying a Tornado for most of his young life, never imagining that he would die in one so soon, shot down by mistake: blue on blue. A young life ended in ironic tragedy.

The marine was OK though. Plenty of wars left ahead for him, plenty of risks to face, but so far, so good. He was looking at his watch, working out how long there was to go before his arrival. This huge man of the Hebrides was about to show his waiting people, his physical presence. So much better than an email or even a video phone call. Whoever met him was going to be relieved and impressed, and probably overwhelmed when the physical contact took place.

It might be a young family with toddlers running towards him and grabbing his neck, the young mother taking a momentary back seat, knowing her time would come later. It might be parents and grandparents, overwhelmed with relief that their son was home safe, even the men unable to prevent fat tears from running down their weather-beaten cheeks. It might be a partner, a soulmate, a true love, a lover. Jack Vettriano would only have painted the latter.

The slow approach to the harbour took the ferry very close to an infamous disaster site. A yacht carrying soldiers back from the horrors of the World War One foundered on the rocks in the harbour approaches, and on 1 January 1919 well over 200 men drowned in the cold, dark, boiling waters. They were within scrambling distance of the rocky shore but they couldn't see it in the stormy darkness. Disorientated and terrified, they slid beneath the waves to their deaths. They had survived the Somme, Ypres, Passchendaele; the machine guns, the gas, the artillery, the air attacks, but they died together, a few yards from home after the peace had been won.

Irony and tragedy, those fated twins. Every village on the island was impacted by that disaster. Such a cruel blow after all the death notices which had already been served on these isolated communities as the war raged on for five years. It had raged on in another world, hundreds of miles away, one which none of those men would ever have visited had it not been for the conflict known as the First World War.

The post-war influenza epidemic killed far more people than the war did, and it killed women and children as well as men of fighting age, but it was this so-called 'Great War' which people never forgot, while the influenza pandemic was quietly reduced to a paragraph in school history books, until Covid came along.

Every battle in that war robbed the remote island of its menfolk; men who in peacetime would only have faced the perils of their native seas. Public school boys blew the whistles and working-class lads went over the top. Crofter's kids, running to their deaths on the whim of a gin-soaked general. These post-war victims survived that lottery of battlefield slaughter but fell foul of an improperly supervised, over-loaded boat when the war was over. Tragedy was never more poignant.

The big ferry drifted safely past the deadly rocks and the shore-side memorial which commemorated the young victims of a particularly cruel fate. The captain had never tired of juggling the big boat into gentle contact with the pier, and after he safely navigated the harbour entrance, he enjoyed lining up for the approach to the jetty. Perhaps this one would be the perfect docking, the maritime equivalent of the super-jet landing without so much as a puff of smoke from any of the tyres.

The crew were an unlikely looking, well-oiled machine, who knew exactly what they were doing. A bit scruffy in some cases, possibly slightly hung-over, cig-in-the-mouth and unshaven, hardly wearing their grubby hi-vis jackets with pride, more to tick a box marked 'health and safety'. Admittedly, they were less impressive than the manicured crew of a super-yacht, but they did everything properly and the boat tied up in exactly the right position to unload, dead on time. There was barely a squeak from the huge tyres which protected the edges of the stone jetty; almost a perfect landing.

The Tannoy boomed out instructions for disembarkation in English and Gaelic, and finally the captain thanked everyone for travelling with him and his crew, wishing them a pleasant stay on the islands. Nobody paid attention to the announcements or to anyone else for that matter. People watching was over; everyone was preoccupied with their own exit from the boat; stepping carefully as legs readjusted to a firm deck after coping with two hours of a moving floor beneath them. Passengers were ensuring that bags were collected, children were being held by the hand, to avoid a lastminute stumble down steep stairs, drivers were looking for car keys as they made their way down the slippery metal steps to the vehicle decks. Those without vehicles to worry about were crossing the lounge towards the pedestrian ramp.

The Royal Marine Commando stood out clearly from the crowd because of his height, his green beret, and his uniform. It was as though he was in high-definition colour and all the rest were in black and white. In the arrivals area beyond the end of the exit ramps there were 57 people waiting, including some taxi drivers with people's names on cards. Two of the cards were upside down and one was held in such a way that nobody arriving could read it at all. One driver had mis-spelt the surname of their client, and realising their mistake, had simply crossed out the error and written the correct name below it.

The crowd was, in most respects, exactly the same as greeting groups at any terminus anywhere in the world. A mixture of ages, a range of clothing choices from smart to practical, all shapes and sizes of human being, different degrees of affluence and different levels of excitement were evident. A crowd only unified by one thing: they were all meeting someone, and the one thing they all had in common was the emotional expectation of that meeting.

Elderly parents met young family members, grandchildren ran up to grandparents and jumped around their necks, young friends hugged and laughed after weeks of separation enforced by university terms, business people were greeted with a hand shake and a rapid walk towards the company hire car.

Nobody was watching for the marine's greeter, but anyone who saw the woman would have known she was his. Jack would have painted her perfectly; standing alone; standing aloof, but with an unmistakable feeling of darkness about her. Tall, dark haired, good-looking in the way Jack would like. Long dark coat, red lipstick, shoulder bag, leather gloves, earrings, Italian crimson silk scarf, red-soles on her black Lubes with impossibly high heels.

She would have seen him from a distance as he came down the ramp, standing out in high definition. She couldn't miss him: his height promoted him well above the bobbing crowd of heads and his uniform was enhanced by the kit he had slung around himself like a paratrooper. The distant sight of him brought feelings flooding back and she fought to control the emotional landslide he prompted by simply appearing on her radar.

As he got nearer the space between them opened out right on cue; people just moved out of the way, as if by magic. He would have seen her as soon as she saw him but he wouldn't speed up because he wanted to savour the moments before they touched. The delicious moment every fortunate child enjoyed at Christmas, the moment before the presents were opened. She wouldn't move at first, almost gasping for breath when she saw him, the burning in her throat almost driving her to sobbing, but she kept it in for a few more seconds. Finally she could resist no longer and she did move, she had to.

She ran at him, rather than to him. Good job his was big, he withstood her impact without flinching; then he was gone too. Just like Jack Vettriano would go, when he saw a woman in seamed nylon stockings with a high heel shoe dangling off her foot, he was gone, and he went the moment he felt her relax into his arms. Her first moment of contact was hard, gripping, tense, almost overeager, then she relaxed, she slumped slightly, he had to hold her up.

He went because it suddenly reminded him of the day his right-hander got hit in the chest by a 3mm round and fell backwards into his arms. The big guy had held his man firmly and lowered him to the ground to treat him but he felt the relaxation and knew his friend had died halfway to the sand. He went because that moment of relaxation said everything about this woman and their precious relationship. His kit fell everywhere, she was in his arms and he held on tight and she sobbed into his chest for a few seconds. Then she lifted a tear-stained face and looked up at him, he had tears too but nobody would see them except her. She put one hand around his neck with perfectly positioned, elegant fingers and pulled him down.

They kissed the best kiss anyone would ever see.

Can't describe it, it would be wrong to try. Jack Vettriano could certainly have painted it, and, if he had managed to capture the magic, it would have been even better than 'Long time gone', and that really is saying something. Everyone should have cheered, but no one even noticed. They eventually left the concourse, arms around each other, and got into a black Overfinch with privacy glass. It fired up, burbled the V8 soundtrack and rumbled off with her behind the wheel.

Some moments of pure magic are best not recorded at all, or least nowhere other than in the memories of the few people lucky enough and wise enough to bear witness. This was such a moment, embedded in their memories but playing no part in anyone else's; a brief moment of pure joy that would be their secret for as long as they lived.

His early life on the islands, his first meeting with Henrietta, their developing relationship, his military service, all lay behind him for now and he could enjoy perfection for a few days, with a person he loved, in a place he loved, never imagining that the Yollumba raid lay ahead for him. But for now, even Yollumba didn't matter.

They drove off into the summer evening, away from the terminal, beyond the airfield, across the low hills and down towards Solas, the home of his distant ancestors, and they entered the place where Henrietta planned their future together. There was nobody else around and bags remained unpacked as more important matters took control and they carefully began to make up for the long time gone.

Solas was an ancient settlement, rich in spiritual history, and the young couple, in the big renovated farm house, added their own chapter to the legend of the place that night. Nothing lasts for ever and they both knew that; all the more reason to be mindful of the moment and the opportunity for sheer happiness it provided for them both.

Nothing lasts for ever, but if moments of magic are allowed to slip by unnoticed, there really is no point in even starting. You may as well accept life's 'Go to Jail' card and forego your £200 reward, even if you pass 'Go'. Far better to buy Mayfair and Park Lane and plan to build on them when you play life's game of Monopoly, and buy yourself out of jail if ever you find yourself in that predicament. Solas people were good at making the most of magic, and they were formidable Monopoly players.

Often, those people of action who died young, had experienced more joy in their brief lives than the longest living of their species, and while the big man knew what might lay ahead, for he had seen it, he was happy to be back home and safe in a place which cared for him spiritually, in ways that had been practiced for centuries. Yollumba certainly lay ahead, and it would test him to the very limits of his life, but for now his ferry trip had brought him to a good place; the very best place to be, in fact. He knew that reaching the best place was something which would not happen very often in life, and for some people it was a goal that was never reached. Some people travelled, and never really arrived, and some never really travelled at all.

He appreciated the luck of his achievement, and he knew that it was all the more reason to savour these special moments of deep satisfaction. He had travelled, he had survived and he had arrived.

The ferry spent two hours refreshing its supplies, unloading its rubbish, fuelling its boilers and changing its crew. It finally sailed into the night with a new cohort of travellers on board, some having a late supper, others settling down to sleep for an hour or so on bench seats. There were no servicemen on board this time, no expectations of emotional greetings at the other end of the crossing, no risk of Jack Vettriano's vision being challenged, no risk of the Uig terminal rivalling Methyl Power Station.

Chapter 4

Status Quo

Georgie Hammond was a fisherman; it was inevitable that he would be. Fishing was in the genes and the family ran their own boat as the boys grew up. Georgie's great grandfather had sailed with other owners for most of his life, but in his final years he achieved his life-long ambition and bought his own boat. The small but sturdy craft brought a deep satisfaction to the old man. He enjoyed the freedom of ownership after a lifetime of serving others, but more than that, he knew that he was now able to leave something useful for his family when he was gone. The Hammonds had owned a boat ever since.

Fishing was as old as the peoples who had inhabited the islands over the centuries. Farming was possible but it would never be rewarding enough to keep the population well fed, and the unreliability of every crop would always lurk menacingly in the background. Disease could wipe out a season's efforts at a stroke and pests could decimate any harvest. A simple but irresistible blight could even render the islands farms unsustainable and cause mass migration, as people went hungry and saw no signs of salvation in their homeland.

One such harvest tragedy occurred just as old Thomas Hammond secured his own wooden boat, and buying it saved his family from starvation. His catches enabled them to weather the storm of famine, which raged across the islands, and to avoid any thoughts of migration. The potato crop had failed and it was fishing which enabled the Hammonds to stay in their home while many neighbouring families took to the Atlantic for one final crossing.

Harvesting the sea was essential in the old days for keeping people well fed, and even now, with ample food supplies secured in the fridges and freezers of the one-stop-shop, fishing was still essential to their standard of living, if not to survival itself. They could survive on frozen food, but it hardly enriched their lives. The income from fishing really was value-added. It secured mortgages, paid for house extensions, purchased the new 4x4 and funded annual holidays abroad. The extra income enabled student loans to be paid-off early and families could realistically dream of big wedding ceremonies and flowers at funerals. Fishing income gave families a sense of secure wellbeing.

In the old days fishing was both a lifesaver and a life taker. It provided vital food supplies, but it took a toll on human life too. Fishing was never a safe occupation. In recent times fishing enriched lives by providing for those extras which made modern life more comfortable, but it was still the same risky enterprise it had proved to be generations before.

The Hammonds were simply following the tradition of generations, but modern fishing made new demands on technology and the lucrative European markets involved stringent quality controls and expensive logistics to get fresh produce across to the continent as rapidly as possible; fishing was a factor in economic survival, and sometimes, still, a matter of literal survival. It did well for them, but it carried its own risks as well as handsome rewards. The islanders knew that the sea had to be treated with respect.

It may have been providing jam on the bread now, rather than the bread itself, but it remained one of the few real threats to survival for the islanders who undertook the daily challenge of the seas but there was no doubt that the Hammonds would continue fishing, whatever the risks.

The only question for the Hammond family was which of the three brothers would get the boat. It fell to Georgie when the twins found that success at school came both easy and early. It's like that for some kids, but, somehow, never for all of them. Georgie was the one it didn't happen for, so when his brothers left the island for college and careers in medicine and law, he took the boat and eventually made his living around the waters of the Minch, and sometimes further out, in the grim suburbs of the North Atlantic.

 But there was work to be done first. The family boat had been laid up for six years since the tragedy, and although it remained sound, it was scruffy and equipment had become outdated. The old-style electrical and electronic gear didn't work anymore and the interior fittings were rusty and mildewed. Georgie took a risk and went for a complete overhaul and as a mark of the change, he decided to rename the boat when he had it refurbished in Stornoway.

It cost half a million, but the bank was happy to invest. He could clear that debt with two years of good catches. The trouble was that two good-catch years could take 20 Earth years. Fishing was a risky business, and you could never control all the variables. It had been rated as the most dangerous job in the country since there were far fewer coal mines and the remaining ones were modern and well-equipped with decent safety measures in place. Mining simply didn't kill miners any more, but fishing still killed fishermen.

Boats were modern and well-equipped with safety designed in as a first priority, but the sea could take any vessel if it wanted to. Nothing was guaranteed to survive a freak super-wave, not even a cruise liner or the largest warship. Mariners were well aware of huge container vessels breaking in half during Atlantic storms. All it took was the right wave pattern and a bit of time.

Fishing boats didn't need a super-wave to sink them. A big storm in coastal waters would do the job. For a huge storm on the deep ocean, it would be like swatting a fly. Despite the risks, fishermen fished. When fishing went well, men were proud that their families prospered, but when it failed, their families took a hit.

Christmas lost its sparkle, holidays were cancelled, loans were called in and the bank might claim the boat, probably selling it to one of the big fleet owners to clear the debt. For the fleet owners, the fishing licence was worth more than the boat. When they acquired a boat, they inherited its licence to fish, expanding their overall fleet catch potential. A licence was money in the bank for the big boys, and every new licence they acquired increased their stranglehold on the industry.

If fishing families lost their boat, they might decide to abandon the islands altogether and take the stormy crossing to a new life on the other side of the great green ocean, just like so many ancestors had done before, when crops had failed just once too often.

But it was going well enough right now. The refrigerated trucks waited at the quayside for the baskets of prawns and langoustines to be winched ashore, and for the lobster to be handed carefully across in trays. Destined for tables in mainland Europe, a catch could make tens of thousands of pounds on a good day. Georgie was more confident than ever that he had made the right choice with *Sally-B*.

His brothers were doing well on the mainland, but he felt he was doing just as well back home on the island. Feelings of failure had almost disappeared, and he felt increasingly proud of his achievement. Georgie's improved boat was an efficient fishing machine, with all the latest electronic gadgets as well as a new engine and safety gear. Clip-on rails covered almost all the deck edges and the crew always wore harnesses.

There was just one stretch where there was a gap in the rails and the boys became expert at clipping off and clipping back on again in less time than it took a pit crew to change a wheel on a Formula 1 car. If they were ever washed off, the harnesses would hold them so they could be pulled back on board; it almost made fishing safe – but not quite.

The storage coolers below decks were accessible via chutes through which the trawl could be accurately emptied, and a crewman could work safely down there, knowing that the pumps would discharge seawater faster than the odd wave could drench him if it found a way to join the fish as they poured down the chute. He worked in oilskins and sorted the trawl into fish-types and packed them quickly and carefully into icy trays. After a few good catches, the room was so full of neatly stacked trays that a man could no longer work in there. 'No room at the Inn' they called it, and it was the sign that it was time to go home.

The more delicate elements in the catch were carefully stored on deck in large plastic trays which were lowered into another cold compartment below decks when they were full. Georgie knew that storage was the most important design feature of the boat and he had given it a lot of thought. Little point in catching fish if you couldn't store them and keep them fresh and undamaged. Dealers soon learned that Georgie's fish were always top quality, and he often sold his entire catch by radio, long before he even reached the fish dock.

Accommodation on the refurbished boat was much better than it had been too. Georgie had a leather covered swivelling Captain's chair on the bridge which enabled him to quickly scan the array of information screens and to see out of the windows onto the foredeck. The crew enjoyed decent bunks and a dining table, just like the ones in a Little Chef, they claimed.

The sound system ensured that instructions would be heard by the deck crew, even over the wildest howling winds and the loudest crashing waves. But for Georgie the amps and speakers had a much more important role. They blared rock music though the stormproof speakers and gave the boat, and the crew, a reputation. The new name for the refurbished boat was the easiest part of the change process.

Young Georgie Hammond was transfixed when Quo opened the Live Aid concert back in the day. He was a young lad watching an old TV in his family's stone cottage by the shore. Everyone else raved about Queen, but for Georgie it was Quo who stole the show, and he'd been 'rockin all over the world' ever since. He always joked about the Barra crews going on about their folk bands, playing their fiddle and accordion music full blast when they sailed, extending memories of happy drunken nights in the lounge bar at the Castle Hotel. For Georgie all that folk-rock stuff was great fun, infectious local fun, but it didn't compare with 'Rockin' all over the world'.

Quo were world class, they touched millions, they gave his boat its soundtrack and its name. On the bow it said '*Status Quo*' but everyone simply called it the *Quo*. Long after it was all over, an American post-graduate literature student from Princeton, used Georgie's choice of the Latin title for his boat's name in her thesis on 'Latin usage in maritime language'.

She heard about the *Quo* during a tour of the Far Isles, and she was moved by thinking of the relevance of its new name. Named after a rock band, perhaps, but also maybe a subconscious reference to the family's association with the sea, and with fishing. 'Status Quo': keeping things the same as they had always been; maintaining the family tradition; 'Same old, same old'. She wondered if Georgie had appreciated the relevance. There was some potential in her theory, but Georgie never thought of it in that way at all. He simply wanted to fish with the family boat and to rename it after his favourite rock band.

Georgie picked his crew of three from a pool of a dozen good friends who were all completely expert at every aspect of the job. They covered each other's boats, and even skippers like Georgie would crew for a mate if needs be, and, instead of taking tens of thousands as the skipper's cut, he would simply fold two hundred quid into his back pocket and say cheers to the guy who paid him. This co-operative, this pool of talent, kept at least three of the local boats at sea almost continually. They worked together and they drank together, they took risks together, and thankfully, it was a long time since they had sampled death together.

Georgie's dad and two other crew were the last to go almost 20 years before. A freak wave broached their boat and it simply turned turtle and went straight down.

Two other boats saw it go, but they only saw one head bob up and it wasn't Georgie's dad's.

It wasn't even his boat. He was helping a mate to put an extra trip in, to satisfy the bank and pay some more off the loan. He wanted to clear the debt before his daughter went to college and Georgie's dad said he would help out. The boat, the *Sarah-G* was never raised.

The family boat, *Sally-B*, was laid up for a while until Georgie was old enough to take her. She rode quietly against the concrete quayside at Killin Harbour on the east coast of the island. Other boats tied up against her and their crews crossed her quiet decks to get ashore, but she never went out to sea herself for six long years. She weathered the layup well enough but the refitting was needed before Georgie took her out again, and that's when the *Sally-B* became *Status Quo*.

It was Georgie's 30th birthday bash when the whole gang last got together in the Oyster Bar at the McTavish Hotel. They just called it the pub, and for all of them it was home from home. The women and kids stayed until about eight then made their way home leaving the crew to laugh and sing, and to get seriously drunk. The humour was predictable, well-rehearsed, but liberating nevertheless. The men all knew that this was lads' stuff, an escape from their real responsibilities, from the real threats that life brought before them.

However well the fishing was going, they still faced the sea and all its dangers, and they still faced the anxiety of the bread-winner. Island life still had its limitations, as did family life, and they all faced the usual complications of human frailty: the inevitable illnesses, accidents and passing's, arguments and personal tensions, plus the uncertainty of their financial futures. Their trade could be wiped out by some vague legislation thought up in Brussels, and living standards would tumble.

Most of all, the men feared losing their children. That would always happen however good the times were, for the islands could never provide enough to keep them all at home. Most of these lovely, uncomplicated kids would have to leave the island eventually, as Georgie's brothers had done. They would want to leave by time they reached college age, and, once they got away, they would never come back for long. Only the academic strugglers would be left behind to carry on with the fishing and the crofting. The one's with good qualifications would seek greener pastures overseas.

Men felt a very deep sadness whenever this thought crossed their minds. Perhaps the male instinct to keep hearth and home together was as primitive as the Bronze Age villages; as deep rooted as the Gaelic language itself; as strong and as fundamental as the wildest Atlantic storms. The boys drank and joked and soon they would sing. They wouldn't sing sad island laments though, like the Barra boys, they would sing the entire Status Quo songbook, absolutely word perfect.

At some point, McClune, whom everyone always called Scouser, because of his fanatical support for Liverpool FC, would do a 'Walk on!', and they would all join-in, walking through the wind and the rain together, with hope in their hearts, pledging their support for each other, agreeing that they would never walk alone. It was usually the last song of the night.

Brogan was more than the bar keeper, he owned the hotel, but he always ran the bar when the boys were in. He was a huge, gentle man. He could hold any two of the crew apart if they kicked off, and he could do it for as long as it took until they calmed down. He never raised his voice, he never raised a fist, he simply commanded the place with his presence. He wasn't an islander but he seemed always to have been there. Some said he was Icelandic, others Norwegian. He certainly understood the culture of the fishermen and got the Gaelic clearly enough to know when he was being insulted by his drunken friends.

He took it all in good part. He loved these men, he looked after them, he felt their pain, their anxieties, and when they began to fall asleep on the floor of his pub, he gently placed cushions under their sleepy heads and carefully covered them with blankets. When they woke up the next morning, he was always gone, but they knew he'd cared for them. Brogan was their minder, their keeper. He would do his best to save them from harm, but even Brogan could not stop their children leaving, and that is finally what they sobbed silently about when they had moments alone; and even Brogan couldn't control the Atlantic storms, any more than he could control the leaving. The big storm which changed everything, began to form even as the men slept under Brogan's blankets.

Its conception was marked by a sudden pressure drop over the Sargasso Sea, over three thousand miles from the pub. Had the storm already developed a consciousness, it would have been amused as millions of crustaceans tightened their grip on their seaweed homes, as the atmosphere lifted slightly above their part of the Atlantic and the water heaved upwards for a moment. The pressure wave that startled the creatures of the Sargasso also tripped the US Coastguard automatic weather buoy Able 110 and it immediately pinged a message to the USCG Atlantic Weather Centre, nearly 800 miles to the north. There were no more discernible changes so the automatic warning was deleted after 30 minutes. The observers assumed it was a glitch, an overactive sensor perhaps, probably nothing to worry about, nothing to worry about at all. They reset the system.

When the storm eventually appeared on everyone's radar was going to be called Kate. It was the girls' turn to provide a name. The previous storm, which was just blowing itself out around Newfoundland, had been named Jake. Jake was a storm alright but he was predictable and avoidable, and everyone coped with him without too much trouble. Kate was not predictable, she was dangerously unpredictable, and everyone didn't cope with her, and she did cause trouble.

The boys left the fish dock feeling less than perfect. Waking up on the pub floor, even with a cushion under your head, wasn't the ideal preparation for six days at sea, but eventually all three boats left together, and Georgie was allowed to lead the way. Quo belted out

'Get down' as the trio pushed out of the calm waters of the harbour approaches and moved into the Minch. The forecast was good enough. Big storm Jake had never even made it across the Atlantic and it seemed to have stalled somewhere off New England; a smaller depression was forming way out, somewhere off the Florida coast, but it hadn't triggered any alarms.

The three skippers chatted over the CB sets and decided to use the weather window to head far west, beyond the headland and into the Atlantic. They would outpace the French factory ships which were hoovering up the fish in their coastal waters, while the fishery protection vessel stood by, powerless to intervene. It was an annoying last effort by the French before new post-Brexit regulations banned them altogether.

All the boys remembered the Russian factory ships of their childhood, anchored up in the deep loch waters off Ullapool. They stayed there while their attendant trawlers plied in and out of Loch Broom with their holds full of fish. It was easy as fishing could get. They brought a mini-boom to the neatly planned little town and local businesses prospered but the boom turned to bust when the factory ships moved on when the herring stocks were decimated, and the gold-rush came to an end as suddenly as it had begun.

The French boats were much worse. Unlike the Russians, these were stand-alone floating factories with no need for a small fleet of attending trawlers like the Russians had employed. These big new factory ships just sucked the shoals out of the sea like an enormous vacuum cleaner. They could move independently to the places where sonar detected the stock and immediately begin to harvest the lot. They rarely made landfall and brought virtually no income to the local shops and pubs.

The islanders called it piracy, and blamed the EU fishing rules, but, ironically, they depended upon the European markets for their own success. The conundrum of Europe always fuelled part of their inebriated banter in Brogan's place and it never led to any sensible conclusions. Even when they were drunk, they realised that banning the French on the one hand and expecting to sell shellfish in Paris on the other just wouldn't work.

All thoughts of Brogan's place and EU fishing rules were behind them as *Quo* led the charge towards the deep water. Within three days she was happily riding the Atlantic swell and starting to make good catches. The men worked for 16 hours, casting the trawl and winching it back almost immediately after it reached full stretch. Each net was full enough to delight the deck team every time it reappeared off the stern and slowly found its way past the guide-plates onto the fish deck. Hauled into the air by the powerful winch, the net was opened and tons of fish cascaded down the chute and into the hold. Bright floodlights illuminated the men and their heaving workplace, and it briefly lit the dark water which crashed over the metal surfaces as waves broke over the deck, highlighting the foam on top of the dark slabs of seawater swilling across their footings before disappearing back into the darkness.

The waves pushed the men around, but none of them lost their footing, stepping skilfully to maintain their balance as water broke over them and rushed beneath their feet. The men were happy; they were in their element; they were in the world which made them feel special. A dangerous world which they had learned to cope with. A world which provided rich pickings for them, if they were lucky. The other two boats were about 60 miles behind *Quo* and hadn't even begun to cast their nets when the warnings started to come in.

A weather warning always grabs the attention of seafarers. It demands action because inaction can quickly leave them with nowhere to go. Delaying a decision may mean that there will be no place of safety within reach. It was always better to move quickly rather than risk just one more catch. For the landlubber, the shipping forecast is usually irrelevant, for the fisherman, out on the water, it is always the programme of choice. Ignored on land, a forecast warning for shipping will raise hairs on the backs of the necks of those at sea. *Quo* was over 250 miles out when the new storm finally showed her true colours.

Kate was still over 2,000 miles from the Far Islands when she had developed sufficient self-awareness to develop a clear idea of what she capable of doing. She enjoyed her ability to think about the possibilities that lay ahead for her in her short life. She enjoyed the thought of being feared. She realised that she would be despised and finally hated, but she cared not. Her psychosis was dominant. She was determined to have her way and she decided to take a life before her powers were spent.

How shocked the humans would be when they, one day, eventually discovered that big storms really did have a life of their own and that their malevolence could be almost human in its intent. Kate's plan was easy enough to formulate: she was going to be unpredictable, changing track to throw off her plotters, making herself seem calm and safe and then quickly change to angry and dangerous, and she was going to take that life before she lost the power to do so.

The first warning came over the radio at midday and Georgie turned *Quo* around immediately. Quickly calculating that the nearest shelter was home, rather than Newfoundland or Iceland, it was obvious that dashing back to the Far Isles was the most sensible thing to do. He didn't like the sound of it at all. There had been no early warnings building up in the forecasts, no warnings at all. The stark message which eventually came through was very clear indeed. A priority warning to all ships, irrespective of size, to seek safer waters, and if possible, to get back to the shelter of a lee coast, or better still, to find a harbour.

The other two boats were much closer to home when they too turned round, warned by the same messages. Georgie knew what they had done and guessed that they would probably make it back before the storm hit, even if it speeded up, but he knew that it would be touch and go for *Quo*. Georgie was paying the price for being in the lead; ahead of the pack. Great place to be most of the time, but always the most exposed place when things went wrong. In any patrol, the man on point was usually the first to be taken out.

When a crew feel the real threat of bad weather, they know what to do, and they do it as well as they can. But they are mere men, and they are up against a much greater force. The *Quo* crew were not afraid, but they were anxious, and their main concern was not for themselves but for their families, and especially for their children. The journey back would take well over 36 hours and although the first hours were easy enough, things began to change as Kate caught them up.

As time passed, and they got nearer to safety, the swell increased to a level of discomfort which disturbed the seasoned crew and threatened their boat. It came from behind most of the time which was tolerable, but occasionally it altered and came in from the side, which was much more dangerous. Kate was playing with them. The pitching motion, as *Quo* slid down one huge wave front before climbing up the next one, was violent and sickening, but the rolling motion, when the swell came from the side was, quite simply, utterly frightening.

Surfing down a steep wave front could put the bow under, but boats could recover from that. A severe rolling motion could easily roll a boat completely over and make it turn turtle, as it showed its hull to the heavens and drowned its crew as it trapped them beneath the submerged deck, or flung them off into the boiling sea.

Quo's last hour in the storm was the worst. They were so near, yet so far. So close to safety, but they all knew, a miss is as good as a mile. Georgie got his boat to within touching distance of the sheltered waters beyond the headland and he dared to believe that they were going to be safe.

Kate was happy for him to do that, to almost make it, before failing. That was all part of the fun. To lead him to believe that he was almost there, then to simply say no. Almost there, is not good enough when lives are at stake. Georgie was feeling confident of survival when he left the bridge under Scouser's control, while he went out to check the forward hatches for damage. He waited in the shelter of the wheelhouse until the rolling reduced with a shift in the wind, and then he clipped-on and made his way forward. She waited until Georgie had unclipped his lifeline for a second, to move across the gap in the rails, then she hit him with 16 tons of icy water.

He was swept off like a feather in a gale. Nobody saw him go, he just wasn't there anymore. Kate kept him under with enough force to overcome the buoyancy of his life jacket. He didn't drown, he died because his heart stopped. The sudden shock completely destroyed his atrial rhythm. Sometimes stress just makes a heartbeat faster, sometimes it stops it dead. He knew it was the end as soon as he hit the icy water and he died wondering how his children would cope with their lives without him. Eventually Kate let him go and the jacket shot him to the surface. When Georgie popped up the crew dragged him in with a boat hook and they did their best to revive him, but they knew he had gone.

For the men who had known him so well, the numbness began and disbelief swept all rational thoughts away. Kate decided to spare the boat and the rest of the crew, she was happy with one life, and she left the scene of her game with a feeling of satisfaction. Destruction, surely being the whole purpose of a storm. Snuff out a man's life and prove who really masters the deep sea.

She moved north-eastwards, towards the Faeroes, and as she finally let the circling winds destroy her pressure cell completely, she simply ceased to exist, but it was all too late for Georgie.

The radio message from *Quo* was brutally brief. Shock hit home across the Far Isles immediately, and gradually the whole nation became aware of the loss, as evening news bulletins carried the story. It wasn't the top report, even in Scotland. Home-rule politics and the royal family grabbed the headlines with equal predictability. The loss of a Far Isles fisherman in a storm at sea was a minor story in comparison to those generated by outraged politicians and aberrant royals. Georgie's death was reported almost as if it were to be expected in such severe weather at sea. He wasn't even named on the news unlike the politicians and the royals were.

A deep feeling of sadness spread across all the islands. The loss of a crewman was like a pit disaster in a mining community. People were numbed into deep, deep silent grief. At the family's request there would be no rock music at the funeral, what the boys did at the wake was up to them, but the funeral was to be respectful.

Funerals are always well attended in the islands and people came from the whole chain. They sailed over from every island in the archipelago and drove over causeways to reach the service. Georgie's young cousin from Vanich, was bringing her new baby who he was never going to see, and boats packed the small harbour as crews came to pay their respects.

The three men he sailed with on that day carried Georgie to his rest, the fourth shoulder being Brogan's. As they climbed the steps to the chapel two of them tripped, Brogan took the whole weight of the casket for a second. The boys muttered their thanks. Brogan said it wasn't the first time he'd had to hold Georgie up, but it was probably going to be the last. The realisation of what he had said hit all four of them and tears streamed down the faces of each pallbearer as then entered the chapel. Four tough men reduced to tears by the loss of their friend.

When the service was over and the men moved forward to lift the coffin Brogan paused. Such was the impact of his stillness that everyone else in the chapel stood fast. Eyes moved towards him. He stood, taller and bigger than the rest, staring at the congregation, one hand resting gently upon the coffin. After a few seconds, the unbearable silence was broken by Brogan's gentle voice, singing:

He sang the opening line from Quo's iconic Live Aid opener, slowly and quietly, then Brogan took a deep breath and finished the job with the rest of the song.

Even Georgie's wife, who wanted a rock-free ceremony, was moved to tears by Brogan's gesture and tears rolled down her cheeks as she sang the lines again, along with everyone else. The boys carried him out to place him in the ground, and everyone picked up the distant sound of Rescue 119 as it hovered in respect, a mile out, rock steady at 600 feet. It would stay there until the right moment and then it would fly over the grave slowly, trailing the Far Isles banner from its winch and then slowly disappear into the west, where Kate had played her terrible game.

Scouser didn't do a 'walk on', but for years afterwards he wondered if he should have done one, and his uncertainty meant that he never tried to emulate Gerry Marsden again, even when he finally got to a home game at Anfield, where he missed both goals because he was thinking about Georgie with tears blurring his vision as the crowd sang their famous song.

Chapter 5

Collateral Damage

For mainlanders, the usual experience of population movement would be the daily commute, and perhaps the annual holiday would provide their only experience of long-distance mass population shifts. Islanders had a rather different experience of population movement, for life on the islands is inextricably linked to people moving about for reasons which have nothing to do with the daily journey to work. Island life necessarily involves isolation and uncertainty, and both factors mitigate against stability. Islanders don't really commute, but they had never been exactly static either.

The spirit of movement had been embedded in island life ever since the earliest settlers landed there. Those early inhabitants inherited the travelling gene from their pre-human ancestors, who wandered about the forests and plains of their original homelands. Eager to explore, the early tribes of hominids spread out to satisfy their natural curiosity, and, as numbers grew, migration became essential to find new hunting grounds and, eventually, fertile soils to farm, once they had mastered the skills of cultivation. The great migrations out of Africa, as Homo Habilis searched for new territory and overcame the Neanderthals in Europe, really set the trend for the human wanderlust, which has never left our collective psyche.

Mass movements are often prompted by necessity. Powerful factors such as war, famine or genocide drive people to seek safety in other places. These island communities suffered their two greatest migrations due to forces beyond their control: one, when the clearances took place and thousands were simply left with nowhere to live; the other when crop failures caused famine and migration was the only way to avoid starvation.

Huge movements don't take place any more, but on a smaller scale the steady loss of young people from the Far Isles became a regular feature of their population dynamics a century ago. It had more to do with a desire to seek better opportunities than anything else, and most leavers didn't return, although they spent the rest of their lives wishing they could.

Scattered families treated reunions on the islands very seriously. They normally planned the next event before the last event was even completed. They talked about 'doing it again' and preliminary dates were put in diaries, promises were given, and plans were made in family groups, to secure the savings necessary to pay for flights and accommodation. The next reunion would mark another passage of time, more grey hairs, more signs of time passing etched on every face, and perhaps they would have to remember someone departed. The changes which time would inevitably bring would guarantee that the next reunion would be less satisfactory than the previous one. There would be more hurt, more damage, more obvious impact of the human changes wrought by time passing.

Sometimes the reunions were huge affairs known as 'Gatherings'. They usually happened every 10 years and the march of time had a dramatic impact on people who hadn't met for a decade. Every reunion required a leader, an instigator, and in the case of Gatherings, an entire committee. The organisation of the tragic reunion at Camas Floe, modest though it was, was no exception. It was instigated by Roddy McKinnon, a successful crofter and proud family man of the islands.

Roddy was in the final years of his long life, and he was determined to bring his family together one last time before he passed. They had grown apart since leaving the Far Isles, driven by the ambition to make new lives across the water.

On the fateful day, he knew that something dangerous was coming because of the colour of the sky and the shape of the clouds during the early morning. In all his time he had never seen such a dawn, and he had never sensed so much threat in the skies above his croft. He had lived for almost 100 years but had never seen anything quite like the combination of colours in the sunrise, nor had early morning clouds looked quite so massive and powerful. He felt afraid of what was about to happen, uncertain about the detail, but absolutely certain about the implications. He just kept thinking: 'It looks like we are in for a Biblical storm'.

He was well used to stormy weather but this one was going to be different. He feared that nowhere would be safe and that therefore, everyone would be at risk. He phoned his daughter, who, thanks to him, was enjoying the family reunion 20 miles away across the causeway, and told her not to visit him later that day as she had planned to do.

She was going to bring all the grandchildren for a picnic by the small beach which she had played on as a child. The sand was coarse and clean and the yellow grains were mixed with shell debris which gave it a magically mottled colour. The coarse sand squeaked with every footfall and she knew the kids would be fascinated. As a child she had called them the talking sands; her brother had called them the squeaky sands. She wondered what her children would call them.

He was looking forward to the picnic; his grandchildren meant more to him than anyone realised. They were the future and he was proud that his life would continue in them. The reunion on the little beach would be a wonderful time to remember for him, and perhaps in time, for them too.

But the sky made him tell her to stay where she was, to close the shutters and sit tight. He told her that he just knew a very bad storm was coming, one like she had never seen before. She took him at his word. He was clearly alarmed. He would not have cancelled the party with the kids for anything. While she set about convincing her family of the danger approaching them from the sea, the line went dead as the first freak gusts brought a pole down on the most exposed section of the main causeway.

Communications were failing across the whole archipelago and soon after they had been abruptly forced to finish their conversation, all hope of further contact was lost forever, unbeknownst to either of them. They were never to see each other alive again. The storm saw to that.

He was killed when the old oak tree, one of less than a dozen left on the island, came through the roof and crushed him beneath its heavy branches. He was already sheltering beneath the stone stairs but the tree weighed over six tons and it simply crushed the flagstone steps down on top of him. His was not the only death.

Three experienced local fishermen were swept away as their boat was overturned by a sudden swell between the sandy islands just off the western shore. It's unmanned remains drifted around in the storm and eventually foundered on the rocky north shore, rapidly breaking up in the stormy swell. The ribs were exposed at low tide every day for the next five years before more winter storms finally dispersed them forever. The engine was destined to remain on the sea bed for almost 50 years, slowly rusting away and attracting its own unique collection of marine life. The site would become go-to area for amateur scuba divers, but the bodies of the fishermen were never recovered.

Three climbers had managed two of the three island Corbett's the day before the storm broke. It had been a perfect walking day and it convinced them that it was worth going for the third top after one more night under canvas. They had walked the first two, but decided to challenge themselves with a rock-climbing ascent of the final peak. They deliberately made an early start on their final day, and after a quick breakfast of cereal bars and coffee they took the short walk to the foot of the infamous rock wall which presented the most difficult route to the top. It was the only E3 on the Far Isles and a prize well worth struggling for.

It was possible to simply walk up to the summit by a well-worn sheep track, but climbers would always go for the challenge of a rock face if they could, and this one was irresistible. They made good progress until the weather changed very suddenly. Neither of them had checked the weather forecast before they left their tent that morning because the forecast was good when they listened to the BBC News on the previous evening. They knew a storm was due later the following day but they expected their final climbing day to be fine and calm, and their climb did begin in dry, calm, sunny conditions.

It all seemed to change very quickly as the storm front began to move over the islands. The darkening skies and the quickening rush of wind across the rock face alarmed them both as they reached the start of the third pitch. They were over halfway up the face. It would be quicker to make for the top rather than climbing down. They both cursed themselves for not bringing sufficient equipment to abseil off the face. Within 10 minutes they were being buffeted uncomfortably, and after 20 minutes the first man was lifted clean off the rock.

He yelled an unheard cry of alarm as he lost his four points of contact and plunged down onto the head of his companion. They both accelerated towards the scree slope below, ripping out the pitons which secured their ropes, leaving them free to the forces of gravity.

They hadn't reached terminal velocity by the time they hit the scree slope below the crag, but they were going fast enough for the first contact to be fatal. It took less than seven seconds for their lives to be claimed by the storm. Their bodies were found four days later by an RAF helicopter search team.

Two climbers, three fishermen and one old farmer. It was a tragic enough toll, but the truly Shakespearian tragedy involved two other generations of the family whom the old man had reunited. Their kin folk had lived on the islands for centuries. The old farmer was seventh generation, the others were eighth and ninth. They were meeting up for a reconciliation gathering. A reunion to heal, as much as to reacquaint.

Tensions had developed over trivial things, and the grandfather wanted, as he put it, to 'calm the waters' and get the family together again. He felt that it was his duty to try, expecting not to live much longer himself. He believed that a happy family gathering and the revival of good relationships could be his legacy. He booked them all into his holiday let on the Atlantic coast by the hamlet of Camas Floe. He wouldn't charge them of course and he was happy to forego the £1,000 loss of a week's holiday rental.

He never squandered money, Islanders never did, but he felt that this was a good investment. He intended to be there when they arrived, show them the ropes, then leave them to it. They knew where his farm was and they could visit him there during their stay, if they wanted to do so. He desperately hoped that they would.

The offer of the gathering was gratefully accepted by all parties; they all sensed the need for re-bonding. Time had driven their lives in different directions. The separation was more accidental than deliberate. Perhaps spending time together, back on the island homeland would be good for them all.

Despite the old man's good intentions, the reunion resulted in precisely the opposite of his best-laid plans. It all began so well, and there was every chance of success, initially. The whole adventure was pleasing everyone; the long journeys were comfortable and exciting for the children and the ferry crossings were perfect.

But the waters were literally to prove anything but calm, and the family was to be torn apart in a most brutal manner, simply by the weather. Irony worthy of the Bard: honourable intentions, within touching distance of a triumphant finale, but resulting in an ultimately tragic outcome.

The old man's holiday house overlooked the Atlantic in a place where there was no shelter offshore. No islands or even sand banks, just the ocean from there to Newfoundland. Unusually, it was a two-storey building with thick stone walls and a recently renovated heavy flagstone roof. All the other buildings in the hamlet were single storey with thatched roofs. Two of them were recently rethatched by a young local man from Lewis who had developed a successful business restoring croft cottages for incomers, but the other four were in a sorry state and they were be likely to blown off in the next big storm. No such problem for the two-storey cottage. The flagstone roof would resist anything that nature could throw at it.

Well maintained, with close-cropped grass surrounding it and a distant perimeter wall which was even older than the house itself, the holiday home gave a feeling of strength and security to visitors and the setting was idyllic.

He was proud of it in a modest kind of way. Only he knew how much work he had put into the ancient croft 10 years earlier when he was already in his eighties. Only he knew how much it meant to him that the income from letting the accommodation, and the capital value it accrued, meant that, despite a lifetime of poverty, he would die being able to leave some sort of financial legacy to his children. It wouldn't be much, but it meant the world to him, simply to be able to leave them something. He had spent most of his life never believing that he would be able to, and nobody ever knew what anguish that caused him. To him it would have been a final failure in a life he felt less than happy with.

Poverty was draining, and passing it on to your children as part of your legacy was guaranteed to break a man's spirit in his final days of reckoning. For most of the islanders living hand-to-mouth became such a familiar process that poor people, like him felt like failures. Those feelings were exacerbated increasingly by the TV programmes which celebrated success and celebrity, usually featuring people who were so lightweight that the mere idea of their being rich and famous offended the hardworking crofter and weather-beaten fisherman in equal measure.

For them, self-esteem did not exist. They hid their lack of self-confidence behind a façade of artificial islander personality, lapsing into the Gaelic whenever they needed to retreat into their islander shells. They imagined ending their lives without leaving any legacy for their children, other than a history of unrewarded toil. They knew that their children would leave the Far Isles and seek comfort in other places. Once they had made the final move across the water, their children could end up on the other side of the world; many of them did. They feared that with their children gone, even their fields would be overgrown with weeds within a year of their death, and their boats would rot, unwanted at the quayside.

For old Roddy, there was a chance that he would at least leave something more than a useless croft to his children. If his holiday let brought enough income, he could easily buy another derelict cottage and leave one to each of them. Roddy began to develop the idea of a minor property empire in his eighties. 'Better late than never,' he used to tell his friends.

Once he had renovated the old cottage and established the holiday let, he thought the legacy it provided would be the thing that he would be most proud of when he breathed his last breath of the island's air.

Even the worst storms the Atlantic could throw at the cottage had no impact whatsoever. In fact, on stormy days he would go over there, go down to the shingle beach to watch the breakers crashing in and enjoy the continual rain of salty spray lashing into his face. The more it blew the more he grinned.

'Man versus nature and man wins again!' he used to shout out loud.

It was a beautiful day when they all arrived and the grandchildren ran around excitedly while the adults greeted each other, betraying not a trace of the difficulties which had developed over the years. He welcomed them and explained how everything worked and they all enjoyed a drink and the shortbread he had made the day before. The get-together was going well as the three generations gathered and talked, played and remembered old times. The old man was pleased that his idea was going to plan, and eventually left them to it and made the short trip across the causeways to his real home, 20 miles away. He smiled all the way home.

His son Tom and daughter Susan were getting on well as he drove out onto the narrow track, and their partners Christina and Richard soon put any animosity behind them, and they all enjoyed seeing the five children playing so well together. Ben was just five, Jake seven, Herbie nine and the twin girls had just had their 12th birthday. They remembered each other well enough but hadn't met properly for over two years; they enjoyed the reunion even more than the adults. The girls made a big fuss of Ben and he revelled in their attention.

Herbie was happy to see his little brother blossoming with his new-found admirers, but Jake felt left out, as middle children usually do. He coped with it well enough though, and tried to interrupt when he could think of something good to say. It didn't always work and Herbie was quick to eliminate any social progress Jake made; he was keen to develop a relationship with the twins and didn't want any competition from Jake to dilute his charm offensive. Ben was a different matter; he was no threat because he was just cute.

The old man was home when the first hint of the storm was given in the shipping forecast. He felt sorry for the family and hoped the weather didn't ruin their stay. In persistent bad weather there wasn't much to do on the island. Hunkering down was an inevitable part of life if you lived there, but it wasn't really what anyone went on holiday for, certainly not for days on end. The tourist board tried to hide the threat of bad weather by claiming that 'if you don't like the weather, don't worry, it changes three times a day'.

All the adults were islanders and no strangers to rough weather. They thought that they were well prepared for any storm, safe in the knowledge that the building was strong enough to shelter them from any gale, and that the sea was a sufficient distance away to offer no threat. This was the 100-year storm though, and it might well have been the 1,000-year storm for that matter. The old man phoned the croft when he saw the glowering sky and gave his daughter the warning. They were cut off after she said, 'OK' but before he was able to answer her question, 'Why?'

The wires across the causeway were the first to be cut as the first tree falls began to hit lines all over the island. An old pine was uprooted on the west side of the crossing and took the telegraph poll down with it, blocking the causeway as well as cutting off communications. The electrical power failed just after communications went dead as the same series of tree falls began to cut powerlines and short-out substations across the archipelago.

Things became immediately worrying for everyone at the croft: no phone; no light; a rising gale rattling the building; things flying about outside in the lashing torrents of rain. Loud, unfamiliar sounds dominating everything. Their world had changed so suddenly and they were bewildered.

An hour later, when the storm surge at high tide pushed the sea over the shingle beach and through the dunes, the sandy hills were simply swept aside and the Atlantic approached the croft at running pace. The sea went easily over the perimeter wall and moved quickly up to the house itself. It swilled relentlessly against the walls of the cottage and began to seek out the weaknesses; the Atlantic wanted to see what it was like inside. Soon water was pouring in around the door and flooding the downstairs rooms with three inches of salty water. It all seemed to be happening very quickly and it became even more threatening when the door was washed open and the ocean simply poured in. The water was soon two feet deep in all the ground floor rooms. It ebbed and flowed with each thundering wave. It was as if each room was a sea, with its own waves and tides, the cold water was swirling around and moving furniture so that it was impossible for even the adults to stand safely.

Their whole world had dramatically and suddenly changed. The real possibility of drowning inside the house, in the lounge or in the kitchen, frightened all of them. In the darkness they could hardly see or hear each other but they quickly sought refuge upstairs, parents dragging children, utter panic only just avoided. The children were crying and the adults were scared. The house shook with each impact and there seemed to be a real danger of it collapsing around them. If that were to happen, they would surely all die in a mixture of swirling sea water and stone. The sound of the sea itself came not from the far shore, but from the very foot of their stairs. The enemy was inside the house and the house was pitch dark.

It wasn't Vikings or Redcoats this time, it was the sea which had come to threaten them. Their holiday home, their place of warmth and safety had been transformed in minutes into a cauldron of horror. The very rooms in which the humans sat and ate, talked and played, became places where they could easily die. They could die in their own house as surely as they could die in the deep Atlantic if their boat had overturned.

The adults argued about the next steps and one half of the family decided to make a dash for it when the lull occurred. There was always supposed to be a calmer moment as the eye of the storm passed over you. A brief window of opportunity before the second half of the tempest came in and renewed the battering onslaught. Sometimes the second part was even worse than the first.

Tom and Christina decided to go and offered to take others with them as they and their two children made their escape. Susan and Richard refused to move. Susan's father had phoned with the warning about the storm and told her to close the shutters and stay put. She told him she would and felt honour bound to do what she had promised. She feared taking the three young boys outside anyway, imagining that they could be literally blown away or washed into the Atlantic by the waves around the house. The wind was certainly irresistible but the real threat was not the wind, it was the sea. Little Ben wouldn't stand a chance and even though Jake and Herbie were good swimmers there was a world of difference between the local pool and the boiling sea which had invaded their cottage.

Tom, his wife and their twin girls feared that their home was going to be swept away and they took the gamble. If they had stayed in their wave-battered house they would certainly have survived. Two days later the house still stood and the upstairs rooms had proved to be a safe refuge for the five who remained throughout the tempest. Susan and Richard weathered the storm with their three boys. Tom and Christina made a different choice, the wrong one as it turned out, but they weren't to know that. That's the whole point about gambling: you never know what the result will be. They took their gamble and they lost.

They waited for the lull when the waves seemed to be breaking on the edge of the garden rather than inside the house itself, and the four of them made a dash for their 4x4. The car had been sheltered enough inside the large garage which was slightly higher than the house. The sturdy doors faced away from the sea and they had not given way. The seawater was two feet deep inside the garage but the car showed no signs of damage. It had a wading depth of three feet and a snorkel extension for the air intake. If anything could weather this particular storm it was their 4x4. It started first time and they all climbed in, Tom leaving the door open as they drove off into the night.

At first, they made good progress, swiftly and safely away from the house through the axel-deep choppy water and onto slightly higher ground. They were just a few yards from the permanent safety of a rocky hill, but as they crossed a small causeway by a low crossroads, a single huge wave appeared out of the darkness and swept them off the road and into a flooded saltmarsh. The car overturned in less than five seconds. Everyone was trapped inside and the outcome was sadly inevitable. Struggling with seatbelts, hanging upside down in the cold dark waves, two generations drowned, struggling inside an Audi SUV, overturned in five feet of stormy water.

The five who remained in the house spent almost 15 hours in an upstairs bedroom; cold, wet, and scared to death. The parents hugged their three children the whole time and kept promising that everything would be alright. For them, it was. For the rest of the family, it wasn't. The sea eventually opened the car up and the lifeless bodies were washed around, sadly scattered and separated from each other in death. The fatal causeway was protected, after the storm, by a stout stone wall to reduce the risk of anything being swept off it again, but it was too late to save the five, and will it probably not be required to protect anyone else from the same fate for 100 years to come.

The storm claimed 10 lives altogether and stories about what had happened hit newsrooms around the world. It was the highest number of fatalities in a single storm on the Far Isles in recent history, and it didn't even involve the loss of any large ships, which would have explained a large-scale loss of life. These 10 victims were caught out in different ways by separate events, exacting identical outcomes. The drowning of the family group was the biggest and most tragic single event caused by the big storm and it dominated the headlines. The other losses: the three fishermen, the old farmer and two climbers trapped on an exposed face on the highest mountain on the isles, were all devastating, but it was the family's fate which shook the island community to its core.

It took the coastguard helicopter a whole day to discover all four bodies. They had drifted far apart once the sea opened the car, pulled out the drowned passengers and swept them away. Somehow the layers of tragedy were compounded by the isolation of the victims in their deaths. Two children and their parents. Even the twins were separated, even they could not hold on to each other in that violent tempest. The place where the tragedy happened was totally unremarkable, and for the next 100 years it would be completely safe. You could drive past it without noticing anything. The sea wasn't even close by. There isn't enough water in the marsh to drown an unwanted kitten let alone a much-loved family of four, strong and healthy humans who had grown up knowing the Far Isles, and until then, coped with everything thrown at them by nature, wherever they had lived. But if you know what happened on that day, you will know that the fiercest sea can reach the spot very quickly if it wants to, and if anyone is around when it decides to reclaim this place, they will probably drown too.

The three generations were buried together in a lonely graveyard within sight of the ocean. They brought the old man over from his farm so that he could lay with the other two generations. Their spirits hear the constant breaking of waves on the shingle beach nearby, and feel the winter spray as the big rollers crash in. There are always flowers on the graves, whatever time of year, but nobody ever sees anyone placing them there. It's almost as if they appear by magic.

The three fishermen are remembered by a carved stone plinth on the dockside close to where they died. The dock is hardly ever used now due to the fishing restrictions imposed by the EU, and the granite cobbles already have weeds growing in gaps between the stones. The plinth is used by gulls as a convenient perch. They will fly off if you visit there but they will reclaim the slab as soon as you leave.

A local woman cleans the memorial every few days to clear the seagull droppings from the engraving, leaving the men's name clear for anyone to see.

The climbing club, which was home for the two young rock athletes, visited the site of their fall a few months after the storm. They cemented a ceramic plaque close to the point where the final, failing piton sprang loose from the crack in the ancient gneiss, unable to withstand the pull of two 12 stone men, pushed outwards by a 200-mile-an-hour gust. The plaque was eased off the face by ice expanding in the gap behind during the following winter, and it fell, like the climbers had, 300 feet onto the screes below. It shattered into pieces just like they had, but nobody collected the pieces of plaque and put them in a body bag, and so they remain there, mingled with the frost-shattered rock debris which has fallen regularly off the face ever since the end of the last ice age, 10,000 years before. Perhaps mingled with the scree where the young men died was a more appropriate place for their memorial, rather than being stuck on the rock face where they had failed to hang on.

The old farmer is remembered every day by his daughter. She had the farmhouse rebuilt and she moved into it with Richard and their three sons. They developed a campsite on the farm with four hookups for motorhomes on the cobbled farmyard and even rebuilt the outbuildings to house the chemical toilets. It almost looked perfect, but there was no oak tree. Susan insisted upon its removal, and there was no sign of even a stump or root. She knows that her father's phone call had saved her life and the lives of her husband and children. Without that wise warning they would surely have left the wave-battered cottage and taken the gamble with the others. Had she taken the gamble there would have been nine bodies drifting around the bay for the coastguards to retrieve.

The great storm had a wide-ranging impact, great storms always do. Shorelines were rearranged here and there, especially the sand and shingle ones. Even the hard cliffs gave up a bit of territory to the battering waves and new blocks of granite and gneiss litter the foot of the tall sea cliffs that only get close examination from the paddlers. Vegetation was altered and whole areas of dune and machair were obliterated. Buildings were extensively damaged and some would never be rebuilt while others had new roofs fitted and windows replaced as they were returned to use. The signs of refurbishment betray the story of wind damage long after the owners have made the repairs and either moved back inside or sold the property on.

In various places the subsequent visitor will see abandoned generators, the size of small cargo containers, rusting in the corner of fields close to the road. They provided power for the local communities in the weeks after the big storm, before the authorities repaired miles of torn-out cabling and splintered poles. Lifesavers at the time, the generators were of no use in the normal times which eventually returned after months of salvage and repair, and they were too big and heavy to warrant commercial relocation. By the time generators would be needed again, a century would have passed, and these monsters would simply be rust stains on the heather.

But the scars which will not heal are those left by the loss of human life and in these always beautiful, and often calm and calming places, there will always be the lurking danger of isobars, pressure differences, the laws of physics and the sudden emergence of the oldest enemy of all: the deadly and utterly irresistible teamwork of wind and wave. Each tempest adds a footnote to the human history of the Far Isles and shapes the people even more than it shapes the physical environment, but, for most people, human memory is short because it has to be, otherwise nobody would ever take a risk. When the next great storm arrives, as it surely will, and if there are still humans on the islands, which there surely will be, people will be shocked beyond measure by the level of destruction, and some of them will probably make the wrong decision.

In the aftermath of a great storm, the Far Isles were a slightly different place, but Susan never fails to take her boys down to the small beach by the farmhouse where she used to play with her brother, and where the five children should have played with their grandfather before nature intervened so dramatically and changed lives forever.

Chapter 6

Catching Flies

On the wild, west coast of the Isles a small group of abandoned Blackhouses were carefully restored in the tight, steep coastal ravine where they were built 300 years before. Unlike the low sand and shingle machair coast with its fragile dune belt, this section was rugged granite with 100-foot cliffs and hundreds of rocky islets. This part of the island faced the Atlantic, seemingly without fear. Unlike the sand shores, which were at the mercy of storms, these solid, rocky cliffs didn't budge, even in the strongest storms. If you found a sheltered place to build a home here, you would never have to move it.

Fish abounded offshore and sea birds teemed around the cliff ledges, ever seeking safe nesting sites with an ever-wary eye for skua. The guillemot brought twitchers to the coast every year but it was the sheer volume of birds which pleased the tourists. The northern tidal marshes provided the landing grounds for migrant birds while the steep rocky cliffs provided the safest homes for their summer residences. Species abounded and there were some nesting gannets, but not as many as before. They once were numerous here but constant harvesting by the local people had reduced their numbers and made the place less safe for the guga than the smaller offshore islands.

The Blackhouse village had housed a simple fishing community and provided very basic warmth and shelter in the steep ravine which, made walking difficult but kept the storm winds out. The thatched roofs were safe from the wind there and, once they were drawn out of the water, the precious boats were too. The homes were without electricity, running water or internal sanitation, but the people had never had any of those luxuries so they didn't miss them.

The small settlement was known as Crogagan, literally the glove which held them safely in its palm. It was well protected by the steep little coastal valley it nestled in, and the community thrived for longer than any other Blackhouse village in the Far Isles. Safety and comfort are only ever relative, and the Black Houses were no exception to that rule. Safe enough to shelter families in bleak circumstances but inside they were black with the soot from over 200 years of peat fires and the smoke, which lingered in the homes and shortened the lives of the inhabitants by contaminating their lungs. The very fires which they longed to sit beside after they battled the Atlantic for fish, or came home from working their small storm-battered cultivated hillside strips for potatoes, were shortening their lives. For them, the peat smoke threatened their wellbeing with far more certainty than the regular storms which they endured at sea or on the exposed hills.

Blackhouses were far from romantic places and the people of Crogagan were pleased enough to abandon them when the new stone cottages were built by the

Laird, along the main road by the top of their sheltered valley. The new houses had running water and electricity, bathrooms and flushing toilets, slate roofs, which would never harbour vermin, and tall solid chimneys. The stacks ventilated every fireplace and took all the peat smoke outside, leaving healthy air inside for the occupants to breathe.

There was little tourism when the villagers moved out of their black houses into the new ones, but there was sufficient love for the old village that everyone pleaded with the Laird to preserve them as a memory of how things used to be. When tourism boomed, years later, the Crogagan community reaped the benefits of the unique Blackhouse village, as it attracted visitors from around the world.

At first the ancient cottages appealed to the tourists even in their ruined form. The Laird quickly realised that that they would be an even bigger source of income if they were restored and put to use. He decided to preserve and restore every building before the storms destroyed their thatched roofs and eventually caused even their stout stone walls to crumble. The work was done by local builders and took almost four years. The Laird gained funding for the project, so money wasn't the problem, but there were too few local craftsmen to complete all the restorations quickly.

The biggest challenge was the thatching; a lost art on the islands. A team was brought in from the Cotswolds and they soon adapted the island's supply of reeds to provide a suitable thatching material. One of the team, a young man from Chipping Camden, enjoyed his time at Crogagan so much that he settled on the island and married a local girl. He became well-known as Thatcher John and was in constant demand across the archipelago, repairing the roofs of old croft houses, which were in great demand as holiday homes.

When the work was finally completed, the restored village of Crogagan immediately became an even bigger tourist attraction. It provided very welcome employment opportunities to the still-isolated new community which had grown up along the island's perimeter road. Local people prepared craft items for the shop and foodstuffs to sustain visitors. Other locals found employment cleaning and maintaining the village facilities and others provided service in the shop and café.

Some of the restored houses served as holiday lets and some as museum pieces, but one had been cleverly converted into the small café which served warm drinks and light refreshments. The regular coach tours around the islands called in for breakfast, lunch and afternoon tea, and the small room filled up quickly, with braver souls accepting the need to sit outside, even braving the rain and the midges.

The café was always busy, right from the start and the site manager manned it with a mixture of local high school students and temporary agency staff from all over Europe. The whole place worked well. Every visitor left with a smile and kind words for the staff, and most people said they felt some kind of magic in the place, as if the spirits of the ancestors were still around.

The café was christened 'munchies' by the local kids, who picked up the slang from Sunday newspaper magazine stories about teenage drug addiction, which they devoured with secret interest. Knowing the slang was as close as the local kids got to illegal substances, but they heard rumours about the kids from the big town, where the ferry called, who were rumoured to be having a go. They thought that they would find out when they went to big school. They all secretly feared the inevitable move to the big school because it would put them at the mercy of the townies.

Lachlan Maguire was 17 and he lived in one of the stone farmhouses close to the village of New Crogagan. As a sixth former at the college, 30 miles across the island, he was as at home in the capital as he was in Crogagan. By local standards he travelled a lot and was regarded by the other children in Crogagan as experienced and worldly wise.

When he had first travelled across the island to the big school, he was just 11 years old. His local primary had 12 pupils altogether and he had walked there in minutes across a field and a stream before crossing the quiet passing-place road which led to the school gate. He enjoyed six happy years there. Big school was a different matter entirely. It meant an early start and a late finish, with a 60-mile round trip on a coach every day; lots of new people to contend with, and, of course, the townies.

Lachlan was descended from Solas people. His parents both came from there and moved north in the islands when they had the chance of a house and a croft.

Like his father he was big; like his mother he was wise. Their house was warm and safe, a happy place where Lachlan and his younger brother, Jake, grew up together. His parents knew that starting high school marked a very big change in their eldest son's life, but they knew he would cope, he always did; he always would. It would take something very serious indeed to knock Lachlan off course. He always woke up early, but on his first day at high school he was ready a full hour before the coach was due. He joined two other local kids on the back seat and settled in for the next seven years.

On the first morning of the first day at his new school he was picked out by a group of the most streetwise townies, a gang from the capital itself – tough local kids who were used to dominating. Everyone was wary of them, even some of the teachers. They mocked Lachlan's pleasantness and mimicked his west-coast accent. When the first boy pushed his shoulder hard, Lachlan simply put him on his back. Nobody really saw what happened. One second the bully was prodding and sneering, there was a blur of movement and then the boy was laid out. Flat on his back or, as they say in those parts, he was measuring his length, simple as that.

Lachlan's swift reaction to the bully momentarily put ideas of retaliation into the minds of his friends. The group of watching kids sensed the moment, half hoping for a big fight. The gang considered their options and, for some reason, just backed off.

No boys ever bothered Lachlan for the rest of his time at school; but girls did. His ability to shine in any sport soon made Lachlan the real star of the school. He coped well academically too, and the staff knew they were blessed with a special one. He played everything well: football, rugby, tennis, athletics, but his real party trick was playing table tennis in the recreation area during the many wet lunchtimes. He was so good that he soon learned to play with two bats against two opponents. The two balls pinged back and forth across the net and Lachlan somehow saw both balls separately and moved his arms and wrists quite independently. It was like the best juggling trick you have ever seen but with the pop, pop, pop soundtrack of bat on ball. 'Like a distant machine gun,' said someone, not realising the prophetic significance of the simile.

Lachlan was aware that girls paid him attention. He knew that different girls did it in different ways. Some of them were obvious: squeezing past too close for comfort, unnecessarily hugging him, arm touching, even pretty obvious attempts to get him alone. Others were more interested in him in a kinder more pleasant way but they were still trying to stake a claim.

Lachlan talked about it to his mother all the time. She got to know the girls through his descriptions and they laughed together about things that happened. Only one of the girls really attracted him, Mary Maguire. She shared his surname but they were not related, even distantly. He was a Maguire of Solas, she was a Maguire from Orkney. Like her namesake, she was good at sport and they became good friends, but he didn't ever think that he loved her. He thought of her more as a sort of sister.

When he was 16, Lachlan asked his mother when he would know he had found the right one, when he would know that he was in love. He would always remember what she said: 'You'll just know Lachy, you'll just know.' He knew, as soon as he saw Henrietta Jacobs.

He worked in 'munchies' for the cash and for the chance to meet new people. She was one of the agency girls at the café, part Spanish part Scottish, the daughter of a British diplomat and his aristocratic wife. Henrietta wanted to be called Henry, it was what she was called at school in Barcelona, and more recently at Cambridge University. Lachlan laughed when she introduced herself with her boy's name. She laughed too; she didn't know why. When he said his name, she laughed again and said Lachlan should be replaced by Robbie, because he reminded her of Robert the Bruce. She had no idea why she said it but in private moments she sometimes called him Robbie from that moment on.

They were soon spending all the time they could together; in modern parlance, they had immediately become an item. Their friendship infected the café with a pleasant atmosphere. Everyone noticed something even if they didn't know what it was. Careful observers would notice the way they smiled at each other, how they touched when they passed close together between tables. They were both pleasant to all their customers but the eyes they had for each other were totally different. It wasn't customer care between them, it was much more magical than that.

On a hot day in the middle of August the café windows were wide open and Henry was concerned about the horse flies droning in and bothering the visitors. She mentioned it to Lachlan and he started to catch the flies. Henrietta was amazed; Lachlan just walked round the café and with his hands working independently he simply snatched the flies out of the air. For the rest of the day not a single fly escaped. Soon customers were pointing flies out to him and the whole café applauded every time he caught one, extra loud if he caught one in each hand at the same time.

As they finished the clearing up at the end of their day Henrietta kept laughing about the fly-catching trick. Lachlan told Henry about the table tennis and she laughed and said, 'You mean just like Forrest Gump.'

He'd never heard of Forrest Gump but he laughed anyway; but she knew she'd baffled him; she always knew when she baffled him. He asked his mother about Forrest Gump that night, and she told him the story. He smiled and didn't feel baffled any more.

Henrietta was tall and dark and she wore jewellery and red lipstick. She was quite different to the island girls, far more complete, even than the more sophisticated townies, and she spoke three languages which was one more than Lachlan. She had travelled and learned a lot in her 19 years, but nothing prepared her for the suddenness with which her fears for her future life, her possible romantic experiences, her elusive quest for self-satisfaction, were all swept away. Quite suddenly there was no more uncertainty.

She had barely started worrying about all these things, when, with one simple encounter, all her doubts and fears were allayed. She believed that her future was mapped out. She wondered what her father would say, but the real liberation that Lachlan provided was that she simply didn't care. For the first time in her life, she simply didn't care about anything people might think of her; and that included her father.

Lachlan spoke about Henrietta to his mother whenever he could. One evening, after a long conversation, she finally kissed him on the forehead and said: 'She could be the one Lachy, she could be the one.'

He smiled and said, 'Maybe,' but he didn't mean maybe, he meant yes, because he knew that she was the one.

When the summer ended and Lachlan turned 18, Henrietta took him out for a birthday meal at the Standing Stones restaurant. They floated on air, and the magic of their relationship caused people to stare at their happiness. They strolled out of the Stones linking arms and walked to the deserted beach beyond the machair. They watched the sunset and stayed together on the sand until it rose again. They left their childhood on that beach.

Henrietta stayed on in the village until the end of September, spending the final two weeks lodging in Lachlan's family home. His parents knew that their eldest son had made the biggest decision of his life, and they were content. That their son and his love shared the same bedroom seemed like the most natural thing in the world to them, as it would have done to generations of their ancestors before them. It was just the natural thing to do when two people were right for each other.

The lovers walked the island together, surprising eagles, laughing at boxing hares, smiling at happy seal pups on nearby rocks, ambling along the lonely beaches while the wind blew the coarse sand grains along, like smoke beneath their feet. Henry understood her Robbie and his island home in equal measure, and she loved them both with all her heart.

One day, when Lachlan's family attended a funeral on the next island, Henrietta walked the long beach on her own. She was used to the bright Far Isles sunshine and the clear blue sky, and she was lifted by it. It was the first time she had been alone for some time and she was enjoying the feeling of freedom in a safe and familiar setting. But her confidence was to be challenged and a vulnerability exposed.

Suddenly the sun dimmed behind the only cloud in the sky. Henry shuddered with a premonition, prompted by the sudden contrast of dark and light. What if she was ever left alone here, what if Robbie was taken from her? Overwhelmed with sadness she sobbed and fell to her knees. The blowing sand bit into her soft cheeks and stuck to the tears. It seemed forever before she was composed by the kind spirits of the place. For a few moments the ghosts of the dark island had taken over. They do that sometimes and their pessimism is almost impossible to resist.

Henrietta and Lachlan spent most of their September time making elaborate plans to ensure that their paths crossed as often as possible, until they could set up home together on the island in the years to come. They both had careers in mind but their relationship would work, and they both knew it. Nothing could stop it working. They were smitten; cast in the kind of spell that the islands never let go. However long it took, they would be together and Henrietta would keep the dark forces of the islands at bay. She knew that her role would be to protect Lachy from their malevolence.

When the day of departure came they travelled to the big ferry port in silence. Lachlan's parents took them to the capital, where both the airport and ferry terminal were located. Henrietta had her bags arranged around her in the Land Rover. Lachlan thought they seemed like a barrier between them. His bags were on the roof rack, covered with a simple waterproof sheet in case it rained.

They parted at the dockside with a timid public kiss; they knew it would be some time before they met again. Henrietta had a taxi waiting to take her to the small airfield, where the Islander waited to take seven passengers to Glasgow, and the international links it provided. Henrietta was flying back to Spain and then back to Cambridge for a second year at King's. She was aiming to score a double first in law and languages; nothing less would satisfy her father. Lachlan was off to Edinburgh once the ferry got him to the mainland. He would be taking up his sponsored place on an engineering course.

As the ferry moved out of sight, she called him on his mobile. Her taxi driver was waiting patiently to take her the airport for her flight south, but she wanted one last word. For a moment he was there, then the signal faded. She texted a message and it pinged onto Lachlan's phone. She wanted to know everything about his plans for their time apart and she had carefully built up a clear picture of what he would be doing, but one thing still required explanation, and she had forgotten to ask.

He had had four offers of financial support for his university course and he seemed to favour the one from the Royal Navy. It made sense, him being an islander.

'You never said which sponsorship you decided to take.'

'Did you go for the Navy?'

'Well yes, but it's not exactly the Navy, its–' and the line went dead for a moment.

'RMC … ' She texted again: 'Who?' followed by 'What does that stand for? Royal Mail Company?'

She laughed at her own joke and texted: 'Will I be marrying a postman?' She put in a laughing face emoji with huge tears rolling from its eyes.

He couldn't text anything like as fast as her, and he always got emojis wrong. He managed to text just as the line went dead for the last time, and then his final text arrived on Henrietta's screen. As soon as her screen gave her the message, the phone said: 'No signal – network connection failed'.

Henrietta stood alone at the edge of the taxi rank, clutching the crush rail with one hand and her phone with the other. She knew at that moment, that she would eventually lose him. The sturdy rail gave her more comfort than the phone had. She stared at the message, preserved in neat white-on-green lettering. She stared as if those final electronic words were all she had left of him. She felt the same burning in her throat she had felt that day on the beach when the family funeral had taken Lachy away from her. She knew what it meant. She walked slowly into the shadows so that she could sob quietly in the privacy which dark corners always provided. She remembered those moments on the beach when Lachlan had been at the funeral and she shivered at the memory.

Henrietta marshalled her thoughts and began to make a plan. Perhaps eventually losing Lachlan was written in the stars, but she would make the best of the time they had together and provide them both with enough happy memories to last until eternity. Romantic nonsense perhaps, and that thought did cross the girl's mind, but Henrietta was tough and totally determined, and she knew that she would do it. It wasn't just romantic, it was necessary. It was necessary for both of them, and it was her responsibility to deliver. Wiping her eyes, she bravely welcomed the magnificent site of the ferry receding into a Hebridean sunset. It had developed a bow wave as it passed beyond the disaster site.

There are no better sunsets anywhere in the world, and there was no sadness in the image for her. She knew that bright dawns followed beautiful evenings after the inevitable darkness of the intervening night, and mindful of her duty to play her part in their future together she accepted the sadness.

The text had simply said: 'RMC, Royal Marine Commandos.'

He was being sponsored to study engineering at Edinburgh University by the most elite outfit of troubleshooters in the world. She had heard them called Special Forces. She almost said it out loud: 'Special Forces'. She thought about the title and realised how appropriate it was. He was known as 'the special one' all though school. Perhaps he deserved the chance to show that he really was special, on the toughest world stage of all.

Henrietta knew that her new love would be bittersweet. She thought that perhaps true love always was. The taxi got her to the small airport in less than 10 minutes and after the briefest of boarding formalities, the noisy Islander lifted off for the 40-minute hop to Glasgow International. Henrietta thought she saw the ferry 2,000 feet below her side-window, but it could have been any ship plying between the islands.

She began to think about Spain and Cambridge, her family and her college friends. She put the headphones on and tuned the seat-back radio into the BBC World Service. They were talking about terrorism in sub-Saharan Africa and the abduction of schoolgirls. They mentioned places her father had worked in: Lagos; Kano; Port Harcourt. She remembered her time in Nigeria as a child; they were mostly happy memories. They began to talk about terrorist strongholds. Places she had never heard of at all. Presumably remote villages in the north of the country, close to the desert border. They mentioned a place called Yollumba, and for some reason it made Henrietta shudder.

She switched the radio off and removed the headphones.

Chapter 7

A Kind of Magic

The Beatles sang about imagination

John Lennon knew Durness but he never went to
Vanich, where the windswept area round the old
military camp still looked like MOD property, even
though the army left there years ago. Decent roads with
urban-style street lights, a bright red post box next to a
freshly painted metal and glass telephone box which
still had a working landline and a directory on the shelf,
strange concrete structures scattered across the dunes,
wide parking areas big enough for small convoys of
trucks, and a mini supermarket in the old NAAFI
building with an ATM in the outside wall.

At the edge of the shopping area sat the huge inverted
concrete cone of the water tower, sitting on its six
concrete legs looking like a surrealist statue celebrating
the arrival of an Apollo command module. There were
some scattered stone cottages, but few of them were
permanently occupied, they were mostly second homes
or holiday lets. Almost all the locals lived on the big
estate in much newer houses from the 1950s: 86 three-
bedroomed, breeze-block semis with flat, felted roofs
and metal window frames, all arranged in regular rows
along streets set out in a grid iron pattern . They all had

post and wire fences and an air raid shelter in the back garden. Incongruous interlopers in the wild and beautiful island scenery, the whole collection of buildings simply looked out of place, but this blot on the landscape was home to almost 400 people, including 215 youngsters, for whom it was the only home they had ever known.

Vanich was easily the biggest settlement on its island. Churchill Road, Montgomery Crescent, Gun Point Avenue and Battery Drive were all evidence of the limited imagination possessed by military town planners in the 1950s. Not only the architecture and the road layout, but the very street names themselves were crass. They could have been Norse or Gaelic, or descriptive of the fantastic landscapes and shorelines right next to the base. But no; it is a military town after all so let's think of a few generals and war stuff for the street names, and the job's a good 'un! The kids invented their own versions of the street names and everyone called Battery Drive, Ever Ready Road and Winny had been the local name for Churchill Road for years. Gun Point was Boot Hill and nobody even remembered why Montgomery had become Donny Osmond, but it had.

Regulation may limit behaviour but it never stifles imagination, and creativity is an enduring human passion, especially with the young. But it wasn't regulation which stifled the kids at Vanich, it was recession and declining opportunity which gradually crushed their spirits. It did so even for the most positive and resilient adults and although impact on the youngsters was gradual, it was inevitable. The air of depression even affected the most energetic, most irrepressible young people, and they were the ones who really needed to dream the dreams if the world was to benefit from their potential.

Even they, the very best people on the Far Isles, were in danger of being crushed eventually. Exhausting young ambition was the worst effect of the base's steady decline. The youngsters of Vanich were as vulnerable as the kids in the mining towns when the pits closed or the fishing ports when fleets were mothballed by European regulations. The young were always the cannon fodder of failure in every generation, innocent victims of adult mistakes.

Politicians tried to reinstate missile testing on the ranges but the live firings had moved to Canada and the testing was done on laptops in Cambridge by brilliant young graduates who had been masters of mathematics since the age of three and who honed their skills in English public schools and Oxbridge colleges.

A skeleton staff remained at the base to operate the radar and maintain the airfield, but the interceptor squadron left when the Cold War finished, and although the RAF still dropped in occasionally, they literally never stopped. Roller landings, and that was it. There used to be hundreds of service jobs, now there were just nine.

Despite the closures, Vanich was still the biggest concentration of buildings and population on the islands and it tried its best to prosper; but it was an uphill struggle. There was little chance of new work, and worst affected were always the youngsters. They moved sadly through their last summer holiday, after years of happiness and hope at school, to the hopelessness of unemployment or emigration. A six-week shock to the system which ruined their final summer break.

The stark choice presented itself quite suddenly: stay trapped in a dying community or leave the islands forever. Tough questions for an 18-year-old. They all secretly hoped for a miracle, but miracles didn't happen there often enough. Islanders had to create their own good luck, and that is precisely what the three girls did.

On the edge of town there was a newly painted concrete building, a unit which had seen different uses over the years. It began life as a small engineering shop where REME fitters fabricated curved body panels for test missiles. The work was specialised and skilled but a cost-cutting government closed the facility and the jobs were lost forever.

Leased to a local garage as a body shop until there weren't enough cars left to provide the trade, it was shared by a riding school office and a hairdresser with two tanning booths, but both the businesses went bust and the owners left for the mainland. The unit was available again and it was offered rent-free for six months. The girls decided to take over the lease just as they were leaving sixth-form. Their logic was sensible: why wait for the serendipity of exam results, college places, gap years and job opportunities when they could try starting a business now and share it between them. Controlling their own destiny appealed to them, so they just did it.

Carole, Stephanie and Suzanna had always been great friends. Different, but very comfortable in their differences. They had that easy, enduring relationship which meant that mutual support was always available. They did share tastes to some extent, but it was the way they complemented each other which enabled their relationships to endure, despite their differences. They called it 'unity in diversity', after they heard the phrase in a geography lesson.

They recognised the strength of their relationship, and as it developed, they even gave themselves secret names. In primary they became the three monkeys and would suddenly cover eyes, ears and mouth in perfect synchronisation. After a particularly good series of literature lessons in high school they became the three witches and snarled at each other with clawed fists and screwed-up faces, inevitably ending up in fits of giggles. After a PTA sixties disco, their embarrassment at witnessing mass parent-dancing for the first time was overcome by an introduction to Motown music. They became The Three Degrees and walked the corridors in swaying formation quietly singing 'When will I see you again?' when they headed for different lessons.

They certainly shared a love of music, but they favoured very different styles. They also enjoyed different types of films and literature, and they always disagreed about favourite TV programmes. They liked different food too, but they did share a real love of great baking, and they all loved dreaming dreams, and that was where the real unity existed. Baking and dreaming; a powerful combination.

They shared, above all, a strong wish to do something different; to somehow break away from the shackles of island culture without actually leaving it behind. They argued about who first used the terms: 'Make a difference' and 'Just do it'; but they were convinced it was them, they just couldn't agree which one of them coined the phrases. Whenever someone on the TV talked about making a difference one of the girls would shout, 'Copycat,' and whenever the Nike advert appeared they would say 'Where's our commission?' in unison, and laugh. Their business venture was launched at precisely the time when their self-belief was at its highest. School was over and the daunting challenges of adult life were barely understood. According to them, they just did it.

They decided that their business would be a new sort of place which would become the hub of Vanich. A sort of meeting place café with great coffee, great pastries and great music. They dared to dream this dream and just for a moment there was hope in the small town that something different might just happen. The three girls took a deep breath, signed the lease, and breathed life into their dream. Once they had moved in, they called the place 'Café Pink'.

Café Pink because they got some awful pink paint, free from a local builder and used it to decorate the outside of the unit. It was hardly subtle but neither were the concrete houses and gun emplacements the military had left behind. They agreed that pink was uncomfortably girly but overcame the problem with the sort of cleverness which youngsters are not afraid to risk. In the entrance Carole hung her poster for 'Pink: The Europe Tour' with pictures of the band. Suzanna added an obscure literature-pink justification by putting her copy of Carrie Fisher's book in the display case where they kept the mugs and car stickers they hoped to sell to tourists. Stephanie just accumulated lots of pink stuff like table covers, crockery and cushions. Café Pink came alive and they loved it and hated it at the same time. Hated it because they were embarrassed by the colour; loved it because it was theirs, and because it was a success.

And so the brand emerged: a great meeting place with cakes, coffee, music, and the girls themselves, who agreed, right from the start, never to wear pink, not even underneath. The whole concept was inspired, but it was the girls themselves who were the key to Café Pink's success.

Carole was a rocker. She already had a child. She didn't marry her man but he provided well enough for them both and she decided to hang on to him, at least for now. She got her figure back quickly and visiting tourists were always surprised when she picked up young Callum with an over-the-top 'come to Mummy' outburst. She did it on purpose for effect, and the hardly hidden looks of surprise on strangers' faces buzzed her up.

'Surely such a slim young girl can't have a baby?'

Once she did it when there were no visitors in the café and everyone laughed and said: 'You don't need to do it when there are no strangers in the place Carole, we know you're his mum, we know who his dad is, and we know exactly where you were when you got up the duff.'

Even Carole laughed at that, and blushed a little at the thought of everyone knowing exactly where and when she'd had her one and only romantic moment, on the night of the Year 11 leavers' do. Carole may have made one big mistake in her young life, but she was a survivor, and both she and her son would make great lives for themselves on the islands.

Stephanie was following a more controlled and conventional pathway through her final teenage years, and as she turned 18, she got engaged to her boyfriend, known to everyone as Radar Pete. He was one of the few remaining military personnel on the island, an Oxford physics graduate who was into electronics in a big way. He worked shifts at the NATO radar station which sat at the top of Yonder Hill, spending more time mending fuses and changing light bulbs than actually looking for Russian planes. He made Steph laugh so much inside when he tried to explain how radar worked, that she became expert, at first feigning interest and then deliberately not understanding a word he had said.

She actually understood more about physics than he ever realised, thanks to a gifted science teacher at school who hooked all the kids on astrophysics, but it suited her to keep quiet about it and to use her knowledge to steer her deliberate misunderstanding in the right direction.

Her favourite moment so far was when he tried to convince her that terrain-following radar was so good it could tell a fast-jet pilot which direction the furrows in a ploughed field were arranged. She pretended to think about it and then said, maybe they should fit it to tractors then. He looked puzzled for a moment as though he were seriously considering this new application of radar technology, then he started to laugh and she did too. It was the moment she decided to give it up. Steph saw something in her radar man during that laughing radar moment which made her decide to be serious about Radar Pete; so she grabbed him and went for it. Pete was never so surprised again.

Suzanna had never had a boyfriend, let alone a moment of passion, but she was the driving force of the group, and she provided them with their moral compass. She was a gifted musician with a strong, sensible, faith and a wonderful talent for baking. She played the violin exceptionally well and imagined a future in some great orchestra. She was always well organised and had already signed up for voluntary work in Africa as soon as it could be arranged, maybe even before college. Suzanna's plans were clear: graduate school, do Café Pink, mix college and Africa for five years or so, and then enjoy orchestral life. She just kept telling herself that her plans would work out, convinced that nothing would get in the way. School had worked out well, a college place was secure, Africa would be sorted, and the café would be fun. She was right. Café Pink was an immediate and popular success.

It quickly attracted local adults who chatted over coffee, local kids who enjoyed the Wi-Fi and YouTube screens, and touring visitors who called in to break their journeys along the island chain. They were always most impressed by the quality and range of the amazing cakes, by the energy and infectious friendliness of the three girls and by the great music, which never stopped.

Music was very important to them. They all loved it, but they did favour different genres. Carole never went softer than Status Quo. Her cousin named his boat after the band, but she would have chosen *Megadeth* if it had been hers. It would have been more appropriate for him, as things turned out. He drowned when *Quo* got caught in a sudden storm. Life could sometimes be cheap on the Far Isles. A storm, a wave and dreams get put on hold for a while. Carole was famous for her crazy rocker-dance routines which amused, impressed and terrified onlookers in equal measure. She wondered about tattoos and piercings, but limited her rocker lifestyle to a leather jacket and ripped jeans for now.

Stephanie went with whichever music rocked up in the charts, and she didn't really care, as long as it was 'now' music. Radio 1 was her musical search engine; if a song wasn't on there, it didn't exist. She always knew all the words of hit songs and mouthed them silently when she had her buds stuck in.

Suzanna was the musical problem though. There may have been some compromise between the other two, but Suzanna the fiddle player only did Island Folk and classical violin; she didn't do Pop; she didn't do Rock, and she thought rapping was a lazy way of singing.

They all wanted music to be a big feature of their café. They all wanted it to play continually, and loud, in Café Pink, driving ideas of boring normality out of people's heads through the power of melody and decibels. The problem was deciding exactly what music to play. Their tastes were so different that it could easily have cause a rift. Carole quickly solved the problem. Her one-word solution, with her baby in one hand and smartphone in the other, was: 'Shuffle!'

Radar Pete agreed to rig up some kit linking their three iPhones into one, unpredictable, music generator, on one condition. He insisted on uploading the whole of the 'Music from Big Pink' album. They knew he was a Dylan anorak but didn't really understand the connection apart from the word 'pink' but they agreed to the upload and the very first track selected by the sync machine was from The Band's first album, the track was 'Wheels on fire'.

That lyrical warning of change set the tone for Café Pink, and from then on it shuffled endlessly and played random tracks for 30 seconds then moved on. Nobody knew what would come next. Sometimes all three girls denied ever downloading the music which seeped into every corner of the café.

'Must have downloaded itself,' they said, 'musical magic in this place.'

Queen agreed with their contribution to the soundtrack.

The music became part of the myth. Great company, great coffee, great baking and great music. Café Pink became the place to be, the hub they dreamed of. Extra seating was squeezed in and a covered outside area added by Carole's dad using up decking timber he had lying around, ordered for a serviceman's family who disappeared from the island overnight; posted to Cyprus. A strong wooden roof and patio heaters meant that the 'ootside', as everyone called it, could be used all year round. Only a really bad midge day would ever drive you indoors if you were a dedicated 'ootie'.

Café Pink was going more than well, but then, quite unexpectedly, simple success changed to absolute magic when Jimmy appeared, in a *deus ex-machina* sort of way. He came, literally, out of the blue, and the mood music switched suddenly from bopping shuffle to a love song which nobody had even heard before let alone downloaded.

Jimmy Idan was a Nigerian Scot, a successful chef and restaurateur, travelling the islands for a well-earned break, but he was also looking for inspiration, and he had found plenty. He was taking back design ideas for his dining rooms, some great artwork and even one or two recipes. He was genuinely thrilled to discover proper Tweed, talking endlessly to weavers in their remote, scruffy sheds. He planned to reupholster his flagship Glasgow restaurant with yards of the stuff, banishing the tartan, once and for all.

'Tweed in!' became his mental mantra, he smiled, unable to stop it echoing round his brain. He tried different versions: 'Tweed good, tartan bad'; Tweed not tartan,' ... but none of them stuck, so he had to accept defeat and 'Tweed in,' it remained.

He had marvelled at the landscapes of mountain and moorland, of lowland meadows and reedy marshes, of machair and deserted shorelines. He watched the ever-changing skyscapes and roamed the empty beaches in soft sea breezes, and he had huddled, collar up, against sudden violent storms until he sought the refuge in his 4x4.

Nature had refreshed him; island culture had inspired him. He was on a sort of high, which, for him, was really good news. A staleness and disinterest had been setting in as soon as he became confident that building up his empire and his reputation had been successful. It shouldn't have been like that, but somehow reaching the top was anticlimactic. He recognised the danger of creative exhaustion and he knew that once the entrepreneur became complacent, the best days were over. His tour round the Far Isles had swept aside self-doubt. The invigorating impact of the Far Isles had excited his ambition and he felt re-energised. At least for now, he had been saved from his demons. He was ready to move forward again, to make the next big effort, and he was surprised by the way in which the islands had given him his energy and ambition back.

He even grew to like Vanich despite its incompatibility; it stuck out like a sore thumb, a strange, almost absurd settlement, reflecting crude and completely inappropriate design ideas, in such a beautiful place. But somehow it was appropriate because it represented a genuine use for remote places; they were perfect for high security functions like radar stations, missile ranges and air bases. He had found military sites in remote places before, so in general terms it was no surprise, but he just didn't expect to find one here in the Far Islands. Its functionality was almost stylish, almost Art Deco, almost inspiring, but not quite. There was something about the brutish forms of the buildings and defensive structures which was attractive, but they somehow made people seem uncomfortably out of place. It was as if the structures would survive any attack they invited but the people would be wiped out. The structures were designed to survive severe impacts, the people were not.

Jimmy thought of stories he had heard about the neutron bomb: humans eliminated; buildings left in perfect condition. The concrete would last much longer than the flesh ever could. He wondered if the Vanich folk were a dying breed, no longer necessary now the military purpose had gone away. Perhaps the islands would be left to the weavers in their sheds and the fishermen with their old boats, risking everything each time they tackled the North Atlantic, which sat just beyond their crumbling harbour walls. The elements would decide what to do with them when they dared to venture out. Lulling them with each safe trip but always possessing the capability to suddenly swipe them into oblivion.

Perhaps it would be right for the islands to return to an earlier way of life because Vanich was an incomer, a stranger to the natural place the rest of the islands seemed to be. Perhaps Vanich had to crumble away after it had served its purpose and the place be left to the true natives who could sustain a living from the land and the sea. Whatever the truth of it Jimmy felt sorry for the Vanich people, for they too must feel vulnerable and, perhaps, inappropriate and unwanted. He wondered how they coped; whether they fought for survival and looked forward to a better future or simply gave up, survived on benefits and waited for something to happen, knowing deep down that it never would.

He imagined the whole place could simply be bulldozed, turned into a wind farm to save global warming, and the people shipped out – like the St Kilda folk a hundred years before. Victims of 21st-century clearances. Jimmy's mind wandered around all these competing thoughts as he allowed the impression of the islands sink in.

He was expecting to be helicoptered out from the airfield, and he parked the hire car outside the pink building right opposite the entrance to the airfield itself. He had been asked to leave the car there because the airport gates were always locked overnight and the hire company wanted access to the vehicle at any time.

He looked at the sign: Café Pink. He smiled at the naivety of the name. He decided not to go in, the helicopter from the mainland was due in 10 minutes and he just had time to check his emails. He reached for his phone but it pinged with a text to say the flight was delayed by an hour due to military activity. Probably a pair of Tornados practising roller landings; he'd seen them do it several times already. Jimmy decided to kill time in comfort. He locked the car with a finger touch, entered Café Pink, and the world changed for two people, one of them being him.

Opening the door coincided precisely with the opening bars of the Italian Symphony. The fiddles gripped Jimmy and everyone else in the place. He was surprised by the quality and volume of the sound. The regulars began to sing phonetic impersonations of the violins. He was instantly struck by the air of absolute delight in the place. To say that it was really buzzing didn't do justice to the energy which the music seemed to release. Everyone was happy, most of them were dancing or swaying in time to the violins, everyone that is except the tall girl behind the counter.

Suzanna wasn't really unhappy, but her face betrayed the fact that she would have preferred just to listen to 16 bars of fiddles before the humans kicked in and sang over it. But she did smile when she wondered what Mendelssohn would have made of it; he might have expected 'The Hebrides' to be a hit here, but not the Italian Symphony! When Jimmy reached the service counter, he was about to order coffee when the soundtrack suddenly changed and Sweet Soul Music filled the place with its brash trumpet intro.

Eddy Floyd ask the regulars a question and everyone shouted, 'Yeah … Yeah.'

Jimmy's face expressed delight; maybe he was wrong about Vanich after all. The place was alive. 'Great music in here', he shouted, 'Is the coffee as good?'

Suzanna was at the Gaggia, her back to him. She turned and smiled. 'Yes, and the cake is even better.'

'Better than Sweet Soul Music?'

'Much better, almost as good as the overture, which always makes them sing for some reason.'

'OK recommend a coffee and a cake.'

'Café Pink regular filter coffee and Hummingbird cake.'

'I'll get the coffee but I'll need convincing on the cake, what's in it?'

'Well, it used to be Hummingbirds but we used them all up so now it's like carrot cake with a lot more than carrots in it.'

'OK, you win, as long as you promise no Hummingbirds were harmed in the production of this slice.' They both laughed, exchanged eye contact for slightly too long, disengaging only when other customers came to the counter.

He wanted to talk to Suzanna about the café, baking and music. But more than anything else he wanted to know more about her. Here was a Vanich youngster who had the sort of spirit he admired. He was intrigued. One of those rare moments of real fascination with a complete stranger – he hadn't had one for a long time but the vibes were unmistakable. Heady feelings after a great trip to the Far Isles. He let the warmth flow over him. Great café, great music, great coffee and an intriguing young woman. Jimmy stayed at the counter, watched her at work and began on the cake.

Bowie's 'Young Americans' suddenly switched to Tom Jones:

The whole café joined in, singing, swaying, arms in the air.

It was a large slice; a wedge sitting perfectly upright on the small plate. It was a 60s Habitat plate; he knew it; he'd bought some. Off-white with a classy pink rim, it was called Kristina, worth money now. He used the hallmarked silver fork to cut out his first bite. Then it dawned on him: pink rim, pink stuff, Café Pink. Clever branding by talented youngsters who were shaping their own future. Classy, simple and obvious; but sometimes really classy things are obvious. That impressed him. Maybe there was hope for Vanich after all; if there was, it lay with these kids. Music rocked the air and the cake began to work its magic.

The whole café cheered and joined in when The Buggles remembered a time before smart phones existed but video changed the music scene.

The cake was light and crumbly but somehow dense enough to transform slowly as he chewed it. He let it rest for a moment in his mouth. Slightly sweet flavours of almonds and orange; vanilla and cinnamon; and maybe a hint of cinder toffee swam through his senses. He was a food expert and this was simply fabulous.

He was smitten by the place, by the music, by the cake and by Suzanna. She watched him eating her cake, she didn't move but her smile told the story. For some reason that she didn't really understand, she was delighted to be pleasing him. She was always pleasant with customers but none had had this effect on her. Carole and Stephanie knew what was happening immediately, and ran protection for Suzanna, diverting customers, dealing with orders and chatting to regulars skilfully. There were no interruptions from customers but E-type provided just the right soundtrack.

The fiddle player and restaurateur exchanged words, smiles, ideas and views on cakes, the universe and everything. Suzanna talked about her fascination with the stary skies that were so clear above the islands. Jimmy said that he'd been impressed by them too. 'Far more stars than in a Glasgow sky,' he said.

Suzanna explained why so many were to be seen there and named the constellations which were always visible above Vanich, which he would never see in the Central Valley skies. She talked about light pollution and the satellites which she regularly tracked across the sky. He asked how she knew so much and she talked about school and a great teacher who loved science. The same guy who had enabled Stephanie to impress and amuse Radar Pete.

Jimmy loved the café and took everything in. He was captivated by Suzanna and saw how she fitted comfortably into island life and into the community this café represented. When they got onto talking about her plans, she mentioned her ideas about volunteering. He offered to help Suzanna with finding work in Africa through his contacts there.

He explained his Yollumba development in northern Nigeria. He was obviously enthusiastic, even excited by what was going on there. She was captivated by his Yollumba story. She wanted to go there. Perhaps it could be the place for her African adventure and he was offering her the chance.

'Two birds with one stone,' she thought, two birds with one stone. If she did Yollumba she might get to meet him out there. She would like that. She liked him. She was fascinated by his outrageous plan to produce Nigerian wine in that remote and trouble-torn region. His big idea was that he could corner the black Afro-Caribbean wine market in Europe and the USA. She was attracted to the facilities he was building there: the school; the technical college; the hospital; the decent houses for the local people who would provide his workforce and the winery itself.

She asked about the terrorist threats in sub-Saharan Africa, which she had read about. He explained that the French were providing military support for the project at no cost. It suited them to protect West African communities and Yollumba was certainly a good cause. The fact that it's emerging viticulture might offer a threat to French wine producers never even occurred to them as a problem. It would provide them with a foothold in the region and a perfect base for both tropical and desert training for their special forces. The French offered to build and manage an airport, which would be both civil and military. Perfect for protection, perfect for bringing goods and people in, and perfect for taking wine out.

Suzanna imagined herself working in the school or in the hospital in a way that simply would not have crossed her mind half an hour before. It almost seemed as though plans were being made. Plans for her future.

He turned the conversation back to the café and to matters of more immediate concern than Africa. He wanted to serve her Hummingbird cake in all his outlets with a good commission for Café Pink.

He wanted Suzanna to bake it here on the island and ship it down to Glasgow every week on the Flybe service. He wanted to make her famous for her baking and he said that he could almost write the publicity script for her product launch. He began to imagine photographs of her in the Far Isle settings he had so admired, holding products against the Hebridean backdrops of mountains and machair, and of cliffs and sandy beaches. He was sensing the very business opportunity he had come to the Far Isles to find.

She just wanted him to stay longer. They talked and talked, smiled and laughed, accidentally touched hands in their animation and smiled even more as she flushed slightly and his mouth went dry. Then the helicopter thundered overhead on its way to the pad, confirming that time had finally run out for both of them. He got up to leave. They shook hands on the cake deal and said their goodbyes. He felt elated, and she felt emptied.

Carefully packed samples of Suzanna's cakes were handed over in an old flour box. Most importantly it contained their entire stock of Hummingbird cake. Jimmy found some cash in his wallet; he pressed it into Suzanna's hand as a down-payment, touching her fingers for a few extra seconds, smiling with his eyes. She grinned and laughed out loud in confused delight.

The Eagles were singing good advice about the pace of life, but taking it easy was easier said than done just at that moment. As suddenly as he had arrived, the stranger had left, but he was no longer a stranger. Elvis had left the building, and for a moment an overwhelming feeling of emptiness overtook the place.

The King had timed it perfectly with his question about loneliness as the Vanich Shuffle worked it magic once more. The thumping rotor sound was soon lost behind the loud music and the three girls huddled together at the counter, amused and amazed by what had just happened. Suzanna was numbed by his sudden appearance and pained by his equally sudden departure. Carole and Stephanie felt like privileged co-conspirators. Suzanna was in a daze but she couldn't stop smiling as the three of them poured over the details of the brief encounter. Then their excited conversation was rudely interrupted.

'You's still serving girls?'

It was Billy, the baggage handler and general factotum from the airfield, their most regular customer.

'Sorry Billy, we've been diverted,' said Stephanie.

'Just like most of your flights!' added Carole.

They all laughed.

'What'll you be having Billy'?' Carole asked with a deliberately strong accent.

'The usual – a skilfully grilled bacon and sausage sarnie with ketchup jus?' added Stephanie followed by more laughter.
'No, Miss Smartarse, I'll have some tea and that bird thing the Glasgow man kept going on about before his chopper took off.'

A moment's pause before they realised what he meant Hummingbird cake!

Then they replied in unison: 'Sorry Billy, we're all sold oot!' They laughed even more.

'Awe bollocks! Story of my life, all sold oot.'

'A jam and biscuit toastie then Billy?'

Billy gave up; he always lost when he took the girls on, but he didn't mind. He didn't need to win as much as they did. When things calmed down Suzanna walked over to Billy's table and sat with him. She leaned forward and asked quietly: 'Flight leave OK then Billy?'

Queen began to sing about magic.

Billy smiled knowingly and squeezed her hand. 'Aye love, it was a piece of cake.'

They both laughed at Billy's joke, then Suzanna smiled and just hoped there would be a next time. It should have been the Stones next, rocking to 'Brown Sugar' according to Radar Pete's shuffle, but something nudged it out of the way and Runrig faded in.

The Café Pink crowd hadn't got a clue about what had just happened.

The customers ate muffins and drank cappuccino, they joined in the music and danced around. They used the café magic to hide their fears of hopelessness, but for Suzanna the world had suddenly changed. Through a maelstrom of confusion and uncertainty, Idan had brought her a lifeline and she clung to the life raft with strong hands.

Heather Small began to search for a hero. Suzanna knew she had found hers. She knew the story would continue because she wasn't going to let him go whatever anyone said. A lot of women say that, but Suzanna meant it. She had found the missing piece for her life's jigsaw.

Suzanna knew that M People were one of her few pop downloads on Pete's sync. She was glad they were there, even though their time on air was limited, and they would surely be replaced any second, but by what? Suzanna waited, for once not wanting Radar Pete's infallible shuffle to work, but of course it did. It was The Italian Symphony again. Suzanna smiled. Pete's shuffle couldn't have done better.

Chapter 8

Helicopter Hero

Remote places always have a character of their own, and whatever it happens to be, it lies at the very heart of their unique impact on visitors. Something provides a unique selling point which attracts attention and draws the traveller in, soon trapping their attention. Forever in their memory, ensuring at least a yearning to return. If threat and uncertainty are sensed, the traveller will quickly move on and never return, but if the place intrigues and attracts an individual, they will be hooked.

Some people prefer crowds, or the confines of the cruise ship or holiday camp. Such people don't like remote at all. They find it unsettling, and would never dream of travelling to the most isolated reaches of the Far Isles. In fact, they would probably avoid the archipelago altogether, and they would never understand why anyone would ever want to go there at all, let alone go off the usual tourist tracks which crisscross the islands. Travellers who enjoy exploration are quite different, and those who do explore, who do move along every narrow road and venture far along and beyond the Land Rover tracks, will eventually find this special place, hidden in the most remote corner of the Atlantic coast. Hiort-Cille is such a place. It is revisited by travellers from all over the world, once it has hooked them.

A man from Canberra spends his time writing speeches for important politicians until he can afford to fly halfway round the world and revisit H-C. He is planning his eighth visit as soon as the bank balance allows it. A family from California with one of the best Lotus car collections on the west coast make a point of returning every three years, coinciding quite deliberately with a couple from Singapore whom they befriended in the Far Isles 20 years ago.

The very name of the place proves that the Celts made their language deliberately impenetrable to outsiders, and however hard the incomers may try, they won't ever be able to pronounce it properly. Pronunciation can be a great barrier, and the Celts use it to the full whenever they name anything. Hiort-Cille is just a particularly good example of Celtic linguistic exclusion, aimed at putting foreigners in their place. It is a very clever trick. Visitors are welcome but they will never be able to say precisely where they have been. They will stumble over the name and probably say it slightly differently each time they try. Mispronunciation is just part of the mystery which these Celtic homelands are so good at providing.

The best way of coping with this situation, if you are an English speaker, is either to invent your own names for things, like for example, 'big rock hill' or 'pretty cute harbour' or by asking a friendly native to keep on demonstrating the pronunciation to you, even though you are most unlikely ever to get it right. Their language, the Gaelic, has a spell on it; it's as simple as that.

All the native islanders speak the Gaelic and by doing so they hang on to something fundamental. A tangible link to their history and heritage, their own language which is almost the same today as when it was spoken thousands of years ago, when the first Neolithic settlements began. It had hardly changed by the time the Bronze Age villages began to emerge. The Gaelic tongue was rich and diverse, with songs and poetry revelling in its richness, and with storytelling gaining power and impact from its diversity of vocabulary and meaning. The lexicon was gradually enhanced by the addition of essential foreign words, but the nuances of emphasis and pronunciation remained unaltered. Hearing it spoken is wonderful.

Somehow, it's never really excluding when the island Celts speak it. They never switch from English to Gaelic just because a stranger arrives on the scene. The Far Islanders speak their language quite naturally and are very likely to switch to English out of good-natured politeness when travellers are there.

Politeness is a sure sign of civilisation and self-confidence. The Far Islanders are under no delusion of inferiority, quite the opposite in fact, they quietly and confidently occupy the moral and cultural high ground and they bask in the warmth of it. The islanders even differentiate themselves from the lowlanders. They are a totally different breed, and should the nation ever allow further independence, the islanders would immediately seek theirs.

Hiort-Cille is a remote and beautiful place even by Far Island standards, and the majority of the small number of visitors are not English or even British, they are intrepid travellers from around the world who discover the place well in advance, and target it, saving up their Air Miles for a year or more. It is home to one of the most isolated guest houses in the land, and it enables the visitor to stay in a level of comfort they would never have imagined could exist in such a lonely place.

The hamlet commands a beautiful sandy beach, contained within a bay, which totally empties of seawater, and then totally fills again, twice a day, as the tides ebb and flow. The water is never more than three-feet deep, and the sand is never disfigured by seaweed or flotsam. It is always completely clean, and the seawater is always completely clear. It is a perfect, minimalistic, sand-and-sea place which looks for all the world like a child's ideal picture of the uncommercialised seaside.

It is a child's drawing of a place, sand then sea, sea then sand, it's as simple and as beautiful as that. A unique and wonderful place, well actually two places. One place when it is full of water and another place when it is empty. Just like every other special place, the bay at H-C is well worth the effort required to get there. Visitors enjoy walking across the bay on soft clean sand and safely wading across it when the tide comes in. Unlike special places nearer to home, the only way you would ever see someone you knew at H-C would be if you took them with you. If you do that, you would have to be really careful that you were taking the right person. Sharing something magical with someone who does not get it, would be a big mistake. On life's list of mistakes, this would always be one of the big ones. So H-C, or Tray Sands to give it the English code name, is one of the wonders of the outer isles, to be enjoyed alone, or with someone you've really made your mind up about.

Fringing the bay of sand, or sea, is a belt of low dunes which were famous for the chess men find, made there quite accidentally over a hundred years ago. Why the ancient game set was there in the first place remains a mystery, and its discovery forms part of the island's folklore. But the attraction of the area went way beyond the scenic location and the local legend. It extended to the people at the guest house and their welcoming provision of human company and creature comforts, which seemed all the more remarkable in a remote place than it would do in a busy and sophisticated tourist destination.

William and Kate, the remarkable hosts spend half the year travelling the world, and half in the Far Isles running their business. Their daughter Rachael stayed in the house all year after 9/11, but her parents still travelled across the Atlantic during the winter season when the guest house was closed. Before the attack on the Twin Towers, Rachael had always travelled with them and she seemed to spend much of her growing-up time in Florida. Kate and William had run the guest house and four self-catering cottages for decades but hankered after life on the East coast of the US too.

They were almost lairds in their own right in the Far Isles, steadily buying up all the properties which comprised the tiny hamlet and building up what amounted to a holiday complex. The family referred to it as The Campus because they thought camp sounded too ordinary, and Hiort-Cille was anything but ordinary. Kate had enlisted local women to help her and Rachael in the guesthouse, and between them they had built up such a reputation for good food that the residents' dining room also opened as a restaurant in the evenings. There were never many spare places at the dining tables, but when there were some, they were snapped up immediately through the pre-bookings which sat on a long waiting list. The dining room was always full with a mixture of residents and visiting diners, and everyone agreed that the meals were as memorable as the views.

The success of the place had slowly attracted ambitious young chefs to the remote location and over an area of 20 square miles there were now more four-star eating places than in most small towns. One of them, the black queen, even had a Michelin star. Residents at the guest house enjoyed massive cooked breakfasts and the huge, brilliantly prepared three course dinners made lunch irrelevant. Wine was racked around the dining room and guests just helped themselves to it and settled up at the end of their stay.

William did the bookings and kept the accounts meticulously, but he never bothered to keep a check on the wine, he just kept the racks topped-up with weekly visits to the excellent supermarket, 50 miles away in the capital. William was a petrol-head. Growing up close to the home of a famous English motor racing team, he became infected with a love for the sport at an early age and he always drove around the islands flat out. On one trip back from the supermarket, with a boot full of Chilean Red and New Zealand White, he drifted around a wide bend he knew well and found a dead deer across the road, recently killed by a local haulier who wasn't sure what to do with it. They lifted it onto the boot-top luggage rack on William's MX5 and took it back to the guest house with him.

Two nights later when he made his usual theatrical announcement of dinner to a packed dining room, he said: 'This evening's main course is venison pie with seasonal vegetables and island berry jus.'

He couldn't resist adding: 'We just call it road-kill pie, but I wouldn't worry about that.'

Most of the guests just laughed, but one or two did worry about it for a moment. There was a trust in the place which added to the magic, and in the 33 years he had operated in this way, he had never been underpaid for the wine which guests had consumed, nor had there ever been a single complaint about the food.

Kate, a slightly less obvious character around the house, commanded the kitchen with her small team of very talented local women, who helped out in varying numbers according to the level of business in the place.

The cooking was outstanding. No meal was ever repeated over a period of seven consecutive days. The breakfasts were, as Michael Winner said after his first visit: 'Historic.'

Despite their excellent teamwork and satisfying companionship during so many adventurous travels around the world, Kate and William had grown steadily concerned about Rachael, because she seemed stuck on the campus now that Florida no longer attracted her. They never admitted it openly, but they both knew that their daughter's future was in the balance. What might have been a glittering international life could now, quite easily, turn into a modern version of the old isolation model, which had limited the potential of generations of islanders who never ventured far from their crofts.

Rachael, in addition to her culinary skills, was a qualified helicopter pilot. She gained her license in Florida during a winter stay there as a teenager, some years before. She had immediately impressed her Vietnam-veteran instructor with her natural sense of balance. 'That's some ass you've got there, missy,' was his way of complimenting her potential, when she first took control of the training aircraft.

'What?' was the best she could do, uncertain of his intentions by making such a personal observation.

'Your ass, missy, your ass.'

'You fly a helicopter with your ass, not your hands, and if you listen to your ass your hands will do the right thing.'

Rachael laughed out loud. 'Oh! I get it.'

'We call it – flying by the seat of your pants!'

'Yea, I suppose that's the polite way of putting it.'

They both laughed.

Without knowing why or how, Rachael controlled the chopper perfectly, right from the start. After three hours of basic tuition, Pete Cong was teaching her some of the old Chickenhawk tricks. He sang 'The Ride of the Valkyries' as he demonstrated the Mekong Delta low-level attack, and he whooped with joy as he performed a perfect Khe-Sanh sideslip landing. When Rachael laughed with delight when he showed her the SAM-avoidance spiral descent, he knew that she was a natural. Rachael loved every minute of it and Pete told her she could be as good as any of his fliers, back in the day. What Pete didn't tell her was that he was one of only three survivors of his original squadron of 16 'Huey-jockeys', or that he had seen every one of the fireballs which marked the end of the 13 other young lives.

Helicopters gave a new meaning to Rachael's life, and she felt very proud of herself for mastering the dark arts Pete told her about.

'I'd have you in my squad any time missy.'

Pete's parting words brought a tear to her eye and she hugged him hard, loving him for teaching her so well, and for giving her a feeling of self-belief that she never thought she would experience. Having dynamic and successful parents was only a limited blessing; children often find it hard to compete. Rachael returned to Florida for a few weeks every year so that she could fly and keep her license up to date. She loved her time there at the flying school and Pete always greeted her like an old friend. Rachael was devastated when she was banned from flying in the US after 9/11.

Despite her years of visiting, despite flying while she put in the required hours to keep her qualifications alive, she was still an alien. She had attended high school in the USA for the winter semester for seven years, but that counted for nothing as far as US Security were concerned. As a foreigner, she presented a potential terrorist threat; it was as simple as that. All appeals for the US license to be reinstated were refused. The post-apocalypse security clampdown was draconian in its implementation, and it was sustained with equal determination by US Security and British Intelligence. There were many unintended consequences of the powerful security clampdown which closed a lot of stable doors after horses had bolted; Rachael's flying ban was just one of them.

Rachael seriously missed helicopter flying. Flying for two weeks in Florida was enough to keep her love of life alive. Occasionally she had been able to spend additional time in the sunshine state and it meant the world to her as she logged-up the hours for three months or more. She had qualified as an instructor during her last long stay, just before 9/11, and Pete had thrown a party for her at the trailer park where he lived, by the airfield. Pete's long-time girlfriend had taken Rachael to one side and confided in her.

'If you weren't just an occasional visitor, I could get seriously jealous you know.'

Rachael was on her guard when she asked the obvious question: 'Oh! why's that?'

'Because Pete likes you too much for a girl to be happy, Rachie.'

Rachael fumbled for an answer. 'He's a lovely guy Maisy, but he's not my type to be honest.'

Maisy looked quizzically, right into Rachael's eyes, and after a few excruciating seconds, she said: 'I hope not Rachie, I hope not.'

Pete broke the tension by bringing them both burger and beer, the country music wafted across the park and the line-dancing began. When Rachael flew back to her island the following day, she reflected on the conversation with Maisy, and thought that things would never be quite the same again over there. Little did she know how right she would be.

Rachael also wondered about relationships and fidelity too and wondered how those things would affect her in the future. She wasn't sure whether she would, or even could, try to take Pete Cong away from his girlfriend. She didn't even know if she wanted to.

She was so right about things never being the same again; but it wasn't a girlfriend's suspicion which spoiled the party, it was the most spectacular act of terrorism the world had ever seen.

In Florida Rachael had easy access to a small fleet of aircraft; she could fly whenever she wanted to, but suddenly the rug was pulled from under her. Back on the island the family didn't own a helicopter and they had no access to one. When the Twin Towers collapsed, it was more than the destruction of two tall buildings and the deaths of so many people; the world had changed for everyone, not just for the unfortunate 2,606 victims and their families. For them, such horrible deaths and irreplaceable losses to cope with; for everyone else, a new way of regarding the world. Fear and resentment swept the globe in equal measure. Wars were declared, terrorism spread in response, and more lives were lost. Families were bereaved and hatred festered. The seismic shocks continued for years; and one woman couldn't fly helicopters any more.

Most people at H-C were visitors who stayed over for a few days, but they often extend their stay if they could, beguiled by the unique combination of attractions. Sometimes the odd person would just call in for dinner, and if there was room at the table William was happy to accommodate them. If there was no room, he would point them in the direction of one of the other nearby eateries and make a booking for them if they wished. It was just such a brief, chance dinner visit, which changed Rachael's life forever.

On a summer's day, when the bay looked stunning in the bright sunlight, and the tide was in, lapping at the lawn edge, a young coastguard officer called in to book a table for that evening. He was introducing his girlfriend to the outer isles prior to his posting to the main rescue base some months later. He was in luck; there were two spare covers. One resident had broken their ankle in an unlucky fall on a mountain walk and they had been air-lifted to the cottage hospital for X-rays and treatment. Their partner had driven up there leaving two spare seats in the dining room that evening.

The coastguard was excited about his posting, and he really wanted his partner to come with him, but it was going to be hard work to convince her. He needed to work a miracle if she was ever to contemplate leaving Chiswick for the wild remoteness of the Far Isles. How could she survive happily without all those smart shops, coffee bars and the general bustle of an upmarket high street? He knew that the scenery alone wouldn't cut it, and when he heard of Hiort-Cille he made it part of his plan. A smart people's restaurant, run by an interesting family, with million-dollar views outside the windows, might just do it. If it was as beguiling as the reviews suggested, it might provide the magic he required to work the miracle.

The evening went very well. The restaurant was full of interesting people, as usual. Most of them were residents and they chatted freely after benefitting from getting to know each other over a few days. A film director was there with his family. He talked confidently about his latest production: a documentary about global warming with some Swedish kid he enthused about but, interestingly, he couldn't remember her name. There was a Glaswegian property developer with his secretary. She was a lot younger than him and spoke with an English accent. They drove a Porsche 911. There was a painter with an immaculate partner whom everyone assumed was his perfect, personal, model. There were two English families with really pleasant kids and they were getting on well with an Australian doctor, who lived in the Yorkshire Dales, and a London GP who talked about once treating Madonna for an insect bite on the eyelid. The coastguard's girlfriend loved it; it was better than the best café-bar on Chiswick High Street.

The coastguard was pleased that things were going so well. He sensed that his girlfriend was loving the place, and he hoped that it would cast a different light on isolation for her. The meal was the high spot of the evening as it always was. The wine racks were considerably depleted and William wondered about an extra supermarket run to replenish the red at least. After the meal the guests spread around the house and lounged in the comfortable rooms; some went outside into the balmy, midge-free, evening air and wondered at the brightness of the sky at nearly midnight. They saw more stars than they ever saw at home, and on that night the air was so clear that galaxies were clearly discernible. They painted their spirals against the dark backdrop of deep space. The night sky was so stunning that people stopped trying to describe it and simply stared, some with a fourth glass of wine, others with excellent black coffee.

Kate finally sat down with Rachael as they both joined William and the guests. The kitchen was shipshape and ready for the breakfast effort, which was just six hours away. Rachael didn't socialise as easily as William and Kate, but she was polite enough to ask the coastguard man if he had enjoyed the meal. His girl was outside talking to the film director. Rachael liked the coastguard guy, he was unassuming, calm, attractive and he looked into her eyes when he spoke to her. She felt the conversation change from good hostess duty to genuine interest when he said what he did for a living.

'I'm a coastguard officer,' he said. 'I'm being posted to the rescue base at the airport.'

He recognised the shift in Rachael's attention as she moved forward slightly in her chair, rubbed her eye, altered the angle of her head, changed up a gear and said, 'So what will your role be at Vanich Base?'

There are some simple questions which have momentous consequences. You don't always realise it at the time but once you've asked them it's too late. Such a question will provoke an answer which homes in like an Exocet, and the impact is inevitable.

'Oh!' he said, 'I fly helicopters.'

The dynamics changed and she was suddenly wide awake. She wanted to find out everything about him. Where he was from, what training had he had, which aircraft had he flown, what adventures would he talk about, what were his favourite places to fly, what was his best manoeuvre, had he had scary near-misses, had he lost any friends, how many lives had he saved? The questions poured out; all the usual helicopter stuff. It was 1am when William allowed the last guests to take their leave and he brought coastguard guy's girlfriend into the room where Rachael had eventually poured her heart out to the only person in the place who could really understand.

The pain of the helicopter ban, her anger that the two causes of her unhappiness, the terrorist event and the security forces' reaction, were completely beyond her control. She shared the hopeless sense of inevitability which overwhelms any victim of an establishment decision, whether it be legal and well-meaning or perfidious, treacherous and life-threatening. She knew that nobody meant to harm her by their actions, but she was nevertheless damaged by the impact of their decisions. Unintended consequences; collateral damage. The coastguard pilot was sympathetic, even empathetic, because he shared her love for the tricky machines which even the fast-jet fliers found difficult to handle, but which he, and she, flew easily and skilfully, as if they were the very extension of their own nervous systems.

The couples said their grateful goodnights, each gaining their own pleasures from the evening. Rachael's feelings were different. She was excited and frustrated at the same time. She didn't want the evening to end, however late it was. It had been a very precious meeting but as she tried to sleep, she kept thinking very carefully about her next move.

Breakfast was a low-key affair; everyone was tired and more or less talked-out. As she began to take orders Rachael found a note addressed to her, propped up on the main wine rack. She took it and unfolded the simple message in the kitchen. It said, 'Thanks for a wonderful night: I'll be back to see you again when I'm posted, I can help, I promise you.'

It wasn't even signed but she knew it was from him. She smiled and folded it again carefully and slid it between the pages of her kitchen diary along with secret notes to self about food preparation and vine vintages. It took almost a year for the note's promise to be honoured. Rachael did not know what the interval would be, but she knew her coastguard would deliver eventually. She secretly hoped that his girlfriend didn't come north with him.

Their story became an island legend when the final act was eventually played out. Like the modern girl and the chessmen; the Solas Warlord; the teacher and the gallery; the pink café; the rock-and-roll fisherman and the girls in the jewellery shop; Rachael entered island mythology when the helicopter returned.

She was sitting in the front garden which had an ancient low wall around it; a strange and telling structure which attempted to separate the small manmade garden from the natural landscape of one of the most beautiful places in the world. An unnecessary barrier, when seamless access between the garden and the real world would have somehow enhanced both. That wall said something about property and boundaries which help to define humans as much as it defined the edge of their property.

Humans: what a strange breed. Surround yourself with beauty then build a barrier. Humans do it with other humans too, not just with beautiful places. People who might provide each other with the perfect soulmate, are kept at just too great a distance for the magic to be consummated. It was as if people are afraid of taking the final risk and exposing everything, even to someone who might really understand.

When Rachael's moment came, William had gone off for the day acting as a tourist guide for a bunch of rich Americans. He was good at that and the income helped his pension fund – the main aim of which was to buy a Daytona Coup. The last one went for £2.4m so he had a few guided tours to get in before he reached that target. Kate was away in the capital, doing the wine run in William's absence. William and Kate were perfect business partners as well as soulmates, and their relationship was much more than one of mere convenience. William and Kate knew they were lucky in love; they just wanted Rachael to find the same sort of happiness.

Rachael was alone in the house, apart from the dogs. It was about 11am. Familiar noises formed a quiet background soundtrack for her thoughts as she sat on the small lawn in the formal part of the front garden. She was four strides away from the endless sands. The tide was out. The clean sand looked perfect. Insects buzzed around, distant tractors grumbled their diesel noises, a transatlantic jet was making its final left turn before heading out over the North Atlantic towards Newfoundland and eventually New York. Rachael looked up and noticed the clear contrail left by the airliner. She thought about Florida and Pete Cong.

All the guests had gone for the day and the staff had finished cleaning up. The house was ready for the next shift. It was peaceful and Rachael was relaxed, comfortable in the almost-silence, surrounded by the familiar, knowing that eventually things would change. She wondered if this was the day William would not return. She had worried about his driving ever since she was a child. She hated it when he said, 'Road-kill' because she had a childhood fear that he would crash one day and join the long list of beasts which end their lives on the ribbon of tarmac.

She thought about her own future, knowing that she was still young enough to restart her life, but she knew that many women thought that 35 was a critical point in the ageing process, even though she didn't know why. Whatever the truth of it, she was approaching 33 and perhaps time was running out for her. Sometimes she dreaded the thought of ageing, wondering how she would cope. She began to think about the care homes which were springing up across the islands as people were living longer, well into the age when they simply could not look after themselves any more. Before her thoughts were interrupted, she suddenly realised that in the old days there were no care homes because people always died before they lost the ability to cope.

Then, with the keen ear of an expert, she picked up the unmistakable sound of the Sikorsky S-92 in the distance. It was far enough out for the breeze to make the sound come and go, but it was undoubtedly a chopper. Soon the noise would be much clearer if it was flying in her direction. It seemed to be somewhere over the sea to her right. She shaded her eyes and strained them to distinguish the flying machine from the gulls, which always looked like aircraft at some stage in their distant flight.

When Rachael saw it, she pointed excitedly and simply said, 'There she is,' to the empty house. It came right up into the bay, dead slow. It was absolutely rock steady and slowing down. She went to the edge of the garden and waved with both hands, her arms describing arcs large enough for the pilot to see, like a child at an air show. She never dreamed that it was intending to land, and she had no idea that her welcome wave was about to be so richly rewarded.

It was Coastguard Rescue 7, call sign Golf Sierra Alpha Romeo Bravo. A familiar sight all over the outer isles, but rarely did it fly right over the H-C campus. It hovered at 200 feet over the still-damp sand, and then, unbelievably, it slowly dropped down and landed. The downdraft was sending ripples across the hard surface of the sand, but the dampness of the grains prevented it from blowing into the air.

The rotors kept turning. A side door opened and one of the pilots jumped out and waved. He was unmistakably beckoning Rachael over. She was uncertain at first but somehow, she knew it was right to just run onto the sands. She didn't stop running until she stooped beneath the rotor blades and threw herself at the pilot. He returned the hug for a long time and they finally peeled off.

She put on the helmet that was passed out to her and she climbed on board. Doors were slid shut, the twin engines spooled up and started to scream. The rotors speeded up to the point when they became invisible once more. The Sikorsky S-92 lifted off in a perfectly steady, vertical climb and rose calmly to 200 feet. After a moment of hovering, the nose dipped very slightly in the direction of the house and she moved forward. The dogs barked excitedly and chased around, already concerned about their sudden isolation.

When you hear this story for the first time, you will want to wave at the departing helicopter too, but you can't, it's long gone. The event has become part of the island's history, and the essence of history is that it tells you about something which doesn't exist anymore. If you had been there, you should have waved your own thanks to the coastguard pilot for remembering everything he learned from Rachael that night in the guest house when all his efforts to entice his girlfriend to the Far Isles were failing. Coastguard man did more than just remember Rachael, he had the determination to come back to make good his promise to rescue another stranded human, who meant more to him than anyone he had ever rescued before. Kate, joined the island's long list of people who mysteriously disappeared, for nobody had witnessed the lift-off, and crewmen never talk.

Rachael and her new soulmate moved to Cornwall where he led a rescue flight for 20 years and where they settled happily with their children. They never returned to the Far Isles; Rachael never returned to Florida. The guest house eventually closed and was converted into a family holiday home by a Dutch financier. The self-catering cottages were purchased by the Far Isles Council to provide affordable homes for four local couples who intended to make their futures on the island. One of them would be a teacher at the local primary school; another was a builder with a young family. He would learn to specialise in lime mortar finishes to stone-cottage walls and thatched roof repairs to cater for the tourist trade and the demands for croft conversions for self-catering lets. The other two would both work online, benefitting from the excellent local internet connectivity, which had been improved by the Americans when they upgraded the ATC facility on the headland.

Government wanted to improve the tracking of all commercial aircraft heading for the US in order to control aircraft movements more effectively and to guard against future airborne attacks. The cost of the upgrade was covered by the NSA, who had demanded better North Atlantic coverage for security reasons. It was another unintended consequence of 9/11 – improved internet connectivity.

Ironic that this significant improvement to local services, which was life changing for two young locals who ran their own web-based businesses, was precisely in the place where a young helicopter flier needed a different sort of help to save her from the collateral damage resulting from that same atrocity, but the Far Isles are no stranger to irony, as every seasoned visitor knows very well.

Chapter 9

The Power of the Sands

Kathryn sat right at the top of the highest dune, head bowed, focussing on her screen. This was the 10th successive laser-drone attack but she jinked nimbly to one side and the beams passed harmlessly beyond her ship's wingtips. She flicked a key with her right thumb while she held two others down with fingers on her left hand. She had reversed the thrust of both engines for a millisecond, slowing her defence ship just enough for the drone to fly past, right into her crosshairs. One quick squeeze and the Droog ship disintegrated with spectacular digital effects. She was on top again. She loved the feeling. On top of the dune; top of the game.

With quick movements of her fingers, she obliterated the final three Droogs and emerged from the mammoth, 60-minute encounter with the virtual garland firmly around her neck, and the virtual trophy heading for her virtual hands. She grinned as the presentation was made to her avatar; the avatar smiled too. She had just enjoyed her best networking game sessions ever, and all while she was sitting on that dune.

She didn't know how or why it had all suddenly clicked; how or why her long, lonely struggles with her competitors, none of whom she had ever met, were finally and spectacularly successful after months of being second best. Since she came to the island, the score counter just kept racking up victory points, game after game. This session had easily been the best yet.

She eliminated her first challenger in less than a minute with a freak killer shot, right into the reactor core of a mother ship. The thermonuclear devastation ended the game instantly. Subsequent matches took longer, but she enjoyed win after win until the final battle. It took almost half an hour, and her opponent was a previous champion. She assumed it was a male for some reason, but of course there was no way of knowing. She had never even got close to beating him before. But she did this time, and she did it without ever losing control of their encounter. Kt1984, for that was her ID, was now the world champion.

She had come from nowhere to the top of the pile, and the beauty was that nobody knew who she actually was. Even better, nobody knew that she was sat on top of a sand dune in a forgotten part of a remote island chain. It was a perfect situation.

Messages poured into the text column at the side of her screen, most of them complimentary, admiring her skill, giving her a thumbs-up emoji. Awesome, sick and respect were the usual words used but a lot of messages were abusive, some promising kidnap, rape, torture, disease and death – but that was to be expected. She was threatened on a regular basis by her invisible watchers and she had regular offers of 'special chemicals' which would improve her fighting skills. Some promised to keep her awake for hours, others offered 'increased aggression'. It was all quite normal.

It was a parallel universe, there at the touch of a touch-screen, while she sat in her real world of school, college, home and family. This was, after all, the internet: the World Wide Web. It provided worldwide access, worldwide opportunity, worldwide praise and worldwide abuse in equal measure. Kathryn was used to it. Her internet gaming community was, what she euphemistically called, a mixed bunch. It was who she mixed with though, more than any group of people she knew, including her own family. She sometimes thought the gaming community was her true family and a dysfunctional family at that. It was her choice to mix with these people, so she happily took the rough with the smooth.

She laughed at the thought of all that bad stuff, and she was totally used to it. It was like water off a duck's back. Her carefully preserved internet anonymity made her feel safe from the 'sticks and stones', and the words would never hurt her. She was so pleased by her own achievements, while she sat on top of her hill of sand in nowhere-land, that even the vilest comments just went over her head.

The lofty location suited her family because they could see her from anywhere on the vast beach, where they played cricket, lounged around and paddled up to their knees, as the tide came in. Whatever they were doing, they could see she was alright, with just a quick glance. They were just so glad she was actually there with them. She could so easily have refused to come on holiday, stayed with her aunt, and surfed the web 24/7.

They knew that she had been drifting away from them for a couple of years, and they shared the unspoken fear that she might just go off somewhere without saying anything to them. They feared for the day when she was attracted by some malevolent online force and drawn away to a remote meeting place, never to be seen again. They imagined the news media losing interest and the homemade posters fading in the windows of local newsagents. As time passed, they would have to imagine how she would have changed as the years flew by. They would probably never know if she was alive or dead, but they would still feel unbearable pain every year on her birthday and at Christmas.

Her mother had secretly planned to keep a spare place set for every meal to keep her memory alive and to offer a welcome should she suddenly walk through the door. They both wondered what they would say about her when the reporters asked the inevitable questions about their daughter. Those desperate parent comments about missing children were always the same. Somehow, they wanted to be able to say something different, but they didn't know what words to use.

Then the darkness was lifted. For some reason she had jumped at the chance of a family holiday in the Far Isles. It was completely out of character, but that just made them even more delighted. Her decision wiped away dark thoughts of loss, at least for the time being. They had no idea why the change occurred, but they were very grateful for her unexpected enthusiasm for family life once again.

Here, in the dunes, they knew that she was happy and safe, and they would settle for that. If she caught them looking in her direction, she waved. Her wave delighted them more than she would ever know. The whole situation suited them. It suited them down to the ground.

It suited her too, because the internet connection was so strong, thanks to a clear and direct view of the air traffic control masts at Storr Point. They carried a bewildering set of small aerial structures beneath the main satellite dishes, several being for mobile phone networks, others for broadband internet connections. The same towers which fed radar data to the Eastern Atlantic Regional Air Traffic Control Centre in West London, also carried cellphone signals to the whole world and an internet satellite link which provided an even stronger feed than their land line back at home.

Connectivity was the key to consistent gaming. Winners depended upon it; everyone was a loser when their connection dropped out. Kathryn revelled in the power of her worldwide reach and enjoyed jousting with like-minded gamers from all over the planet. She also revelled in her sudden acquisition of improved virtual fighting skills. She assumed that she was just comfortable in her remoteness, while still connected to her family and her virtual world. She assumed that feeling comfortable somehow freed up her playing. She had no idea that the power came, not as she suspected, from being comfortable or from the Storr Point masts for that matter, but from the sand itself. She had no idea that it was the dune which gave her the new power. That a force which had grown over time, was giving the sands at Tray Bay their secret powers.

It was a power which had been noticed before. Some of the local people who felt the magic called it the fourth dimension. 'There's length, breadth and thickness, then there's the feeling you get on the dunes.'

Others just called it the force. Some never sensed it at all, and wondered what the believers were talking about. When she first heard it mentioned in the guest house, she assumed it was just part of the local folklore. She knew that time had always been a powerful force. She knew that it was more important because it went unnoticed for most of its unrelenting, continuous, never-ending existence. She knew that time was the one force which, according to gamer Harry Jacob Samuels, 'continually affects everything and ultimately allows everything to change'. She remembered him saying, 'Time is the only thing that really matters.' She often thought about that.

Time continues even when there is no gravity, no action or reaction, no friction, no mass. Once, when Kathryn read those wise words by HJS, she crossed out allows and wrote demands. Allows or demands? Depends how you look at it, she decided, and she thought that her experience told her that the mighty force of time demanded more than it allowed. Time seemed to demand things from her, sure enough, but she knew that it also allowed things to happen too.

Kathryn loved what she called, a thinking challenge, and wallowed happily in the uncertainty of such personal, internal debates. She regularly undertook them with herself without anyone else ever knowing. They assumed she was just miles away, and actually, her mind was. She was sailing at more than light speed through an infinite space which allowed her thinking to expand without the restrictions of external criticism. She decided that time both allowed and demanded, and that it was the one force in the universe which touched everything and everyone, at every moment: in fact, she decided, time was the only force which operated all the time. She laughed at the thought and became fascinated by time, and its relationship with the conventional forces of physics.

She had had some interesting discussions at school with a young Taiwanese physics teacher who had defied her family to move to England, seeking a teaching post to improve her English to a level which would gain her residency, and a place in a university research team. She aimed to be an astrophysicist. She had replaced a man who had moved away from the north of England to these very islands, some years before and he was apparently a very hard act to follow. The young woman rose to the challenge and quickly became one of the strengths on the teaching staff at the Grammar School, role-modelling opportunities for women in science perfectly.

Kathryn had reached a point in her thinking which placed time ahead of all the other forces. Newton would not have agreed, but Hawking probably would. The force of time had certainly played a part in the power which had fed her gaming skills in that remote place. The fact that she had decided to come here with her family was a direct result of her temporal reflections.

She realised that her life would move on, and that soon she would literally move away from parents and siblings. She decided to do one more family holiday before it was too late, and by making that decision she unwittingly exposed herself to new forces which even she could never have imagined.

The powers of the sands were real enough though, and they came from a chess piece buried there over almost two thousand years before, and the chess magic had increased steadily as time passed. It was strong enough now to make a difference to things, and it was time for it to be noticed by the young English girl.

The foundations of firm sand beneath the shifting dunes were laid down back in the pre-history of the place. The rising sea level slowly engulfed the coast, depositing a layer of shingle and coarse sand in the shallows of the bay. The successive layers of sediment buried all signs of the rocky basement.

In time it was overlain by fine clean, yellow sand, formed by the previous million years of grinding ice, and brought in by coastal currents to form the perfect surface of Tray Bay.

The wind steadily winnowed out the finer grains, blew them beyond the tidal beach, and formed the vast dune belt. The very lightness of those wind-blown grains meant that the dune shifted constantly, despite the best efforts of colonising vegetation to anchor them.

Shifting sands could easily bury things, and the source of the force which helped her gaming was buried beneath the very dune which Kathryn occupied for her gaming sessions. She chose it because of its prominence. The force chose her because she was the right one to receive its help. The chess piece, from which the power emanated, was the sole survivor of a complete set, revealed by chance, as these things often are. Kathryn's game was Droog-megadeath, but the original game played in this place was chess.

The digital game was as fascinating to the young English girl as chess had been to her alter-ego, thousands of years before. The games were separated by a millennium of technology, but the common thread was the young women who played them, and the disapproval expressed by their elders. These coincidences all lined up, through time, eventually enabling Kt1984 to become a world champion. The www.universalchampion@droogmegadeath.com.

The exhumation of the buried chess set was the result of a storm, which blew deep into the high dunes and shifted the sand in a place which was usually well protected, even from the strongest gales. Freak eddies in the airflow moved sand far enough to reveal the long-buried artefacts, and a local beachcomber saw them the morning after the tempest ceased. He would have settled for driftwood, but he found treasure instead. It was a chance discovery and the crofter knew it. He could so easily have missed it. He spotted the pieces with his keen eyes, but he did not sense the magic.

Magic is often sensed by people who are completely unaware of their own powers of reception because they have never been awakened before. Kt1984 was completely unaware of hers. Such people are gifted with a sensitivity which transcends generations and which sometimes goes completely unnoticed even by the possessed, because if they never encounter magic, they will never realise their powers of reception. But as soon as magic reveals itself to them, they will sense it, and their sensitivity will be revealed too.

Some would call such gifted people: Shaman. The gifted are usually cursed with difficulties in situations of social competition, which less talented people find easy to cope with. Gifted people usually prefer their own company, or the company of people who recognise their value and are grateful to receive their friendship. Such people are rare though, and it may be years before one is encountered.

Gifted people abhor the rituals of point scoring interactions, the self-aggrandising normality of everyday life, but they love the discovery of new things which challenge conformity and they revel in enlightenment. They always have a love of learning, and Kathryn was exactly like that. A social outsider, a slightly off-piste skier on life's slippery slopes, an embracer of new ideas and a champion of all things downtrodden. Kt1984 was a NewGoth. She invented the title herself. It described a person where the inner-Goth was masked by a more conventional outer-self. NewGoth described Kathryn perfectly. New-Gothism suited her, and without them realising it, it suited her parents too.

They knew she was different inside, but they were grateful that she didn't appear to be particularly different on the outside. Kathryn was quite different from her siblings. Unlike them she would never enjoy adventure parks; she would never go on a cruise; she could never join a uniformed organisation or enjoy sleeping in a dormitory. She would love a split-screen VW Campervan, a Jet Boil and a billy can. Kathryn was comfortable in her unconformity, and she had developed a sufficient range of skills to ward off too much attention from normal people. Happy in her own version of the world, she went along with family things only to avoid alarming her parents too much, and she was relaxed about her siblings calling her weird, because they did it with affection, not malice.

Such kindness did not exist at school though. Her difference marked her out for abuse. She was ignored by boys and known as 'freak' by the other girls. Teachers wondered about her special needs and there was talk of the spectrum. Kt1984 was aware of it all but coped quite easily in the knowledge that time would pass and she would be able to join a world which welcomed and appreciated her for what she was; like her family did.

She was secretly thrilled about the family holiday to the remote islands which she had noticed once in an atlas at school as she was browsing through it during a boring geography lesson about paddy fields. The teacher, a rather inadequate, jock-strap of a man, poked fun at her when he saw the page she was on.

'It does rain rather a lot in Scotland Kath-er-ine but you won't find any paddy fields there.'

His deliberate mispronunciation of her Christian name amused everyone, and the class laughed at her. She grinned in grim acceptance, but she stayed on the same page, ignored the teacher and carefully memorised the outlines of the islands and some of the place names. She silently promised herself to go there one day. It all seemed so remote, but remote was good, and Kathryn was really looking forward to experiencing remoteness. Remoteness would suit her.

Their rental cottage was right next to the coast and the huge expanse of flat sand was perfect for playing. The guesthouse had a restaurant which they could book into for any meals they wished, even breakfast. Beyond the small group of buildings the high dunes fringed the sands and formed a belt almost a mile wide. The dunes were certainly remote and few people ever visited them due to their isolated location. The small number of tourist visitors were impressed by the sands but none had ever really explored the dune system, and so none had ever experienced the power.

A sensitive extraterrestrial would pick it up straight away because the spirit of the place is different from most other places on Earth, and the anomaly would stand out immediately to the inquisitive outsider, if they had sensors which could probe the planet's emotions. Most humans simply didn't have the capacity to notice. They would see the name sands and think sands, they would see dunes and simply think dunes. They would not see beyond the stereotype; most humans never do.

Kathryn did have the capacity to notice though, and as soon she walked the dune belt she began to feel the magic; the magic which came from the ancient burial. She knew nothing about it, she hadn't been prepared for it nor was she expecting it; it just happened. She knew immediately that this was where she would play her games while the rest of the family enjoyed the flat sands. They would enjoy that, and she would enjoy this. Her parents were happy that she was not staying in her room at the cottage. She may not have been enjoying the cricket, but at least she was in the fresh air.

She wondered if the feeling had anything to do with her enjoyment of the place and with her sudden improvement in WarCraft Survival10 – Droog Megadeath. She had read the guide books and she knew about the chessmen but didn't think they had anything to do with her own gaming activities. She cared about them, but she didn't connect the ancient artefacts with her electronic gameboard.

She was indignant about the removal of the chessmen to mainland museums, and she thought about the Elgin Marbles, and wondered about the scale of first-world plundering. She daydreamed about leading a campaign to restore artefacts to their place of origin. It just seemed right to her. She didn't realise that the power she felt came from an unlikely remnant of a life long gone; carefully carved in walrus ivory.

The storm, which had blown for almost a week without any break in the gale force winds, exposed three pawns at first but then revealed more pieces as the winds ate more deeply into the damp sand, which formed the very foundations of one big dune. The local crofter, walking his dog, and looking for firewood, glimpsed the exposed pieces, pulled them out and told the police about his discovery.

The press picked up the story and there was immediate archaeological interest. After a much-publicised dig, almost all of the pieces had been discovered and removed, but there was a mystery over the missing black queen. Questions were aired in the media: Was it simply lost, or was it stolen by the beachcomber, or was it deliberately held by the last player, thousands of years ago, so that no future plunderer would ever enjoy the full set?

By keeping the queen, perhaps the final victor had ensured that their last game really would be the last game, or perhaps it was just kept as a trophy of a final victory. For that final player, the black queen would have been their trophy of success, their garland. It would be their proof that they were top of the pile; the chess champion. Whatever the truth of the matter, speculation about the black queen helped to boost the tourist trade and it was considerably embellished by the guides on the coach tours. American tourists lapped it up.

A local family made replicas of the lost black queen out of moulded plastic and sold them from their garage gift shop for £5, including a neat plastic see-through box. As sales grew, they began to make complete chess sets in the same way, following the designs of the original pieces exposed and removed years before.

Everyone had their own ideas about the disappearance of the black queen, but nobody knew the true story. Nobody had ever heard of the rebellious native girl, Freyja Grainscript, who loved the chess set and played whenever she could. If Kathryn had an alter-ego, it was her Dark Age forebear, Freyja.

Kathryn and Freyja were separated by 2,000 years of time and history, and their lives were very different. But time knew, that despite their differences in lifestyle, the two girls actually had much in common. They were really the same young woman, millennia apart. The dunes were a place where magic had happened, and Freyja's story was the source of the power.

Her story was handed down for a few generations, by word of mouth, as storytellers recounted the tale, but it was finally lost in the sands of time, forgotten during the so-called Dark Ages, when little of historical detail was recorded. Freyja's story may have been lost to human memory, but the power of the sands in the dune belt around Tray Bay were created by that young woman, over 2,000 years before, when she made her rebellious decision, deep in the dune belt which fringed the bay of sand then, as it does now.

Speculation about the chessmen and the missing queen came and went. Whenever the tourist board or the media chose to reignite the debate, the same speculations occurred. People speculated about their placement under the sands and wondered if they were lost or hidden. Each explanation has its supporters and detractors. There was just as much speculation about the lost queen herself.

Lost is easy enough to understand; shifting sand covers things quickly and leaves no clue as to where a buried treasure is hidden. Deliberate burial is an understandable way of hiding and protecting something of value which might otherwise be damaged or stolen. Accidental sand burial is an altogether darker thought than deliberate concealment. If it was an accident what happened to the players? Was it a catastrophic event which buried people as well as artefacts? Simple carelessness, a deliberate burial to protect a valued artefact from thieving raiders, or a dark and catastrophic event?

As time passed the story went cold again and the world moved on. Local people quietly kept their interest alive, occasionally speculating about the burial and the missing chess piece. Every year they were reminded of the power of large sand dunes to bury things quickly. They would read of some kid disappearing under shifting sand after excitedly digging a tunnel or a trench. One moment they are there, the next moment gone, suffocating beneath an apparently smooth surface. If you looked very carefully you might just see a ripple, a slight disturbance, a final sign that things were ending.

If the chessmen were simply lost, they would have made no complaint about their burial. Suffocation was not a threat to them for they didn't breathe in the normal way, although they certainly possessed a life of their own. For them there would be no physical damage as the sand gently enveloped them, in fact sand burial would help their preservation. They could rest, unblemished, for centuries awaiting their chance exhumation.

When the chessmen were eventually found and quickly went to the museums on the mainland, there was a brief local outcry, but crofters stood no chance against the Edinburgh elite and all but the lost queen left the island for good. But the magic lay in her, the lost queen, and she stayed on the island, and so the magic remained.

The set was in remarkably good condition considering its age and it was a highly prized museum exhibit. Efforts were made to find the lost piece to complete the set, but despite careful sifting, the missing piece remained hidden beneath the dune, just where Freyja had hidden it, and right where Kt1984, eventually found it.

Freyja had perfectly normal parents for her time. They loved their daughter and were desperate for her to remain safe and healthy, and they tried to encourage her to conform. Conformity was vital for survival. The tribe was suspicious of change, afraid of new things, and could be easily led towards a suspicion of witchcraft if people appeared to be different. Witches were stoned to death and their bodies were burned. The practice made conformity essential.

At first Freyja's parents were pleased that she liked chess, because it seemed a harmless, if rather unusual pastime, which she would surely grow out of. It was a complex and demanding game which they didn't understand, and it was not one for children and certainly not one for girls. Chess was male thing, a warrior's game, a wise old man's game. Something they played when they were too old to fight. No women played it, no girls played it, but Freyja did, and she played it well.

They talked about banning her from playing chess because it seemed abnormal. It threatened the order of things. A girl playing chess was a freak. But Freyja loved the pieces and the complexities of the rules of movement, which enabled the player to consider strategy, forcing them to consider the consequences of particular moves, and making them plot their way to victory; just like Droog-megadeath. Freyja was a natural.

At first, she just watched the old men and held the taken pieces for the players, so they didn't get lost. Eventually the men let her set up the board for their games and she quickly learned where all the pieces went, and by carefully following games, she worked out the complex ways in which pieces were allowed to move. Gradually she plucked up the courage to ask for a game.

She lost at first and the men humoured her. One cruel champion player mocked her continually, but most of them enjoyed her company and often asked her to play, knowing she was easy meat. Freyja gradually worked out some strategies for winning after she realised how important the first moves were. She immediately began to win games. The men became increasingly irritated as she defeated them one by one. She finally defeated the cruel champion. His anger drove him to demand her banishment.

Her father was aware of the growing unease amongst the menfolk and his discomfort was confirmed when he was told to keep her away from the chess boards completely. She had no choice but to stop attending the games, but she continued to play alone. Not wanting to defy her father, she found a compromise by staying away from the men and walking out into the dunes with a set by herself, to handle the ivory figures, arrange them on the board and enter the gamer's world single-handed.

She hid the set in a special place beneath a small flat stone which she found near the beach and hid it all beneath a clump of marram grass, high on the big dune. She walked there to play in the quiet hours. People gradually realised what she was doing during her trips to the dunes. She had to cope with wagging fingers and wagging tongues. She became the black sheep of the tribe, the family failure; the you-will-come-to-a-sticky-end girl who only really wanted to play chess but who, by doing so, had caused a real problem for her community.

The abnormality of girl-chess gave her tribe the excuse they needed to categorise her and eventually separate her from her chess set forever. Non-conformity was a threat. It could not be tolerated. She held on to one important thing before they crushed her spirit; she hid the game more deeply beneath the dunes so that only she would ever know where it was, and she separated the black queen to improve her chances of survival, should the rest of the pieces ever be unearthed.

The black queen was Freyja's favourite piece. Freyja thought that she was the black queen. That secret knowledge gave her the strength she needed for the rest of her life. She reluctantly conformed, never played chess again and she took her gaming knowledge to her grave. She told no one of the buried pieces and knowledge of their very existence died with her.

Her father never understood the damage he had done to her, nor did he ever think that he might have missed an opportunity to help her to grow into something new; a person who could lead the tribe forward and inspire new thinking. He was so embarrassed by Freyja's behaviour and her chess obsession, that he banned her very name for future generations and there were no more Freyja's on the Far Isles for almost two thousand years. The power of the dunes was the power of self-determination and independence exemplified by a young woman who, thousands of years before, was determined enough to preserve her love for a game. The power remained there with the capacity to permeate and inspire Freyja's spiritual descendants.

Kathryn was just such a descendant. She was the kid who sat in the dunes with a MacBook ignoring the family's shouts to play on the sands. She, the iPad girl who preferred ear-buds to earrings, did not know why it felt so right to sit there playing her game; she could not explain the feeling of comfort and enjoyment. She looked at the far masts and domes on Storr Point and wondered, but she never worked it all out. She had played the game hundreds of times before, she was totally used to it, reasonably good at it actually, but somehow it felt different on this dune in Tray Bay, and she was certainly better at it here than she had ever been at home.

Later she described the feeling as spooky to her brother; she would never realise how right she was to use that word. The power of the surviving queen was enough to inspire the modern gamer, and leave her with strong thoughts of independence and magic.

So that's the truth of it. The chessmen, not lost, but hidden. Hidden by a young woman who was so far ahead of her time that her people were frightened by her and forced her to conform, but they never broke her spirit. Her spiritual descendant was no blood relative and she appeared two thousand years later. A slightly punky, Gothy, mildly rebellious girl from Manchester, confident enough to translate family holidays into her own language.

She was the 21st century kid sitting in the dunes with a MacBook, politely ignoring the family's shouts to play cricket on the sands.

Kathryn played the game better than ever, reaching higher levels than she had ever reached before, and gradually realised that there was something special about gaming in that sandy place. She was unaware that Freyja's ghost was the reason for her success in the dunes. The vesper power from a rebellious game player thousands of years before, guided the iPad girl to victory in the drone wars and to world championship.

Freyja enjoyed watching the electronic games being played on the bright screen, even though she did not understand the magic of Kathryn's technology. She wished that she could solidify herself and sit next to the girl and learn how to press the small square buttons that she seemed to be using to play her game. It wasn't her beloved chess, but Freyja wanted to learn the new game anyway. Girls like her are never satisfied simply watching. Freyja was determined to enjoy the new sort of game somehow, and true to form, she found a way.

The day before the holiday ended Kathryn went onto the hill for the last time. She was sad that it was all coming to an end, but time was making its inevitable demands. They all needed to get back home as work, school and college would soon be making their demands too. She logged-on and Kt1984 prepared for a final challenge from whoever happened to be online. The site immediately pinged her a challenger ID.

She could not be challenged for 21 days by anyone she had already beaten, so the challenger had to be a new combatant. She read the name out loud: 'FreyjaG'.

Kt1984 had chosen her number quite deliberately. It came from the dystopian fantasy concocted by a tortured soul on another far isle. She always thought of hidden cameras and 'big brother' when she signed-on with 1984. She loved Orwell as much for his dystopian predictions as she did for his exposure of working-class poverty, just like she loved Dali, simply for his melting clocks. Dali understood the fickle nature of time as much as she did. She had a melting clock as her screen saver.

Here, on her dune she was well clear of Orwellian prying eyes and the only person judging her performance was this new challenger, who could have been literally anywhere in the world, or maybe even off-world. She smiled at the thought.

But Dali's clocks were still melting and she knew that time would always win. She needed to get on with the game. Kathryn flicked return with her thumb to announce her acceptance of FreyjaG's challenge. She stretched her legs out and buried her feet into the soft warm sand in anticipation of the game, and as she did so she felt a small hard object with her toes.

Chapter 10

The Girls in the Jewellery Shop

Islands are no strangers to migration. The movement of people was always part of the essential dynamic of island survival. In bad times people moved out, in good times people moved in. Temporary migrations are usually the result of something being required which the islands cannot supply: advanced medical treatment; higher education; employment experience; hot beach holidays.

Temporary in-moves are usually the result of a craving for a taste of island life, as unsettled mainlanders believe the solution to their problems lies in beautiful isolation; such moves rarely provide answers and usually end quickly.

Safer, short-term inward movements involve conventional holiday visits, wildlife explorations, research projects, or field trips, and those temporary migrants bring money to spend and add value to the economy of the whole archipelago. Some of them brought business opportunities to the islanders. They bought the cloth and the foodstuffs, the whisky, and most recently, the gin. Islanders quickly adapt to the temporary trade opportunities and add to their income by serving the needs of the passing tourists, providing building services for those who seek to refurbish and resettle and by making the best of new trading deals offered by the travelling entrepreneurs.

The Craft Centre was a perfect example of just such an opportunist enterprise in days gone by, and it had benefitted from the travelling trade for hundreds of years. More recently it had grown with the new technology and significantly expanded its markets. It lies close to a place where, in modern times, keen birdwatchers congregate twice a year to spot rare wader migrants on the mudflats. It was a twitcher's paradise. In late September the sheltered, shallow bay provides the first suitable landfall for thousands of birds moving down from the Arctic to more temperate latitudes. A first place of rest after a long and dangerous flight across increasingly stormy waters.

In autumn the mudflats provide a place of safety, a welcoming haven for the nervous birds as they breathe a sigh of relief and look forward to a safe winter in the relatively benign conditions of the British coast. When they move back north, in the springtime, the same salt marshes and sand bars provide the final staging post before the long flight back to the Arctic breeding grounds. They are no longer a welcoming and safe arrival place, they are the final risky stepping stone to the start of the long flight north, a last chance to feed up on lugworms and sand eels before braving the still stormy Atlantic. Rather than welcoming a safe arrival, the marshes were now the birds' departure lounge. Migration for them is part of their natural cycle of movement. A regular event, a natural part of their lives.

Seasonal mass movement is essential to their way of life, vital to their very survival.

Sometimes this has been the case for humans too; essential movement away from danger and towards safety, but now it was more likely to be a temporary move which brought people to these places. Jimmy Walsh migrated there twice a year, on business, and he always visited the Craft Centre during his island trips. He called it 'The Jewellery place'. He went for a coffee and a cake, and to remind himself how special the staff were. Jimmy's biannual migration was really just a couple of long trips which are not enforced or even risky; he jokes about migration but he knows that it's really an inappropriate reference in his case. He was just a visitor. Jimmy knew full well that true migration had always been a very different experience for the island people; much more significant and life changing than a casual trip could ever be.

Migration of people wasn't always a natural movement, like it is for the birds, and it wasn't always a pleasure, as it was for Jimmy Walsh. For the native islanders it was often enforced. For them, it was usually a reluctant choice; an unwelcome disruption which went against all their natural instincts to nurture their families safely, and to root their generations in a well-known and much-loved homeland.

In the past, for many of their forefathers, it was a once-in-a-lifetime decision forced upon them by the politics and economics of a greedy and unforgiving world. Migration was as much a part of the culture of the people of the Far Isles as it was for the waders. The islands had been a stepping-off point for people for centuries; the human equivalent of the springtime launchpad for the birds heading north. The migrating humans headed out over the North Atlantic too, aiming for the New World, hoping it would save their desperate lives and give their children some hope for the future. Like the birds, not all of them made it.

On one of the islands lies the mass grave of over 100 men, women and children who drowned when their emigrant ship foundered near the shore. Near enough for the bodies to wash up on the next tide; just too far out in the stormy water for anyone to get to the safety of dry land. Close, but not close enough. Their lifeless bodies would have been mingling with the remains of the dead sea birds, also overcome by the ferocity of the same storm. They would have drifted in together in the tidal flow, rolling and turning like logs in the water with every passing wave. Risky business migration.

The Craft Centre began life as a jewellery workshop, generations ago. It had existed, in some form, as a centre of island crafts for almost 500 years. It had witnessed the famines, the clearances, the emigrations and even the drownings, which marked the island's history. Initially it was a simple, thatched, stone cottage. An original Black House, housing a family of jewellery craftsmen. They began by making religious artefacts, for that was where the best market was to be found. The church was happy to spend the parishioners' money on such things to glorify their god. The craftsmen specialised in Celtic crosses, decorative chains, fasteners, rings, altar candle sticks, platters and quaich.

During the better times, when islanders could spend small sums on themselves, without offending the church, the craftsmen made kilt pins and broaches, bangles and earrings. During the poverty and famine, and while the clearances were shifting families away, they simply reverted to serving religion, hoping that God would eventually reward their diligence and afford them a little comfort once again.

As tourism slowly developed, the jewellers made more of the personal pieces and less of the religious products as the church's demands pretty well dried up. Good planning by the current group of craftsmen-owners, led to the development of an internet presence, and demand for their jewellery grew as a result of the new markets which went way beyond the islands. As they grew, they began to provide their busiest outlets with personalised display cases, manufactured by a small start-up business on Orkney. They provided cabinets for other island craftsmen too, and their small factory, on a bleak industrial estate on the coast by the Scapa distillery, was working flat out.

The jewellers offered the display cases to shops who were willing to stock samples of their full jewellery range, anywhere in the world. It was a marketing masterstroke. Soon their rings, and other items of personal jewellery, could be found in these attractive cabinets in places as far apart as Edinburgh and Sydney, New York and Shanghai. They were even carried on upmarket cruise liners to provide celebrating couples with the opportunity to buy each other expensive gifts to commemorate their trip of a lifetime.

The stone-built farmhouse was converted, by careful stages into a complex consisting of living accommodation, workshops, a showroom, a gift shop and a café. The courtyard and outbuildings had been developed into a parking area, garage space and secure storage rooms. At the core of the site was the same farmhouse, which had stood for almost 400 years. Welsh slates had replaced heather thatch, and with water and electricity being reliably supplied, the black-house interiors were cleared of peat-smoke stains and brightened up. The café was just the most recent of a series of extensions.

The jewellers managed to combine a modern, businesslike style with a feel for the old and traditional, and the atmosphere was one of open friendliness, reflecting the genuine welcome which was to be found all over the Far Isles. Carpe Diem could have been invented by islanders, who knew, more than anyone, how important each day was, and how wise it was to enjoy every waking hour. This simple belief created the welcomes and the pleasantness which characterised the people of the Far Isles.

The craftsmanship was conducted in the workshop, only to be glimpsed occasionally through the heavy chain curtain which hung across the internal doorway, designed to keep flies out but allow humans to pass through. The workshop contained its secrets well, screened-off behind the shop counter. There was a newer, bigger workshop on a nearby croft, attending to the internet orders, and there were plans to open another, even bigger facility in an old MOD unit which was going on a cheap lease near the airfield. It had been a café but the young women who ran it had recently left the island.

The bigger workroom would help them to meet the ever-growing demand to keep their worldwide cabinets fully stocked, and to respond quickly to internet orders from their growing band of loyal customers. What a tool the internet was. What an impact it was having on the Far Isles. It switched their market from a few hundred annual tourist visitors to hundreds of millions of potential customers.

Maintaining the website was demanding, but it took just one person, working for about two hours a day, to keep hundreds of millions of people fully informed of their products and prices. It was truly a revolution, and one which could secure life on the Far Isles in a way which it had never been secured before. It would be no longer necessary to migrate away from the islands to make a fortune, or even to simply achieve economic stability. It would surely now be possible to enjoy a future in the calm beauty of the archipelago, in the sure knowledge that the future was reasonably secure.

Despite the boom in business, the old, original showroom was small. The real showroom was the website and the showroom at the Craft Centre was just for personal visitors. It displayed a lot of jewellery, with a few other bits and pieces for the less wealthy tourists. Fridge magnets were good sellers, and kids usually went for the pencils with the jeweller's name printed on the side.

The small café was next to the small showroom, just down two wide steps. It took up about half of the entire shop floor: half showroom; half café. The café was started almost accidentally at first. The jewellers took pity on the soaked and shivering twitchers, and started to offer hot drinks to them. The service lasted for a few weeks each year, but it proved to be popular, and even slightly profitable, so the business-minded craftsmen decided to make it a permanent part of their service.

At first, they served the few regular birdwatchers and got to know them personally. The islanders were amused by the variety of English accents and they privately imitated them once the twitchers had left. One of the girls in the café did a perfect Lancashire accent which the rest of the staff found hysterical. They were forever asking her to do an 'ee-bye-gum'.

The café served hundreds of tourists every year, and it was usually very busy, whatever the weather. Coaches began to call in regularly once the café was opened almost all year round, and the provision of toilet facilities, as well as light meals and cakes, proved to be a winner with the tour operators. Most of the tourists were from the cruise ships, which were migrating thousands of people at a time around the coastal maps of the world. Mostly, the passengers just saw the sea, but when they made the occasional landfall, the cruise company depended upon local organisations to provide the all-in day-trip packages which added interest, and more importantly, added income. Island entrepreneurs soon cottoned on. With a decent coach, a good local guide proving the commentary and a couple of stops off to provide food, drink, toilets and a chance to buy local products, they provided exactly what the cruise companies wanted.

The jewellers formed half of the 'Celtic Crafts and Standing Stones' package. One coach would arrive in the morning and the other in the afternoon. Two was really their limit. If the cruise company had more demand for day trips than the jewellers could cope with, they would add: 'Standing Stones and The Gallery by the Sea' to their itinerary and send a coach or two in that direction.

The café was an important part of the Craft Centre's success, and although the jewellery business depended more on internet and international franchise sales, the island home was still at the heart of the business, and the only problem was keeping up with demand. The demand for gifts and the demand for refreshments.

Staffing the Craft Centre was not a problem. The local youngsters were naturals, and anyone from 16 onwards would be more than capable of handling tables and counter sales. None of them were bad at it, but some were better than others, and the two girls at the jewellers were absolute naturals – probably the best on the islands. They charmed everyone and always got generous tips off their cruise ship customers.

The two girls move easily and confidently between all the front-of-house functions. Anything from making drinks to serving up a Coronation Chicken panini. All the café demands were dealt with equally well. There was no problem the girls couldn't handle. Slightly more challenging jobs, like carefully explaining a product range, were delivered with knowledgeable confidence. They often answered product questions while customers ate and drank in the café, carefully steering them towards the shop to purchase their gifts later.

If they had time, the girls would accompany customers to the shop personally and deal with the demonstrations and product sales. If they did that, one of the shop staff would quietly move down into the café to take on the service role while the sales pitch unfolded. It was perfect teamwork.

Clearing tables was easy enough, but it was the meticulous attention they paid to the needs of clients which marked them out as gifted workers. Good people always do the simple things well. They handled what they called the clearances brilliantly: no crockery noise, no spills, a gentle word and a winning smile. Clearance was essential if they were to make the best of the limited space they had, balancing the need to provide customers with a seat as soon as possible, without rushing the people who had just finished their food and drinks. They never pushed clients out but they hovered, politely waiting to move in, to make a table clear and clean for the next customers who would be waiting patiently by the door. They could advise the queue on likely waiting times as they monitored the progress of groups eating scones and drinking coffee, and they were usually right to within a couple of minutes.

They were able to take payments by card, even when the connection was poor and other people failed to make the machine work; they seemed to have a magic touch. They were happy to advise on the best maps to buy, the most appropriate post cards, and the best non-jewellery gifts to take home for friends and family. Their real expertise was related to the jewellery though.

They had both inherited an understanding of the metals and their magic, descended as they were, from the original jewellery craftsmen, 400 years before. They were always able to find the right rings and pendants to please clients, and they were brilliant at suggesting the right earrings for women who were careful about their appearance.

When Jimmy arrived on one of his regular visits, they were carefully managing a fitting for a young couple who wanted to buy each other Celtic rings. It was a quietly conducted affair. A very personal service which treated the couple with special care and attention, and they obviously appreciated it. The girls were making a special occasion even more special with their purely natural people skills. But there was more to it than that. They knew this was a chance to plant a gift in their choice of rings. A surprise which they would only discover many years later. It was time for a handful of island magic to be sprinkled over a young couple who were starting their life together.

The young German students had just graduated from Heidelberg and they had come away together a month before. They wanted to make a memorable trip, an adventure, to commemorate four years of hard work. Africa was out of the question because of the high risk of terrorism or criminal violence. They considered the classic Far East and Australasia trek, but decided to stay in Europe, which they felt would be the safest thing to do. They chose the north-west coast and the Far Isles, for some reason, and they never regretted it.

They were friends, good friends, but nothing more serious than that. They would have a tent as well as an old VW Split-screen Camper Van which they christened The Migrant, and painted the name on the doors with a hippy-style flowery font. They knew they might be thrown together more closely by any sort of unexpected turn of events: an accident or illness for example; bad weather, a ferry cancellation perhaps. They easily agreed clear ground rules even if they had to share a room in an emergency. They wouldn't sleep together and they would never share a toothbrush, but they might share a towel or a track suit top. No problem sharing almost everything, in fact, but nothing else would happen, it would never be everything. They knew how to look after each other and would share all the work and all the costs. There would be no, absolutely no, complications. They would simply enjoy the adventure together as old friends, watching each other's backs.

They had spent four undergraduate years without any complications, and that's why they chose to go travelling together. Supportive and safe; good friends;

simple as that. They would wander round the remote hills and islands without any particular plan; just travelling around like migrants from one campsite to another as the fancy took them. It was a bomb-proof plan.

One week, just seven days, is all it took. One week on the Far Isles and the ground rules evaporated. There were just too many sensations, too many totally magical moments. They were both battered into submission by the magic of the islands. The sunrises and sunsets, the deer roaming close by, the soaring eagles and the quartering owls, the hunting harriers and the tumbling waters. They were mesmerised by the landscape and by the sudden appearance of huge cliffs and breaking waves, crashing rocks against the stacks and arches. They were fascinated by the ancient settlements and burial grounds, and by the enduring island culture. They wild camped whenever they didn't need campsite facilities. They marvelled at the fields of barley swaying in the wind as if it was commanded by some magical remote control which made the crop mimic the waves on the sea.

They couldn't believe the way in which the dark skies revealed the richness of the universe, with more stars than they had ever seen before. They were hypnotised by the people and their ancient culture, by the sense of timelessness and mystical tradition, and most of all they fell in love with the beaches; huge, lonely places, bordering both the land and the ocean. Flimsy lines of yellow sand marking that most fundamental boundary; land and sea, life and death, safety and danger, almost solid separated from ever-moving liquid by a simple strand line. They fell in love on a beach too, and they simply forgot about the ground rules. In just seven days they had been transformed from two into one.

That's what the Far Isles are capable of. They can take your life or make your life. They can make you fall in love or tear someone dear away. The islands will choose what to do, you won't have to ask and you probably won't have any control whatsoever over the outcome.

The die was cast; the only question was how to mark the moment when the rest of their lives had just been determined. The young Germans thought that island rings would be the best symbol of the new and unexpectedly serious relationship, because they knew that it had developed under a Celtic spell. They spotted the jewellers and walked in without discussing the matter; it just seemed to be the right thing to do.

The girls knew, as soon as they saw the couple looking at rings, that there must have been a backstory and they wanted to help the pair celebrate their relationship with a suitable touch of magic. They signalled the jeweller and he just nodded in understanding. He brought out the tray of special rings from the high shelf in his workshop. His colleagues noticed and smiled; something special was about to happen. They hadn't sold one of those for years. The last time it was to a young member of a very famous family, looking for something special for his grandmother's birthday.

This time it was two young Germans, who fell in love unexpectedly, and decided to share some ancient Celtic symbols of allegiance; they really wanted rings, so rings were what the girls presented to them. Cleverly establishing the amount the youngsters could afford, the girls fixed the price exactly to match their available funds. The rings were a perfect fit for them both. They were the perfect customers for the girls' thoughtfulness.

Decades later the Germans would discover that the rings were purest gold, and that the intricate knotted pattern woven into their surface, was over 1,000 years old, the earliest examples being found on the stone circle monoliths beyond the causeway. The Germans would be reminded of their moments of magic on the Far Isles every time they saw the rings on their fingers, but only realise their unique value decades later. They would plan a return visit to celebrate their retirement, four decades after their first visit to the Craft Centre. When they eventually returned, the girls would be long gone, but the jewellers would still be there and the true story of the rings would be carefully explained to the former students who decided to spend their lives together during their first visit to the Far Isles.

The two girls were a great team and they covered everything easily with the lovely western isles accent lilting its way around every syllable, but time moved on and eventually they would too. They talked confidently about anything and everything but they never talked about the big storm when their friends died just up the road, right where the waders found safety, right where the twitchers competed for a sighting; that's where their friends died.

They never mentioned the tragedy even though they knew all about it. They lived it and they felt it, but they didn't ever talk about it. They didn't because they knew the family so well, and the twins were their best friends. Talking about it never helped; people said it would, but it didn't. They just didn't talk about it, as if that would make it go away. It didn't, and even Jimmy Walsh didn't know that, even though he found out more about the two girls in the jeweller's shop than most people ever did.

Jimmy Walsh was always drawn back to the jewellers. It reminded Jimmy of the place in Lochalech on the west coast mainland where you could get the best pies in Britain at the end of a 50-mile road to nowhere. Not just the best pies but 20 varieties of the best pies. The coffee was very good there too, and the people made you feel so welcome. He tried to think of a word to describe it: he thought incongruous would probably do it.

Jimmy loved that; when you have no right to expect brilliance and suddenly, there it is.

Whether it's a coffee, a pie, a slice of cake, a perfect malt or an outstanding gin. It may be a word, a gesture, a genuine handshake or gentle kiss on the forehead, it could be anything, but if it takes your breath away because you never expected it; it is brilliant! The Craft Centre did all of those things as far as Jimmy was concerned, which was why he loved the place. But most of all Jimmy wanted to talk to the girls and he was so pleased that they enjoyed talking to him.

He was staying nearby for a few days, re-exploring the isles, crossing all the causeways, and calling in every day for a coffee and maybe a bite to eat. He had upgraded the aerials at Storr Point for the second time. His new communications company had secured ministry contracts. He expected to be working at the radar stations the following year and probably at the airfield too. He was making a lot of money and hoped for international contracts over the next 12 months. This time he also wanted to buy a proper gift of jewellery from the Craft Centre.

The girls remembered him well enough from his previous visits and treated him almost like a friend. He knew about food and the ways that cafés worked. He didn't say anything about his own work, or his successful electronics empire, because he wanted to learn innocently, like a layperson discovering the way things were done. He smiled at the thought of being under cover.

One quiet morning they joined him at his table when he had finished his full-Scottish. They brought their sourdough toast and smoothies with them and, smiling a little awkwardly, pulled two chairs out. They weren't sure if they were doing the right thing, but they felt that they couldn't sit separately as he was the only customer in the place. Neither of them joked much, they took life very seriously behind that pleasant professional front, and conversation was rather forced at first.

Jimmy risked asking them some simple questions about themselves. There were two of them, so any embarrassment would be diluted by sharing, and there was little risk of offending them with his curiosity. He would never have approached one of them in this way, but as they had the numerical advantage over him, he felt he was on safer ground. They reacted positively and talked about school and hopes for college places on the mainland, and they talked about island music and the annual folk festival on the southernmost island.

The Far Isles Folk Festival was a causeway and two ferries away, and attending it required overnight stays for three nights. For them, it was the absolute high spot of the year. It was a pity they had to wait 12 months for it to come round again. It was like waiting for Christmas, or your next birthday. When the magic day finally arrived again it could not be the same as the last one because, as each year passed, the participants became one year older, with the passage of time bringing different expectations.

Time passed, and there were inevitably consequences. Different shape, different size, different face, different skin, different tastes, a different set of experiences and, probably, a very different set of expectations. Jimmy guessed that drink and boys would be playing a much more important part this year than three years ago, when they first went to the festival, and he wanted to warn them about the new risks, but he had no right to do so; so he didn't.

They politely asked about his plans for the weekend. He admitted that he would probably give the festival a miss. They laughed. He said he wanted to visit local graveyards as part of his research into Far Isles history, tracing Clan names and looking for famous local figures. He said he was interested in victims of World War Two who were washed up on the island shore, more than 70 years before. Perhaps after an aircraft went down or the U-boats sank a convoy ship. They knew of some sites and advised him how to find them by following the War Graves Commission signs.

He told them that he knew about the family tragedy nearby during the big storm and thought he would look for those graves too. They smiled shy smiles, said nothing and then looked away as if to close the conversation. The sudden closure surprised him, but he sensed a personal sensitivity on their part and he probed no further. He had business elsewhere on the island for the rest of the day and he left them to it.

By the time he returned, the Craft Centre was closed for the day and the whole area was deserted. The girls were off to enjoy their three days in the world of music festivals. This was their Knebworth, their Glastonbury, their 'Who Live at Leeds'; Jimmy hoped they had their 'Queen at Live Aid' moment.

He left his lodgings after the evening meal and went looking for the local graveyard. It was easy to find. He parked the Land Rover at the end of the track which led to the place and he found that it was right on the coast, with the Atlantic waves crashing in, down on the shingle beach about 100 yards away. There are two types of beaches on the Far Isles: beautiful, deserted golden sands, like the one that beguiled the young Germans, and beaches like this one. Unattractive grey shingle, littered with the flotsam of the busy North Atlantic. Not beautiful perhaps, but nonetheless impressive. Perhaps these were the real 'working' beaches of the Far Isles, littered with old floats and broken netting, old ropes and washed-up remains of timber planks, splintered by the sea and sprinkled with a selection of plastic, ranging from drinks bottles to protective sheeting, blown off some container ship miles away from this resting place.

For him, on that day, the weather was beautiful and calm with barely a whisper of wind. These breaking waves had been generated days ago by some mid-Atlantic storm over 1,000 miles out, 100 horizons away from there, but such was the energy of that storm that these waves reached out far enough to crash against this lonely Hebridean shore. Even on a calm day, they provided an impressive and appropriate soundtrack for Jimmy's homage.

Sometimes people do something big, like that storm did out there, and the ripples go on for ages and wash up all over the place. Collateral damage; unintended consequences; very much a part of life. Sometimes the original actions go completely unnoticed while the unintended consequences are noticed by everyone. The outer ripples of a storm can affect far more people than the original event.

He wondered who remembered the long-dead servicemen and whether their final acts of sacrifice had any impact on the outcome of the World War Two at all. He found the graves of the sailors and aircrew immediately; the standard ministry headstones were always a giveaway. Concrete slabs with their regimental insignia moulded into the surface. He read the names of the 12 men and noted their ages. The aircrew were particularly young; none were older than 23.

After reflecting on the lives of young men lost in war he moved on and soon found the resting place for the family drowned in the storm just a few years before, long after the war was over. These were the graves the girls didn't want to talk about. Unlike the austere war graves, these were decorated simply and beautifully with fresh flowers. The twins were so young, much younger victims of the Atlantic waters than even those young airmen had been. The graveyard was deserted but the flowers on the family's resting place were obviously a very recent gesture. Jimmy read the headstones and then placed his flowers gently down beside the others.

Anyone who has ever loved another person in their lives would have been moved by the simple headstones, engraved with the girls' names and recording the length of their brief lives. The perceptive visitor would realise that the soundtrack of the nearby ocean explained these tragic deaths more clearly than any words, and it was that realisation which moved even those with the hardest hearts to tears.

The place is almost always deserted, and it let you show your emotion without embarrassment, without witness. It was a good place to grieve in private, not just for this unfortunate family but for everyone in your life you have ever loved and lost, and for everyone you do love and fear losing.

A small local fishing boat chugged by, about half a mile offshore. Jimmy thought he heard rock music for a second but it was carried away on the wind. The music reminded him of the two girls and the music festival. He wondered if they danced to rock music. The music drifted in again and Jimmy realised that it was coming from the boat.

Back at the lodgings Jimmy had a whisky with the landlord and they talked about the great storm because he didn't mind talking about it. He was involved in the search and recovery, and could explain clearly what had happened and what had gone wrong. He ended up repeating, repeatedly: 'It should never have happened, it should never have happened,' and shaking his head with tears in his eyes. They had another drink to get over the emotional moment and they both recovered well enough, but the truth was, the islands never completely recover from any tragedy; each one leaves its mark forever.

Jimmy realised that the girls were somehow close to the storm victims, and like his landlord, who will never recover, the two girls will never recover either. Three days later Jimmy called in for a farewell coffee and to buy a jewellery gift for a good friend of his. A woman who meant a lot to him but was no longer part of his life. He had no idea what to buy. They asked him to describe his friend.

He admitted to the girls that he couldn't really do it very well, and said their questions reminded him of that Elton John song where someone can't remember the colour of a friend's eyes. Both girls smiled at Jimmy's attempt to be cool. They knew the song and sang lines of it just to prove how well versed they were in Elton discography. Hot from Barra Fest they were on a high and keen to help.

They asked Jimmy to describe anything about his friend but he found it too difficult. He simply could not put his clear mental picture into words. They said it was difficult because he didn't really want to describe the image in his head. Some things, they said, are better left as mental pictures, living in our imagination, never being articulated, never exposed to the stark light of day. Jimmy basked in the revelation they had unwittingly shared with him. These great young women had learned to survive by holding onto mental pictures and protecting them from the cold light of reality.

They finally picked him a Celtic cross on a silver chain and hoped that the gods would smile on the wearer and bring her good fortune. They knew it was a special item, fashioned from very old silver, which had been traded in the islands 700 years before. Jimmy would never find out; his friend would never be told. When she received the gift through the post, she knew it was from him even though the cryptic note wasn't signed. She knew because of the postmark and the message. The handwritten note simply said: 'Every man is an island.' She told her partner that she'd bought it from an online jeweller, which was almost true. She sensed a strange feeling whenever she wore it; a feeling of contentment, a feeling of peace, which came from the metal itself.

Sale complete, the girls came to the door and waved Jimmy off. 'Till next year,' they shouted and laughed.

'Yes, till next year.'

They both leaned forward and kissed Jimmy on the cheek. It was the first time that had ever happened, maybe things were changing. As Jimmy drove along the causeway and left the beautiful, sad place behind, he glanced at the twin radar domes on the ridge and wondered if the girls would still be around when he returned to service them in 12 months' time. He was glad that he had failed to describe his friend to the two girls; he didn't want to leave any vestige of her there for the powerful elements and omnipresent ghosts to play about with. That could be dangerous.

Jimmy never returned to the Far Isles. He was killed in the Russian airline disaster six months later, travelling from Estonia to Italy in order to explore the possibility of expanding his electronics business in Eastern Europe. Most of the passengers were German and Polish, so

Jimmy featured on the British media because he was the only UK victim. There was some speculation about terrorist activity, as there always was when a Russian plane went down. British Intelligence suspected that it had run out of fuel. Russian intelligence knew exactly what had happened and began to hunt down the responsible parties immediately.

When the story broke and Jimmy's picture flashed on the TV screen in the Craft Centre café, the girls were too busy serving tourists to notice. They waited for his return for the whole of the next summer season but assumed he had lost interest in the Far Isles when he never appeared, never suspecting that he had no choice in the matter any longer.

Chapter 11

Another Last Supper

Tommy McKinnon was cruising towards bedtime and everything was going well. He had lived his whole life on the Far Isles and now he was finishing his time off in the capital. He had always lived more remotely, in small villages by the sea, but the capital provided best for his needs now, so that is where he ended up. It was hardly a demanding life because he was used to the routine of the place and every important thing was set up for his convenience. It all just worked, like a well-oiled machine. He still had a part to play of course, but the pressure was off now. Other people did so much for him, and they would do even more as his own capacity diminished; that's what he paid for.

He was slow and awkward with aching joints and uncertain balance, and he always felt unsteady on his feet. There were limits to what he could do for himself, but the room and the furniture helped him to make the best of it when he was alone. Tommy was content; he could so easily have not made it this far. He could cope with his physical limitations in this benign environment. He didn't like it, he would have preferred to be young again, but he could manage perfectly well and he knew that he was luckier than many people of his age.

The idea of being 'in a home' would have shocked him a few years earlier; he would have said: 'They'll never get me into one of those places.'

Neither of his own parents had ended up in a home. One died in their own home, and the other in hospital after a very brief stay. Both had harboured illness quietly until the inevitably fatal point was reached, without their GP ever knowing. Tommy had learned from their suffering, and decent medical support had kept him well enough until old age began to wear him out.

For all his problems he was pleased with this place. He was well cared for and able to maintain as much freedom as he wanted. Most importantly his presence here made his family feel better. They did not have to cope with him, and they could get on with their lives knowing that he was safe and comfortable and in the hands of good people. On balance, thought Tommy, it was all for the best.

The most difficult part of each day wasn't the immobility, limiting though it was, the hardest part was the thinking. When he was sound asleep, he dreamed very clearly, and he always woke up happy and refreshed, almost as though he had lived a full life while he was sleeping, and he was always ready for another day of rest; but daytime thinking was another thing. It was increasingly hard for him to keep his thoughts in order and to stay focused on any job to be done. He sometimes struggled to remember things like names: names of people; names of places; even the names of some objects, like the makes of cars or types of breakfast cereal.

He was finding it increasingly difficult to take an initial idea all the way to a reasonable conclusion, and even if he read for a while, he couldn't always remember where he started from. He once said to his son that if he read a newspaper from start to finish, he could start all over again because he would have already forgotten the first story.

He was always reaching for thoughts, but often failed to grasp them. It was as if they were just a little bit too far away. He knew they were out there somewhere, but often he couldn't quite get there. It was like gradually losing sight of a landscape as the mist rolled in. It was frustrating, but he was used to it; it was part of the endgame that he knew that he was playing.

Sometimes very clear memories would suddenly come into his head and he seemed to remember every detail. He remembered faces, names, places, incidents and outcomes, as if they had just happened. He really enjoyed those moments of clarity, and he wondered if he was always able to remember things so clearly when he was younger; but of course, he couldn't remember. He just assumed that his mind used to be like that all the time – sharp.

He often tried to remember his mother. Sometimes he could hear her saying, 'Our Tommy's been in the knife box again,' when he said something funny which made her laugh. A strange expression which he took for granted as a child; he took it as a compliment, an acknowledgement of a quick wit. He remembered that he liked to make his mother laugh; it was good to see her happy. That expression about the knife box was one which had stuck in his mind since childhood, but he had never really understood what it was supposed to mean.

Did it just mean clever, or could it mean hurtful? Did it mean he was making funny remarks which amused her or did it mean that his remarks were wounding her in some way? He would never know; she wasn't there to ask any more.

Memories of his mother sometimes made Tommy cry quietly; he was already much older than she had been when she died of cancer, and he knew that his life, hard though it had been at times, had been much easier than hers. She just had the family. No spare cash, no good clothes, no holidays, no car, no job, no meaning beyond the four walls of the small council house. Tommy's mum had never eaten a meal in a restaurant in her life. She had never had a decent break at all in fact. Surviving the war and getting her husband back was the first real achievement in her life, and looking after her family for 30 years was the second.

He felt sorry for her and wished he could have done more to help her but it was far too late for that. He could only enjoy the thought that she had wanted him to do well, and she died believing that he had started a better life than she had been able to have. It was her dream that each generation would do better than the previous one; she told him that. It was the only dream she shared with him; it may have been the only dream she ever had. He had done better than her and his children were doing better than he had. He hoped that his grandchildren would fair even better still: be even happier, even healthier, even safer, and even more successful. When he thought like that Tommy felt that he was helping to keep his mother's dream alive and he smiled.

Tommy's rooms were comfortable, convenient and practical, but they also had personal touches which made them more like home than rooms in a home. Those personal touches were enough to make Tommy feel at home, albeit not as at home as really being in his own house. Some of the furniture was his, many of his books were there, his outdoor clothes hung by the door and even though he would never use them again they reminded him of walking and bird watching, on remote Scottish islands and on Normandy beaches.

He still used his own crockery, including his favourite mug and an old plastic plate which he bought from a camping shop almost 70 years before. It was the one survivor from the set they used on camping holidays when the children were young, and it always brought back happy memories of family times in Scotland during long summer holidays. When it sat on his tray, he only needed to look at it and something came back to him.

Yesterday he suddenly remembered eating heated-up hot dogs from a tin with local bread rolls sold in the site shop at Sango Sands, and how much the boys enjoyed that simple camper's meal. There were always families with bigger tents and some with small caravans, but none of them had managed to achieve as much in the time they had as Tommy's family did. They prided themselves on doing interesting things, on taking that last walk in the twilight while other families watched their TV sets, and being rewarded with the sight of a barn owl quartering nearby fields or an otter squirming along the banks of a ditch as it made its way home.

There were always bats to be glimpsed out of the corner of an eye, and even when they were very young, Tommy's children could spot a bat a mile off. It turned into a competition with the first spotter saying: 'Bat,' and pointing with an arm.

'Where?'

'Over there.'

'Seen it, and there's another.'

Tommy used to pretend not to see them and the boys excitedly tried to get him to spot one. When he sensed that interest was waning, he would suddenly shout: 'Seen one.'

He was never sure whether the, 'Well done Dad,' was an expression of congratulation or irony; but it didn't matter, it was just a game of engagement after all. Happy memories; Tommy was glad that bats were protected, they deserved to be.

But it was the photographs which wore the really personalising touch. Tommy looked at them most of the time; more than he watched TV, more than he looked out of his first-floor window across the park where young families played and people walked their dogs. Some of the photographs were on the wall and some were on the book shelves, but his current favourites, all of his grandchildren with their newly acquired dog, were either on the table next to his chair or on the small bedside cabinet next to his bed. He liked those photographs because they were the future, and soon he would be the past, in fact, he often felt as though he was already the past.

His grandchildren were fascinated by one old photograph of Tommy's father working on the construction of the causeway they drove over every time they visited him. Whenever they came, they asked him about their great grandad working with the construction gang and he made up stories about it. They listened, with rapt attention, to his tales and believed every word. Some of it was true, and remembering things his father had said during his own childhood provided a firm basis for the stories he invented to amuse his grandchildren. Storytelling provided a welcome break in the predictable daily round.

The ritual schedule of Tommy's day dealt with all those necessary personal things associated with getting up; getting washed and dressed; toileting and doing simple exercises. They were the basic stuff of life now and Tommy was used to being helped in increasingly personal ways by the staff at the home, and especially by My Lai, who had become very important to him.

Tommy saw his family members quite often. The home was chosen because it was reasonably close to where they all lived and it was easy for them all to get there from time to time, to see him, but he saw My Lai every day and he felt that he knew her better than he knew anyone now. She cared for him and respected him; she looked after his personal needs when he could not manage to do so for himself and she cleverly enabled his independence to survive too, as far as it could. Perhaps, most importantly, she made mealtimes very special, especially the most important meal of the day for Tommy, the final ceremony before sleep – supper.

He did not always eat alone. Sometimes he went down to the lounge for lunch and sometimes family members joined him and shared a bite to eat, but he always had supper in his own room, and he knew that My Lai would always be close by, and sometimes she would sit with him if he wanted her to.

His favourite shared meal was with his grandchildren and of all the family visits he enjoyed his grandchildren's visits most because they were such good company, and they were the future. They were the future his mother had dreamed of. Perhaps one day they would have children too, and the world would continue to spin through space with good humans on it. He knew that he would never see great grandchildren, but he still hoped to have them.

His own children were very much the present. They were the epitome of the fully functioning, working adults who kept the show on the road. They were the money-earners with mortgages and pension plans, lease cars and holiday bookings two years ahead, they were the planners and influencers, they were the very stuff of established social order; part of the establishment in fact. The establishment which all civilised societies inevitably required so that things actually worked. There was a price to be paid for that sort of life though; the price was hard work preoccupying your time; a businesslike approach to everything; and a relentless focus on career. Whenever his own children came, they were always preoccupied with something else: the next thing to do; the bills to be paid; the domestic improvement to be organised; the holidays to be booked. Tommy understood all that. They were busy people with complex lives. He smiled at what he thought of as irony: the more successful the family is, the less successful the family is.

His grandchildren were not like that at all. They were still experimenting with life, learning the rules, changing their ideas, slowly establishing their values and beliefs and consistently challenging the expectations of their elders. They would eventually become the next establishment, but for now they were wonderfully naive and unpredictable, unafraid to get things wrong, unaware when their simple comments betrayed enormous insight, well beyond the capacity of hidebound adults, whose thinking had already been carefully schooled. The grandchildren were eager to learn about life, and because of that they were a joy to be with, and like My Lai, they treated him with respect. His age and frailty did not matter to them; he was just Grandad.

Sometimes they shared a lunchtime meal with him but more often they would sit around and share his tea.

My Lai would make extra ham sandwiches on white bread with the crusts cut off and no mustard. She would secretly provide prawn cocktail crisps, rich tea biscuits and thin scones with butter and jam. Once she made biscuit butties and they immediately became the firmest favourite of all. There would always be Battenberg cake when the boys joined Grandad for tea and they would each get a plastic tumbler full of blackcurrant cordial and a small bowl of cashew nuts with slices of freshly peeled apple; always Pink Lady. For all of them it was a real treat, a much-loved ritual. The boys thought it would last forever; Tommy knew it wouldn't.

Tommy loved tea with his grandchildren but, if anything, he loved supper even more because it was a luxury, an indulgence, something he could survive without; a luxury rather than a necessity. Any sort of luxury was a treat. Tommy never took luxury for granted, simply because he had rarely experienced it. His life was nowhere near as hard or as limited in its scope as his mother's had been, but it hadn't been easy either. He had lived from bank loan to bank loan and always worried about his mortgage and his rights to his croft. The day he paid it all off and secured his tenure, he felt the weight lift from his shoulders. Supper was a simple luxury, but it was a luxury nevertheless and that is why he enjoyed it: a simple luxury every day. A good way to end a life, he thought. Weight off the shoulders and a bit of luxury.

He needed breakfast to kick start his metabolism, his body expected a lunch in order to quell hunger pangs and a light tea was a traditional part of his eating habits which the home dutifully maintained, and it had developed into a sometimes very pleasant ritual with his grandsons, but supper was something new; a special occasion which My Lai insisted on preparing for him and one which he had grown to love. He had never had supper before he came to live in the home.

He didn't remember who was first to call it 'not the last supper', but they both laughed about it. My Lai referred to each ceremony as just supper, even though she knew what 'the last supper' meant. She was rather superstitious, and using a term which even hinted at finality was something she simply could not do. Tommy on the other hand enjoyed the gallows humour so typical of his generation, so 'last supper' was no problem to him, in fact, it made him smile.

They both knew that Tommy's life would end in this place, they didn't know when, but they both knew it would. They knew that if he died in his sleep, which they both secretly hoped for, then, one day, his final evening meal would really be his last supper. Tommy knew that as each day passed, he became less relevant. Each passing day slid him a few more inches into obscurity. Each passing day meant that people would pay less attention to what he had to say and would increasingly forget everything that he had done. Time was the enemy of life, and eventually there would be a last supper.

Quite independently of each other, both Tommy and My Lai prepared for supper in the full knowledge that it might be the final ceremony before going to sleep forever. Tommy was completely comfortable with the idea. He had embraced what was fashionably known as 'mindfulness' ever since he became seriously ill for the first time. His almost complete recovery simply reminded him how fortunate he was to experience each day. His life became a series of days, each one to be enjoyed, each a series of moments to be appreciated. The end of each day was a ritual which he and My Lai carefully respected.

It always began with a soft knock on the door, after which it opened slowly as My Lai carefully entered. She always looked in to make sure Tommy was comfortable to receive her. Tommy looked up and smiled at the young Cambodian refugee, who had been granted residency to protect her from traffickers.

My Lai was a qualified nurse and carer, and her professional abilities would probably secure citizenship for her eventually. She had impressed Tommy's family with her genuine and touching relationship with their dying father, and they had enough power and influence between them to secure her future in her new chosen country. She more than deserved the reward. Tommy thought that she was developing a slight island accent to her English; he hoped she was catching it off him.

My Lai bowed slightly and put her hands together, Tommy smiled and did a thumbs up. They both laughed. The different greetings neatly reflected their cultures which came from different sides of the world, but which came together perfectly in this private place. My Lai carefully pushed the trolley into the room and parked it close to Tommy's chair so he could see everything on it, but far enough away so that she would have to wait on him and transfer the plates and cups across to his table. It was part of the ritual. They both had roles to play and they played them well.

That evening it was one of his favourite suppers: toasted teacake with butter, warm white toast with marmalade and tea. It would be English Breakfast tea, Normandy butter, Frank Cooper's Fine Cut Oxford Marmalade, and Warburton's small White Toastie bread, all served with his red plastic camping plate and the Calmac mug. The butter reminded him of many happy trips to France and the tea and white bread had been family favourites for years. The marmalade was the only one they had ever used, ever since it first appeared in local supermarkets. It seemed special, somehow better than the normal stuff, and his boys had collected the jars to keep pencils in, carefully washing the empty jars so the labels were preserved.

Two sat on his sideboard with his youngest grandson's crayons in one of them and black fibre-tipped pens in the other. They weren't used much now but they would remain there as reminders of past times when pictures and drawings were coloured-in here and neat writing was practiced and, sometimes, important homework was completed at the last minute, during a teatime visit.

But this was supper, not tea, and there were unofficial rules to be observed. My Lai served the teacake on his own plate and poured the drink for him. The toast was ready for the marmalade and he asked her to put it on for him while he enjoyed the first sip of tea followed by a quarter of the still-warm teacake. Tommy savoured the familiar taste of the crisp toasted surface of the teacake and the mingling of the bready part, the sultanas and the smooth French butter. He decided to sample the toast and marmalade before finishing the teacake and My Lai served him both slices onto the camping plate.

Tommy sipped more tea and slowly ate the toast, enjoying the familiar taste of the marmalade and staring at the jar which reminded him of so many things. My Lai offered him more tea but he had had enough and he had one more sip before finishing off the teacake. Another last supper was almost over. Tommy licked his finger and used it to pick up a few crumbs of toast off the plate so he could eat them. It was an old camping habit which made washing up easier. The last crumbs of a last supper.

He took a final sip of tea, looked at My Lai and said, "Thank you, that was perfect."

My Lai cleared the plates back onto the trolley but left his Calmac Mug; Tommy liked to go to sleep with it next to him on the bedside cabinet. It helped him remember so many good things and led him into happy dreams of holidays and adventures with his family. She would wash it for him in the morning when she brought his breakfast.

She knew that one day soon she would not have to give him breakfast and she always felt sad at the thought of it. One day it really would be the last supper. The same unspoken thought always occurred to Tommy as he prepared for sleep, but Tommy knew that he was fine. He would only ever know when it wasn't his last supper, for waking happily after a night of dreams would show that he was ready for another day, and that the previous supper had just been supper; the best meal of the day, and he would have to wait for the real last supper.

Chapter 12

End Game

One predictable disadvantage of remote island life will always be the lack of advanced medical services. There were decent GPs and a pharmacy within reach of most settlements, and on bigger islands there were small facilities for dealing with minor ailments and injuries, usually located at a local clinic or at a community medical centre. These services were insufficient for critical cases, and they would usually require airlifting to a mainland hospital.

The Far Isles archipelago was fortunate in respect of its medical provision. The capital had a small, modern hospital as well as easy access to the ferries and airport. It also had the only significant collection of shops and the only proper supermarket across the whole island chain. There were three pharmacies, one specialising in the mobile distribution of medication to all parts of the island chain. There were sufficient cheap hotels to accommodate family members when patients required longer stays in the hospital and day visits were impractical.

The capital also provided the main secondary school, the only tertiary college, four petrol stations, a taxi service, car hire, a coach company and more coffee shops and ATMs than all the rest of the islands put together. Home of 'the townies', the capital often entertained foreign seafarers and most of the islands' tourists, including the thousands of annual cruise liner passengers who paid a small fee for the lighters to take them the short distance from the deepwater anchorage to the quayside. The tourist money supported jewellery shops, gift shops, local fashion outlets, three restaurants and several pubs which served decent food. It all conspired to make the capital quite different from anywhere else on the rest of the island group.

Local fishermen made safe money by providing trips to see the marine wildlife, hoping that the local dolphin pod would turn up on time, and secretly praying that an orca would at least show its back for a few seconds. Their sales cabins were adorned with pictures of killer-whale fins and near-surface images of basking sharks, neither of which were usually spotted on the tourist runs. The more successful outfits provided oilskins for their clients, knowing that even if the rain stayed away, the spray would be too much for the average tourist's waterproofs.

The hospital just formed part of the services which the capital provided, and like all hospitals, it could suddenly play a vital part in someone's life, having gone almost unnoticed until it was called upon to perform. Hope Hospital was small, but the facilities were good enough to scan and to X-ray, to perform most types of surgery, to deal with accident and emergency traumas, and to provide effective isolation for critical disease cases.

The small coronary unit was well used to dealing with heart-attack cases. The predominance of old people on the cruises resulted in more than the national average of cardiac arrests on the streets of the town, as weak and weary folk enjoying their 'holiday of a lifetime', suddenly clasped their chests and collapsed onto the wet cobbles. The cardiac team was perfectly capable of dealing with anything short of major heart surgery, and they secretly joked about, one day, performing a transplant.

For the islanders themselves, the Hope was usually called 'The Cottage' because it started life as a cottage hospital and traditional titles were long-lasting in the Far Isles. Tommy Mac went into The Cottage for cardiac investigations. They had a new scanner and the young cardiovascular team were keen to use it. Tommy laughed when they told him that he would be injected with some radioactive stuff which they would track as it was pumped around by his heart. He asked them whether there was any danger of an explosion with him disappearing under a mushroom cloud. They laughed but told him, seriously, that he shouldn't hug any children for a few days.

He had to lie still for 15 minutes on the scanner bed while the machine made its video of the isotopes flowing round his body. Tommy managed it easily by falling asleep. He enjoyed lying on his back and he enjoyed sleeping. He began to dream of a film with someone riding on an atom bomb as it headed towards its target, but a nurse woke him up before he could see the ending.

They decided to keep Tommy in for a week or so to carry out more tests and perform what they described as a minor procedure. His report spoke about serious concern over heart failure, but they didn't tell Tommy, nor did they tell him that they were arranging for his transfer to a mainland hospital for further surgery. It was at that point that everything changed.

He was surprised when he was suddenly sent back to the care home; the cardiac team at The Cottage were dismayed because they knew he would become a casualty of the forces which were changing their world completely. Barriers between doctors and patients were being swiftly erected, new hospital rules imposed and plastered all over the buildings on huge posters. Tommy was caught in the middle of a pandemic.

He went back to a completely changed care home; changed because it had transformed from a place of familiar, friendly safety to something precisely the opposite. A place of barriers and distancing, which turned out to be incubating death; shortening life rather than prolonging it. Tommy was surprised to find some of the staff wearing plastic face visors and rubber gloves, but not all of them did, and he heard them talking about social distancing and deep cleaning.

Tommy returned to his care home without the minor procedure having taken place, without expert medical attention or modified medication, and without the knowledge that his future had been determined by forces as far beyond his control as the wild Atlantic storms which had ended the lives of so many of his friends. It was another sort of storm which ended Tommy's life, and in its own way, it depended upon a series of unfortunate coincidences to produce the end game, just as a death at sea does.

There would always be miraculous survivors and unfortunate victims, differentiated as much by chance as anything else. A freak wave, a failed lifeline, a malevolent storm, versus a lifesaving rescue from a mountainous sea or a one-in-a-million air pocket trapped beneath an overturned boat. Tommy was discharged before the lifesaving stents could be fitted, and before appropriate medication could be calculated, formulated and issued. There was to be no miraculous escape for Tommy Mac this time.

Tommy's place in the queue for heart surgery on the mainland was cancelled and he was discharged from a place of safety and hope, to a place which unwittingly exposed him to fatal danger, as surely as a tempest on the high seas. The care home he left a few days before felt like a totally different place now.

He didn't see My Lai at all for the first few days. The staff who helped him were somehow different from her. Not just different people, as they had a different attitude too. The friendliness was gone. He felt as though he was being treated by people who didn't know him. Tommy slowly deteriorated in the care home for three months, until the combination of the virus and his failing heart brought him to his final day, his end game.

***

He lay quite still, on his back, his arms and legs in perfect symmetry.

He controlled this position deliberately.

He found comfort in the simple achievement of symmetry.

He enjoyed sensing the first signs of asymmetry creeping in, and he enjoyed applying small corrective movements to get the geometry right again.

He could feel the bed beneath his shoulders and heels, and he could feel the pillow beneath his head. He knew that he had bedsores, which were treated every day, and he found the treatment painful and humiliating, but they were not hurting him now and he was grateful for that.

He was in a state of calmness and contentment. He knew it would not last for long, but for now he was happy, and enjoying the moment.

He always had been able to make the best of things, even bad things. When others defaulted to complaining at the slightest opportunity, he had always been able to see the bright side.

'Grateful for small mercies,' his mother used to say.

Grateful for small mercies indeed, he thought, and smiled to himself as he remembered her words.

He was unable to open his eyes for some reason and his breathing was shallow. He could hear it rasping in his chest and he was making more of an effort to breathe than he usually had to.

He was completely unaware of the virus which was sweeping the world and he had no idea that it had found its way into his care home through a lack of knowledge, careless hygiene and the absence of effective protective equipment.

His carers began to use face shields, but because they completely misunderstood the nature of droplet and aerosol infection, their shields simply directed their exhalations down onto their patients, effectively ensuring cross-contamination.

The virus came to the care home via a cleaner, whose daughter had caught it in a Glasgow night club during a drunken hen night.

She was asymptomatic, but was eventually identified as the island's first super-spreader.

Her mother was mildly ill but by the time she was tested and diagnosed, the damage had been done.

There were millions of copies of the virus infecting Tommy's lungs now, and there was nothing he could do about it as he steadily lost the fight to provide his own body with sufficient oxygen.

Care home staff were as helpless as he was, and the visiting doctor from the local general practice had predicted a fatal conclusion within a few hours. She said he had not suffered cytokine shock, which was good, but his lungs and heart would not cope for long.

The young GP scrawled 'no revival' on his paperwork, forgetting what the proper term was for the patients who were to be left to die. The word resuscitation had completely escaped her.

She was traumatised by the impact of the viral outbreak on the islands and she was struggling with the heartless new protocols. Her world had changed from one she loved to one she hated.

She remembered her triage training during her final year at medical school in Liverpool, and how she had hoped then that she would never have to use it. During Tommy's last few days, triaging was dominating the work of hospital doctors all over the world and it was a nightmare for all of them.

Through her own carelessness at his bedside, the GP contracted the virus from him as he breathed towards her, vaguely aware of her presence, but completely unaware of the threat he posed to anyone who inhaled the air he had just breathed out.

Carers had unwittingly condemned him to death, and unwittingly, he was returning the compliment.

Close to death, he was still capable of dealing death, like a mortally wounded soldier with a finger still on the trigger and just enough strength to squeeze it.

He was conscious that someone was holding his hand but he had no idea who it might be. He could still hear some sounds.

Some footsteps, some rattling of trays or trolleys maybe, some muffled conversations. He remembered hearing someone say:

'Family can't get here right now, hope they're not too late.'

He wondered whose family, and too late for what? Too late for visiting time maybe.

He readjusted his symmetry.

He heard someone in the distance say something like: 'With these new regulations the family may not be allowed to see him even if they do get here.'

He didn't understand it, and he thought they might have been talking about a TV drama or a film maybe. He sometimes heard people talking about stuff they'd seen on TV.

He thought of films and let the images flicker through his thoughts like a badly threaded 16mm reel back in the old days when he had projected movies in the Town Hall for the local film society.

He suddenly remembered, with absolute clarity, the time when he had laced up *Wild Strawberries* too loosely over the optical sound head, resulting in an electronic mush of sound instead of dialogue.

He thought that was part of the show until a genuine Bergman aficionado angrily pointed out the problem. He remembered correcting it by holding a pencil in the film loop and pulling it tight.

He didn't understand why these embarrassing memories came, uninvited, into his head. He didn't understand why they vanished just as quickly, leaving no trace.

He wondered if it was like that life-flashing-by thing he remembered people talking about, and for some reason he associated that thought with the phrase: 'Out of body experience.'

Then he completely forgot what he had just been thinking about.

As suddenly as it had gone out, the light in his brain came on again.

He remembered the picture flick-books of his childhood and wondered if that was what was happening with the memories in his head.

The thought disappeared quickly and a few seconds later he could not even remember why he was suddenly thinking of strawberries, then he remembered Bergman.

He had a clear image of death playing chess with a knight in a gloomy black-and-white world. He remembered, with absolute clarity a woman, whom he had once thought he loved and lost without her ever realising it. She always talked about film-noir with a knowledge and enthusiasm which impressed him at the time.

It took him ages to find out what film noir meant. He went to the library and took down the relevant, heavy volume of Encyclopaedia Britannica to look it up. Even that had taken much longer than he thought it would.

Something made him think of the word 'Google' and he thought of his grandchildren talking about Googling. He wondered what it was.

His breathing was still steady, but even slower now and the gentle rasping sound seemed to echo around his head. He could sense the symmetry of his position and remembered that he used to do it deliberately when he was a young man in the belief that it helped his to sleep.

He suddenly thought of the words foetal position.

He wondered why he was so comfortable in this 'symmetry position' when he probably started life all curled up sucking his thumb.

He remembered the term recovery position and some first aid he had learned at sea.

He remembered a young nurse being embarrassed when she explained something called the kiss of life.

He smiled to himself and his watcher saw the smile cross his lips. She smiled back, even though he couldn't see her, and she squeezed his pale hand with hers, then she wiped away a tear from her face.

He thought of *Blade Runner* and that line about, ' ... if you could only know what these eyes have seen,' or something like that.

He thought of the replicant woman and the different endings the film had. Memories were clear for a few seconds and he remembered the words: Director's Cut, but did not know what it meant.

The thought slipped away and he wondered why he suddenly thought of places called Stepford and West World. He tried to remember visiting them, but he couldn't.

Thoughts were keeping him awake and he wanted to sleep before his next round of treatment. He suddenly remembered, ' ... to sleep, perchance to dream.'

He smiled to himself and remembered a friend who loved Shakespeare even more than he did. He felt his hand being squeezed by the person holding it. He tried to open his eyes but he still couldn't. He realised he could make the person who was sat with him into whoever he wanted them to be.

He could change them if he wanted to. He realised that not being able to open his eyes was fine; it meant that the identity of his companion, whoever they were, could be whoever he chose them to be.

At first, he wanted it to be that film-noir person. He wanted her to be there in black and white. Then he changed his mind and he imagined that the person holding his hand was his mother, and he smiled.

Then he wanted it to be his wife, who had died some years before.

He hoped he would meet her again.

The watcher noticed the smile and squeezed his hand gently once more.

Tommy remembered the film *2001*, and how they had made a special trip to a widescreen cinema to see it. The word Cinerama came into his mind for some reason but he didn't know why.

He remembered arguing about the film afterwards; he was the only one who enjoyed it.

He remembered the apes and the slabs of stone. He saw the huge, white rotating wheel of the half-finished space station and remembered the weekly comics of his childhood, which always showed space stations like that; huge rotating wheel-shapes.

He suddenly remembered that his favourite comic was called 'The Eagle', and he clearly remembered the names Dan Dare and The Mecon. He remembered Hal, the speaking computer, and thought of the flashing light which showed that it was working.

He remembered Hal's voice slowing down as it died, and he remembered the light going out. He knew that the arguments about the film were difficult, and how the arguments made him think differently about his friends.

He lost respect for them because they didn't understand it. He remembered a baby at the end of the film.

Hal's calm, machine-like voice was now talking to him. He tried to listen to Hal but he kept being distracted.

He heard two voices in the room and one kept saying Zoom. He didn't know who it was, or what Zoom meant.

Then he heard someone say: 'Not too long now.'

'You can never really tell.'

'Indicative vital signs diminishing.'

'No more medication.'

'Shall I keep the drip up?'

'Yes but no re-suss.'

'We can't allow visitors.'

'Just let it happen.'

He wondered why Hal was saying these things, then he remembered it wasn't Hal. Tommy's confusion was complete. He didn't understand the words anymore, and he didn't even know who was saying them.

Hal's light was now flashing orange. Tommy began to hear a slow and regular thump, thump, thump sound.

It reminded him of some deep, deep memory. The regular thumping was very comforting and it blotted out the gentle rasping of his breath. He thought of a heart beating but he had no idea that it was more than just a memory.

It was the memory of the sound of his mother's heartbeat which dominated his senses before he was even was born. The memory was being emphasised by the sound of his own, faltering heartbeat.

He thought of the curled-up baby in *2001*.

He became irritated by the perfect symmetry of his resting position. It didn't seem right any more.

He tried to shift onto his side but he didn't have the strength to do it at first because something was keeping him confined. He couldn't move his arms any higher but he found that he could push his legs against the confining material of the sheet and blanket.

Tommy worked the bedclothes loose with his feet, and in his final moments of self-determination he began to turn his body. He let go of the hand which was holding his, rolled onto his side, brought his knees up to his chest and he brought his free hand up to his face.

Tommy realised that the thumping heartbeat was fading. He thought he was walking towards an old bridge with a tower at the side of it. Tommy's last thought was that the heartbeat was his own.

Hal's voice slowed to a drawl:

'Here … we … go … I … think.'

The thumping stopped altogether.

Hal's light went out.

* * *

When they were sure Tommy had gone, they filled in the cause of death section on the printed paper sheet which hung over the bottom rail of the bed on an aluminium clipboard. The top of it was curled backwards on itself so that it fitted perfectly over the round tubing of the top rail at the foot of the hospital-style bed. It was a perfect arrangement. The sheet could be inspected casually at a glance, and if a more careful analysis was required the clipboard could be easily lifted off, the sheet read in detail, additional comments added, and the whole thing quickly replaced over the rail. When Tommy's clipboard was replaced, the sheet simply said 'CRRF' in an almost indecipherable scrawl. It was their lazy, shorthand method of summarising the way in which a rich, long life had finally been curtailed: CRRF. 'Covid-related respiratory failure'.

Abbreviation was power; jargon was as self-aggrandising as an ID badge with a carefully selected picture on it, hanging from a corporate lanyard. Abbreviations were part of the stuff which excluded people who weren't experts and made the experts feel more important. The well-meaning but under-qualified people who had let Tommy down, added the final insult by summarising the end of his life with an abbreviation:

'CRRF' and they couldn't even write it neatly.

Tommy's family did not arrive in time, but they wouldn't have been admitted to the care home even if they had. This was lockdown. Family life was just part of the collateral damage wrought by the new virus. Tommy McKinnon was remembered as a statistic, briefly reported within the daily summary on the national news, lost amongst an avalanche of data about infection rates and fatalities.

Much later, after the public enquiry, Tommy's death would also appear as a digit in the 'collateral damage list' of people whose lives might have been saved had they not missed-out on critical care because of the Covid-19 diversion of medical services. People who might not have even been infected in the first place, if health care workers had been properly instructed and equipped.

Tommy was lost in a new national obsession with data, poured over by experts on every newscast, and increasingly lost on a cynical and baffled public, who were keener on pubs reopening and booking holidays to a hot beach, than they were on understanding what had happened to the world.

As Tommy left, news was breaking about something called the 'care home scandal', and politicians were defending their policies to 'protect the NHS and save lives'. Tommy's place of safety had simply ceased to be safe, but nobody realised before it was too late for him. Whatever the politicians and experts had managed to do between them, however successful they had been at salvaging their reputations and boosting their careers and bank balances, it hadn't worked for Tommy Mac.

His funeral was 'Covid-safe' and hardly did justice to the man's life, but eventually a small group of old friends invited Tommy's family to a simple service of remembrance on a lonely island beach. The waves gently shifted the shingle as they shared their energy with the land for one last time and then allowed their water to suck back through the millions of pebbles which marked the strand line. Words were shared and tears were shed. The gentle sound of waves and rattling shingle formed the perfect background music.

An airliner drew a perfect white line across a patch of blue sky, a helicopter flew towards a small fishing boat about three miles out, and flock of waders skimmed the sea. Tommy had crossed his final causeway, but island life went on without him, almost the same as it always had. If Café Pink had still been there, Radar Pete's shuffle would play us out with Talking Heads asking us questions about time going by, and if the shuffle slips up and plays the whole track, you might agree with their conclusion.

Postscript

Time has passed since these stories were recorded and as Kt1984 would say: ' ... time demands more certainly than it permits.' Of course it does both, but the demands of time cannot be avoided, whereas the permissions are opportunities which allow an element of choice: they can either be accepted or rejected. Choice in life is a blessing but the irresistible demands of time are always steady, powerful and irrevocable. Nothing is ever exactly the same for long, because time passes.

People age and, eventually, people die – some of them far too soon. Increments will be shaved off even the toughest granite cliff faces by wind and weather, and by the relentless power of the waves. Some things will seem to be almost the same, but in truth they will have been at least slightly altered.

Tray Sands are still magnificent and the tide still flows in and out twice each day, but high-water mark has risen slightly each year, as global warming steadily melts the polar ice. The black queen still lies safely beneath the dunes where Kathryn decided to leave her, protecting the memory of Freyja Grainscript. Her final and most memorable game with her new opponent, FreyjaG, ended in an unheard-of draw. The first and only time a Droog-megadeath encounter had failed to find a winner. The high dune remains almost exactly the same, bound by the magic, but like all the other dunes, it changes its shape with every breath of wind as time goes by.

Kathryn has not yet returned to the island, but every day she promises herself that she will. Freyja Grainscript patiently awaits her return, with a calm determination matching that of the Warlord at Solas, who looks forward with calm patience to hearing the next story. Udal still lies there, under its own shifting dune belt, quietly waiting for the next storm to expose it briefly for the islanders, and maybe for a lucky visitor.

Shutty and Reyja still run the Gallery together and open it three days a week. William's grown-up children have returned to the Far Isles. They were both unhappy about their mother's decision to leave him and, unknown to each other, they made promises to themselves to go back to him when they could. Shutty developed new skills in computer graphics and began to produce photographic artwork based on digital images taken by Reyja with the Canon D1 he bought her for their first Christmas together. They have cemented the future of their business by selling artwork online, and the computer they use for it carries the same screaming-beach screen saver as the old laptop which first brought them together.

The Macs still live at Solas and Simeon has managed to return almost every year for at least a few days. He has noticed them getting older and, during the pandemic, he stayed away altogether for fear of literally killing them. They spend much of their time quietly remembering the past times they have enjoyed together, hoping that they will see Simeon and Mairead once again before they pass. They both secretly hope they will come together and share a room for a few days in their house at Solas.

Simeon spends time with Mairead whenever he can but they haven't moved in together yet, even though they both secretly believe that they will do so eventually. He has bought the Chiswick flat after securing a lucrative deal with Channel 69 to produce a series of travel documentaries entitled 'Remote'.

Brogan can still be found at the Oyster Bar at the McTavish Hotel – the pub, and he welcomes tourists with hearty pub meals and good local beer. There is never any trouble there. Georgie Hammond's widow moved in with him two years after the drowning. She was so moved by his performance at the funeral that she saw a side to the big man she never imagined existed. It was enough to make her believe that his strength could be part of her recovery process and so far, she believes that she was right.

Roddy McKinnon's croft is still there and his daughter and grandchildren enjoy the memories as well as the setting. Their camp site has flourished and is now an all-year-round facility with proper toilets and showers. During the summer season the children run a small café for passing motorists and walkers. The family is as happy as it can be after the tragedy of the storm, and Susan is strengthened by the fact that she and Richard have rebuilt her father's house, rejuvenated the croft, and created a business which their children can eventually inherit, if they choose to stay on the island.

They sold the holiday cottage by the sea because of the memories it held, but they regretted their decision immediately, and bought it back three years later, as soon as the new owners from London grew tired of island isolation. They let it for most weeks of the year, but if there is ever a gap in the bookings, they travel over the causeway and spend time in the cottage to help the healing process.

The girls from the Craft Centre have moved on and rarely return to the island, but the business is still thriving, thanks to online orders, despite the drop in tourist traffic and the decline in direct sales. The café closed completely during the lockdowns but it is ready to reopen at a moment's notice, with plenty of local youngsters ready to staff it. The girls are still unaware of how Jimmy Walsh lost his life in the air crash, but the Russian security services were well aware of the cause and they released one of their top assets to hunt down the terrorists, who are led, they believe, by an English woman whom they intend to eliminate. He has a vested interest in the mission for his brother was on the plane.

The Café Pink trio have quite different stories to tell, and the building itself has experienced its own changes. It is currently a fabrication unit, manufacturing display cabinets, and there is no longer any kind of hub for Vanich, since it closed its doors for the last time. The new occupiers even painted out the pink walls with a dull grey finish, which matched the local concrete gun emplacements better, and the new visitor to the small settlement would have no idea about the vibrancy that once existed there.

The old military airfield is still there, maintained by the MOD, just in case, and Billy still takes care of the commercial activity and manages the smallest baggage collection conveyer in Europe. Fewer planes practice roller landings now but fast jets still echo around the hills practising low-flying and radar-avoidance tactics around a well-defined circuit now known as the Mac-Mach Loop by the aircrew risking their lives for national security.

Radar Pete trained as an air traffic controller and manned the tower at Vanich for a couple of years but moved on to a mainland airport for much more money, and he took Stephanie with him. Steph started a coffee shop in the small Cheshire village where they settled. It was close enough to Liverpool John Lennon (where Pete became senior ATC) for him to manage an easy commute across the Gateway. Steph called the coffee shop Causeway.

Stephanie put some picnic tables out in the ancient cobbled yard at the back, and she called it the ootside. She was always glad that there were no midges in Cheshire whenever she served coffee out there. Every time she sold a piece of Hummingbird cake she thought of Suzanna and Jimmy Idan, and every time an EasyJet flew over, she thought of her Radar Pete, and the look of surprise on his face that day.

Carole moved to the capital with her son and his father, but they haven't married yet. They are now running a car and van hire business from the small industrial park next to the ferry terminal. She is a governor at her son's school and plans to run for council on an 'Island Independence' ticket as soon as she organises enough people to vote her in. Her son would eventually secure a place at Oxford University to read PPP and go on into a political life himself, eventually moving much higher up the political food chain than his mother.

Suzanna thrived on her relationship with Jimmy Idan, although she nearly stumbled into an overcomplicated relationship with Lachlan Maguire, who she knew from school and always admired. He was already well-attached to the glamourous Henrietta, and everyone knew it. They accidentally bumped into each other in a narrow corridor at Café Pink one day, and they were literally thrown together in the confined space. It was one of those moments; they just hugged and then kissed for a long time, as if they had been longing to do it for their whole lives. Then, as they both suddenly realised it was impossible to take their instant relationship any further, they disengaged, blushed and went their separate ways exchanging some harsh words.

Suzanna went to Africa after securing an open scholarship to the Royal Northern College of Music, and she stayed in Yollumba for a year. She returned there after graduating, staying until the terrorist event occurred, and by a twist of fate, she met Lachlan once more. That meeting was even more dramatic than their brief encounter in the corridor, years before.

Henrietta remained in Solas. She kept the house ready to welcome Lachy home for a final time, hoping that he would still be alive when he made his final return to the islands. If you visit Solas and see her in the Co-op one-stop-shop, you will know it is her immediately, and you will think Vettriano.

At the site of the hostage drama, two years after the buildings were abandoned and demolished, a young local boy, scavenging for scrap, found the three fatal bullets in the rubble. He held the flattened slugs in his hand and wondered if they were worth trading with a metal dealer. After weighing them in his palm for a few seconds he decided that they were of no value and threw them back into the pile of bricks. He had no idea of their true significance.

My Lai had sat with Tommy McKinnon in the care home and enjoyed many a supper with him, but it broke her heart when he died from the virus and she sat at his bedside, holding his hand until the end. Tommy Mac's family did look after My Lai but she did not want to stay on the islands anymore, preferring to return to her homeland with the income which Tommy's family had secured for her. It didn't seem much in European terms but it was a more than comfortable pension for a Cambodian.

The Far Isles continued to attract what the islanders called 'big ideas', and they provided food for thought even though most of them came to nothing. The massive wind-farm proposal never progressed beyond a handful of huge, isolated turbines. There was no commercial or government interest in laying the complex and expensive under-sea link to the mainland. Wave and tidal power were another matter though and there was talk of research facilities being developed at Vanich. The council hoped that alternative energy work might revitalise the place which had never recovered from the closure of the ranges. The radar domes were never converted into futuristic holiday homes and Vanich runway was never extended to take large aircraft in need of an emergency landing strip.

The closed-roads motor rally proposed by Carole to the island council never materialised, despite her car and van hire business offering sponsorship, and her son's passion for fast cars. The new cruise-liner facility at the main ferry port remained on the drawing board and the liners were still happy to anchor offshore in the deepwater harbour, sending the tourists ashore in lighters.

The islands were still rather divided on the sanctity of Sunday. More businesses than ever operate all weekend, but many were still firmly closed on the Sabbath. For some islanders, religion was still the most powerful force in their lives, for others it was completely irrelevant.

Populations continued to move around, youngsters moved out and new settlers with dreams moved in – usually not staying for long. There is still a regular discussion about affordable housing for islanders who want to stay, an annual argument about deer culling, the threat of the mink and everlasting disagreement about Sunday ferries. The cruise business provided a viable tourist trade once the threat of Covid-19 was manageable and the growth in motorhome ownership across Europe had an impact on both the roads and the campsites across the Far Isles.

Time passes and things change, but the crime rates on the Far Isles remained low by any standards, even though the local free sheet still manages to produce headlines worthy of any mainland city newspaper. But the shock-horror only exists in the minds of sensation-seeking journalists and editors; the Far Isles remain one of the safest places in the world. The Russians were no longer a nuclear threat since the radar sites closed and the Far Isles were no longer a prime target, but their spy boats still explore the coastal deepwater troughs for NATO submarines, and the Royal Navy still keeps a constant look out for the Russian submarines which exercise regularly as close to the coast as they can get.

An unusual earth tremor, which rattled cups and plates on sideboards across the archipelago, prompted the local newspaper to speculate about geological-plate movement. The journalist, who had discovered the Far Isles 20 years before, during an undergraduate geology field trip, claimed that the Atlantic plate was on the move again and that islanders should expect volcanic eruptions and lava flows, before the Far Isles disappeared forever beneath the ocean floor.

Whether or not that most unlikely scenario ever works out, such speculations have nothing to do with the day-to-day life of the islanders. They continue to cope with the challenges of isolation while enjoying the advantages of their unique environments and dreading the loss of their young people through migration.

Technology seems to be providing a new way forward for the Far Isles and the Far Islanders. The internet has revolutionised opportunity for isolated peoples around the world, and the shrewd inhabitants of those remote places are increasingly aware of distance-learning, virtual business practices and, more so, of the massive potential offered by the huge worldwide market that the internet presents for their products as well as for their services. At the press of an on switch and the flick of a few keys on the qwerty, the world is their oyster, and the Far Islanders are famous for making the best of that tasty mollusc.

Plans to replace the old causeway, with its famous escape tower, were shelved after strong local reaction to its demolition and replacement with a concrete alternative, and islanders continue to drive over it slowly, in respect for its ageing woodwork. In order to protect it against further threats the council unanimously agreed with Carole's proposal to grant it the legal protection of a Grade 1 listing.

Causeways continue to provide vital links between isolated communities but local people are wary of them, knowing that there are powerful forces which can sweep mere humans away in an instant, even from the apparent safety of a sturdy causeway.

If you are ever tempted to use a causeway to take you to the place where you think you want to be, remember the dangers, and make sure you know where the escape tower is.

Chapter 13

The Yollumba Raid

'No pestering, no stalking, no unwanted attention, just leave me alone … ' Lachlan's last conversation with Suzanna had been a disaster, he hadn't intended it to be anything like that at all, in fact he didn't even intend to meet her, let alone talk to her when they bumped into each other at the back of the café.

They knew of each other, of course, but she was away so much with her family doing the missionary-medical stuff all over the place, that they only really caught fleeting moments, usually in a school class when she made a temporary appearance. He always liked her for some reason, and even in primary he remembered finding her somehow attractive. He liked her energy, her smile, her kindness towards everyone and her musical talent, but she appeared and disappeared so quickly that he never really worked out if she could be the one.

Then, in High School, he realised the utterly undeniable power of her physical attraction and relished the end of term, when she tended to turn up for a few days. She played music with carefully considered brilliance and beguiled audiences with her fiddle playing. Even the realisation of her physical attraction didn't change anything in practical terms; he didn't *do* anything, he didn't even think of trying, but it was there, nagging away at him.

Nothing ever came close to happening between them until that chance coming together at the back of the café, but the potential was always there, and it had always been an undeniably powerful potential. All it needed was a chance.

He knew that she had returned for a longer stay on the island, as her parents had retired from missionary work and taken up GP posts in the main port. She would eventually return to Africa herself of course, but for now she teamed up with two old friends to run the Café Pink. He guessed that Café Pink provided a purpose for her and he knew she would enjoy the music, the baking and, most of all, the camaraderie which was the main attraction of the place.

By the time Suzanna reappeared on the island Lachlan was totally and utterly committed to Henrietta. They had spent very deep moments together and developed an understanding and affection which most people don't ever know. Their partings were always painful and when Henrietta left on the big ferry to meet her parents on the mainland, and Lachlan had only his own company to enjoy, he was in bad shape. He was experiencing physical and emotional sensations that he simply didn't understand; he didn't like it, he felt uncertain; vulnerable.

He told himself that this temporary parting would be good practice for their longer separation which would soon come when they both left the island for different universities; but that thought made it worse, not better. He watched the ferry nose out of the harbour, beyond the shipyard, beyond the breakwaters, beyond the lighthouse, beyond his reach. He walked back to his car without remembering how he got there. He drove out of town and instinctively pointed it in the right direction; there were only three ways out to be honest but at least he picked the right one.

He knew that Café Pink was sure to provide friends, and he drove there directly. It took two hours, three causeways and a small ferry but he made it by lunchtime. He parked round the back by the air-conditioning cabinet and saw that the service door was ajar; he strolled in and bumped straight into Suzanna by a stockroom door. There was nobody else in the corridor and they had come together pretty hard; their faces were level, their eyes and mouths were close, they were momentarily pressed firmly together and neither moved away, they both reached out to regain their balance after the collision, their arms touched, hands went round shoulders, their eyes closed and they kissed each other without a word being spoken.

Potential – such a dangerous thing, potential. All it needed was a chance, and here was the chance. No one will ever know how long it lasted, but it was a very long and a very hungry kiss. There was a lot of time to be made up; a lot of potential to be realised. They eventually pulled apart, shocked and uncertain about what to do next. Suzanna spoke first.

'Sorry, sorry, sorry I shouldn't have done that, we shouldn't have done that, I know about Henrietta of course, everybody does, it's the talk of the Island, your relationship, like a Mills and Boon, the perfect romance, every ordinary folk's dream, true romance between two lovely people, out of the blue, and here's me spoiling it when her ferry is only halfway across the Minch. Sorry.'

Suzanna walked away, back towards the café, Lachlan tried to follow, he tried to speak but she beat him to it: 'No pestering, no stalking, no unwanted attention, I promise, and you must promise too.'

She was giving him instructions as she walked away; she didn't turn around to look at him, she just waved a hand over her shoulder towards him, palm held up in a stop signal at the end of a stiff arm. She kept walking away and then drew her hand in to wipe tears from her face. She disappeared through the door and it swung shut on the automatic spring like the saloon doors in a cowboy movie.

He turned and left the building. He drove home across the deserted island he was soon to leave and he cried himself out behind the wheel, in the sure knowledge that the eagle, which briefly peered into the car, and saw the state he was in, would tell nobody. He thought he would probably never see her again, and he never returned to the Café Pink.

All that was almost 10 years ago. Lachy may never have seen Suzanna again but the pain never left him. He was happy with Henrietta and she was happy on the island. He returned quite often between operations and, since those early days in the Commandos, he had risen to command positions in his regiment, so he often saw active service.

He was eventually chosen to lead a new Special Forces unit created to deal with specific terrorist threats which were destabilising British interests, especially in Africa. His new responsibilities made the demands upon his time even more flexible and less predictable than before. Henrietta had given up living on the bases where he happened to be posted, preferring the beaches and mountains of the Far Isles, and she waited there longingly for him to return.

They always met at the pier in the capital. He always came in uniform; sometimes dress, sometimes fatigues, and he always carried his kit himself. He always looked extra big with the kit on and the bags hanging off him, like a well-drawn comic book hero. She always drove the black Range Rover, they always kissed in the arrival hall and it was always a showstopper.

This time they had only spent three days together before the red phone rang. The PDA was actually battleship grey but everyone called it the red phone. When it pinged you took it seriously; there were never any trial runs with the red phone; it was always for real.

When it sounded and they both woke up with a start; Lachlan was straight out of bed reaching the device from the windowsill where reception was strongest. He flicked the screen onto full illumination and read the message twice. He then pressed rescan to double-check the validity of the message and there was no doubt. He stood up against the window as first light was showing through the thin curtains, flicked to voice, put it to his ear and spoke into it.

Henry felt excluded; this was nothing to do with her, this was the price she paid for being in love with him; she knew the score and she knew that he would keep going until he was stopped. She would never stop him and he would never stop himself, but there were people out there who would.

She remembered the day of the funeral in their early times together, when she walked alone on the beach and felt the terror of premonition. The terror came flooding back, it gushed through her body, she shuddered and cried into the pillow, jamming it into her mouth to control the first sobs. Her duty was to be well put together by the time he noticed her; she had a few seconds.

'This is Premier Alpha Golf Uniform 1, day code Marmalade.' Henry's sobbing suddenly turned into laughter; she bit the pillow even harder. Marmalade, fucking marmalade, what kind of code word is that?

Lachy just kept saying Yes, and OK, and Understood. He finished by saying: 'Confirm Zulu 10 hundred; ATC mast.' He turned the red phone to standby and put it back on the window sill.

'Sorry', he said. 'I've got to go; something has happened in Africa.'

Numbness, silence, brave acceptance, huge fear, they held on to each other for a few seconds then he was off: bathroom, packing, dressing. By the time she had prepared a bite to eat he was in full kit with both his bags fastened tight and ready for anything.

His pickup was by helicopter from the Air Traffic Control Masts which were about 12 miles away on a steep headland at the end of a single-track road. The local police would provide armed cover and he expected them to be already informed and on the way. Whoever came, they would know each other and although not fully informed, the cops would know exactly what was going on.

They were both in the car when the police arrived in their Defender. There were two of them, his brother Jake and Mary Maguire. Jake didn't make a joke, which he would normally have done, because he knew what his brother did, and knew it must be serious for him to be dragged off leave like this. Jake knew that it was probably a life-threatening situation and that Lachy's intervention would put his life at risk. Mary knew that too – she still loved Lacky as much as she had at school and she hugged him before they all drove off. She had married his brother, but sometimes she secretly wished that she had married Lachlan.

The police Defender waited half a mile from the masts, to give the helicopter a free run, and both the armed officers got out and watched, with their automatics slung from their shoulders. There was nobody else about, but this routine was well-practiced and had to be caried out properly. They all knew that a terrorist intervention would be sudden and probably totally unexpected. They had to be ready for anything, even in this remote place.

Henrietta drove right up to the masts and parked on the concrete hard standing where Lachlan assembled his kit and waited to be lifted off. She said a brief, brave, goodbye and drove back down the track to where the police waited. The masts connected every aircraft crossing the North Atlantic with Air Traffic Control; vital to the safety of thousands of people and billions of pounds worth of aircraft in the air at any one time. Take out these masts and aircraft would get lost or collide or just fall into the ocean. Utterly vital equipment just concreted into the headland at the end of a single-track road on the very edge of the Far Isles. As incongruous and as wonderful as the prize-winning products of the remote Lochavet pie shop, world-class Far Isles Gin, and Hummingbird cake at a café on an old RAF base. All examples of the wonderful juxtaposition of remote island serenity with real-world reality.

The morning was calm and sunny and both Henrietta and the police officers got back into their vehicles. They waited with the windows down. The chopper was due and sure enough there was the unmistakable sound of a Special Forces Chinook. Once you hear it you know it will only get louder until you see it, and then it gets even louder until it is over your head. The Chinook landed on the missile platform, which doubled as a landing pad, a hundred yards away, the large yellow 'H' giving it a very decent target to aim at. Lacky waved and then walked over to the chopper. Strong arms pulled him in and it took off immediately.

The Chinook was heading for Machrihanish, where the four Hercules transports would already be in the final stages of setting up for their trip to West Africa. Four aircraft, 200 Commandos, eight Land Rovers, and a full suite of assault weaponry, including drones and two helicopters – a big show by any standards. The sheer scale of it made him apprehensive. If it went wrong, the whole world would soon find out; he had to lead this event to a successful conclusion, there would be no hiding place.

Major Lachlan Maguire was happiest in small raiding party operations. It was what Commandos were supposed to do. Small elite teams who knew each other well. In and out before anyone realised what was happening. Hit and run; butcher and bolt. But 200 men – that sounded more like an infantry operation.

Lachy knew both the soldiers in the Chinook; he'd worked with them before and he was glad when they confirmed that they too were going to Yollumba. Both of them were attached to the SAS with original experience in the Parachute Regiment. Suddenly the professional confidence returned. Royal Marines, Paras, SAS, Special Forces Chinooks and Hercules; this was what he trained for; this was what he did best; this was something the UK forces excelled at; this was an operation that would go well, even though it was a bit too big for his liking. They shared what knowledge they could in the noisy confines of the chopper's main cabin and had a pretty good idea of what they were in for.

Touchdown at the massive airfield on the Mull of Kintyre was classic SAS style: high angle of attack, bang in, roll rapidly forward along the ground to the safest location, ramp down, troops out. There was simply no need to do it like that on a friendly airfield but the aircrew couldn't help themselves; once they had trained to do it, that was the way they always did it.

Everyone met up in the terminal hanger which had been set out to accommodate a presentation: raised stage for the speakers, chairs arranged in theatre style, very large maps on big wooden frames, digital projector screen. After 30 minutes they all knew exactly what to do and 200 men boarded their designated aircraft.

Everyone knew full well that even the best plans were the first thing to go out of the window once the fighting started. They all knew that their survival depended upon their ability to handle the inevitable surprises which the action would present them with as soon as it began. The Yollumba Raid, codenamed Operation Release, was simple in its intention. The British and Nigerian citizens who were being held hostage by the Boko Haram terrorists were in mortal danger.

The 'Boks' were more than capable of abusing and killing women and children. They specialised in abducting schoolgirls from village schools in order to force them into so-called marriages. It was their chosen method of combining their future population supply with an on-going reputation for unfettered, vicious, terrifying action against helpless populations. They seized the winelands of Yollumba because of the income they could provide for them. Once they controlled them, they could blackmail the owners in the same way that *they* blackmailed the oil companies when they highjacked the 100,000-ton tankers off the East African coast. Piracy was becoming risky as ships were being staffed by special forces sharp-shooters, but Yollumba was pretty well unprotected.

The French were there, with a few fighter aircraft on the nearby airbase, but they were not a threat to the terrorists. Only ground forces could really shake the Boks, and they were ready for that. Any attack would result in the immediate execution of 18 British citizens and over 120 Nigerians. In order to prove their determination, the Boks had executed Jimmy Idan and posted it on Facebook.

Idan was ready to fly back to his new European HQ which was to be opened by the Swedish Prime Minister in four days' time, and he was saying his goodbyes to his British staff, when the Boks arrived. Suzanna was going with him but neither of them made the flight.

The terrorist group were well trained. They were an elite squad carefully prepared for this event by the elusive English woman who had emerged as one of the key players in sub-Saharan Africa. Charlotte Bingham-Pierce was over a thousand miles away when the event began, but she knew how it would develop and she knew that it would end in death. She didn't care whose death, that wasn't the point. The aim was simply to hit the headlines across all the world's media, and abductions, torture, extortion and gruesome deaths certainly guaranteed headlines.

After filming Jimmy's execution and posting it, they fortified the main building and blew up the sheds around it to create lines of fire. The rear was covered by three machine-gun nests and a mortar team. Antipersonnel mines were scattered across the open ground to the sides and front. Airborne surveillance was inevitable, but an air attack was unlikely because of the hostages. What they were prepared for was an attempt by special forces – either French because of their interest in the territory, or the SAS because of the large number of British hostages.

A ground attack of any sort would end up as a shootout, and it was Charlotte's simple instruction that, in the end, everyone should die. All the Boks knew what would happen to their families if they failed. They were ordered to sacrifice their own lives for the cause and thereby save their wives, children, parents and grandparents from certain execution. That was how Charlotte worked, and that was why she was one of the most effective terrorist leaders in the world.

The Hercules had to air-refuel twice before they reached the small French airfield 20 miles from the scene of the event. The squadron of nine Rafales was parked well off the single runway to give the big transport aircraft room to manoeuvre.

Lachlan called an O-Group inside the hold of the first aircraft, after it disgorged its Defenders with their trailers full of weapons and ordnance. He invited the intelligence group to bring them all up to date and what they revealed chilled him to the bone.

'Probable 19 UK hostages held in fortified main building, clear fields of fire all round.'

'Approximately 100 Boks, heavily armed, seem to be a death squad with the usual CBP connections.'

'One man, IC3, executed for publicity, likely to be the UK business guy who ran the place.'

'List of names of known hostages here.'

The list was passed to Lachy. He scanned it not expecting anything other than a list of names of people who were going through hell and would probably soon die. Bok death squad groups were everyone's worst nightmare. They were the kamikazes of the terrorist world; their first event was always their last. Lachy's eyes froze on one of the names: Suzanna Morgan. He knew it was her.

The same name could be a coincidence but everything suddenly lined up. He knew she had intended to go to Africa, and he knew she had been there, come back home, and then returned. He realised that the executed IC3 would be Jimmy Idan, and he knew Suzanna was a close friend ever since that famous meeting at the Pink.

He remembered his meeting with her in the corridor and how they had parted.

'Unfinished business.'

'What boss?' asked the right-hander.

'What do you mean, 'What boss, Jacko?' asked Lachy.

'You just said, "unfinished business" boss, I wondered what you meant.'

Major Lachlan Maguire was unaware that he had spoken out loud.

'Oh! nothing Jacko, I mean we've got to get on with it and finish this business.'

Jacko knew Lachy well enough to leave it at that, even though he knew something had just spooked the boss.

The assault team formed up two miles short of the target with a three-mortar firebase to support the attack and two machine-gun pits ready to cover their retreat. The aim was simple: a surprise frontal attack by three men to take out the guards, followed by an immediate full unit charge to take over the buildings.

Lachy surprised everyone by announcing the order of battle. 'I'll lead the three-man spearhead with Jacko and Tommy as my wingmen. The rest of you attack close behind with your full troop strength: X behind me; Y on the left; A on the right; B in reserve. H troop to remain at the firebase to liaise with all comms and cover any withdrawal when we release the hostages. Give us just enough time to down the guards and reach the building before you break cover, then charge like hell.'

'Any prisoners boss?' asked Tommy.

'Unlikely, to be honest, these guys are ordered to die, so most of them probably will, but prisoners could be useful to intelligence if we manage to bag any. Prisoners are not our priority – the hostages are. And if Boks get in the way, tap them twice.'

Inside the building all the British hostages were in the main reception lounge right at the front of the ground floor. There were 15 guards inside the room and four on guard out at the front. The rest of the Boks were 200 metres back, sleeping on the ground around the mortar pit.

Lachy began the silent walk towards the veranda from about 400 yards out. He was between Jacko and Tommy with about a gap of about 20 feet between them. They carried their individual assault rifles high across their chests with the 30-round magazines fitted and the safety catches off. Each C8 carbine had the shorter 10-inch barrel fitted for close-quarter action and each man had a sub-compact machine gun across his back and a 1911 in a thigh-holster. The tabloids would later describe the trio as armed to the teeth, and to be fair to the headline writers, that was a pretty accurate description.

The drone was feeding a high-definition picture onto Lachy's headset screen and he could see that the four guards were asleep in chairs which faced forwards, towards the waist-high rail across the veranda front. Lachy had led his men to within 30 metres of their target when Tommy stood on a mine. He heard the click and said, 'AP Mine,' into his headset.

The trio immediately accelerated into a sprint towards the guards, leaving the mine as far behind them as possible before it leapt up into the air and sprayed its ball bearings in a lethal cloud.

Two of the guards were stirred by the noises of boots on the ground and they were shot dead as soon as they moved. The killing had begun. The mine went off with a loud bang which brought the other two guards to their feet a split second before they too died instantly from gunshot wounds to the head. The men knew exactly what to do now that the guards inside the building were alerted, and they knew that X Troop would be up and running about 20 seconds behind them, so it was now a matter of getting into the room and shooting the bad guys.

They unofficially called it 'room clearance with care', and it really was the most difficult thing they trained for. They couldn't just throw grenades in and then go in shooting everything that moved. The hostages would be mixed in with the terrorists, possibly even attached to them, and some may already have explosive vests wrapped around them. There could be kids with necklaces of grenades around their necks. Any level of horror could await them on the other side of the windows.

Jacko fired a stun grenade through the window on the extreme left, where they believed there were no people at all. If there were any, the grenade could easily kill them. A strong adult might survive, but a child would almost certainly die if it went off close to them. Jacko didn't give it a thought as he watched the dark green canister fly precisely though the glass pane. The loud series of four bangs preceded their entry by less than two seconds, as the individual charges carried by the canister went off in quick succession. Things were going to plan.

Lachy was first through. He vaulted the rail and leapt through the large window, smashing glass and wood into the room with the sheer speeding bulk of his body. His helmet, mask, gloves and body armour pushed the sharp fragments aside and he began his work in the hostage room. He scanned quickly and his night-vision goggles revealed five obvious terrorists immediately, one of them was holding a long-haired white woman with a gun to her head.

Lachy recognised her as Suzanna and shot the man through the head, spinning him away from her as his final muscular spasm fired the weapon into the ceiling. He shot three more of the terrorists in quick succession, all of them frozen in time, open-mouthed with surprise, wide-eyed with terror.

Lachy became aware of Tommy and Jacko in the room and saw other bursts of fire going in. As the reality of the event sank in, they all saw terrorists exiting through doors at the back of the foyer. They kept running through the room, picking off targets as they went. Lachlan told his wingmen to follow him into the back rooms to complete the clearance, leaving the hostages to the men of X Troop who were about to enter the building.

They knew that timing was everything and if X Troop were late there would be a moment when surviving terrorists could do their worst. X Troop were nine seconds late.

Suzanna was shaken to the point of paralysis by the noise and the sudden appearance of the science fiction fighting-men, in their black uniforms, masks and helmets, and who burst through the wall and began shooting at people. She felt her tormentor loosen his grip on her shoulder and realised that the gun was no longer resting against her temple. She saw his body at her feet and the gore spurting from a headwound. She saw the handgun and reached for it to prevent him from using it, even though he was probably already dead. That simple, impulsive, act was unnecessary. None of the terrorists posed a threat any more.

Dougal McDonald was the youngest member of the unit. At nineteen and a half he was barely out of training, but his talent was unmistakable and after graduating top in every class he was a natural choice for Lachy's commando. The fact that he too came from the Far Isles added to the irony of the unfolding events.

Dougal was one of the first two X Troop men through the wall.

They knew they were slightly late due to antipersonnel mines taking out three of their lead runners, but the second men made it after a delay of almost 10 seconds and went through the wall. They had been prepared for a delay during the briefing and knew that the main result would be that any surviving terrorist would have had time to recover from the shock of first-entry and would be likely to present a threat.

Dougal was bristling with expectation as he scanned the room and caught Suzanna's movement out of the corner of his eye. He turned his head and looked at her full on. White woman holding a Glock, black guy with headwound at her feet. Dougal knew this was a Charlotte Bingham-Pierce operation and assumed that the white woman swinging the handgun towards him was the terrorist leader they all called Queen-bee. She was wanted all over the world and there were official contracts out on her pretty well everywhere, including the UK. Suzanna continued to swing the weapon towards Dougal.

He made an instant decision, honed in the shooting gallery rooms in the training estate at Bunarkaig, where cut-outs of people popped up and trainees had to make an instant good-guy/bad-guy choice and decide whether or not to shoot. He had achieved the highest success rate ever recorded on the course. He hadn't put a single shot into the wrong target. It was an achievement which helped secure his membership of Lachy's team. Dougal made the first wrong choice of his shooting career and put two shots into Suzanna's chest. She was dead before she hit the ground.

X Troop began to evacuate hostages and march them to the side now secured by B Troop in order to avoid the minefield. Two helicopter gunships were approaching from the west when the terrorist mortar team began to bomb the building and one of the machine-gun nests opened up and sprayed the intervening ground with short, accurate bursts of fire. Tommy went down first, with serious leg wounds, as the gunners found their first target. He was soon attended by a medic from B Troop who applied tourniquets to the bleeding limbs, injected morphine and wrote 'M' on his forehead with a Sharpie from his map case before the unconscious wingman was removed on a stretcher.

With two men still running towards them, firing their assault rifles accurately from the hip, one of the loaders ran for it and was immediately hit with two shots in the back which sent him tumbling forward, head over heels. He left the ammunition belt flapping loosely at the side of the PKP and his triggerman knew he had only a few shots left before the belt ran through and the gun became useless. The gunner squeezed the trigger for the last time and sent fourteen 7.62mm rounds straight at Major Lachlan Maguire.

The bullets had a killing range of well over a kilometre and at less than 100 metres they still had the muzzle velocity of 825 metres per second. It took 0.1212 seconds for the three shells which hit Lachy to reach him; just over one tenth of a second. Such a short time to end a life; no time to contemplate; no time for life to flash before your eyes. Alive and then dead, in less time than it takes to blink an eye.

The shells penetrated his body armour, penetrated him, and came out through his back with sufficient power to kill anyone who was unlucky enough to be behind the falling major. There was nobody there and the shells passed harmlessly through the X Troop force troops following the trio, lodging themselves in the brick wall of the hostage building.

The ammo belt ran out before the gunner could find Jacko, but he had stopped his run anyway as soon as his boss went down. As Jacko reached his fallen leader, the first gunship rocketed the mortar pit and machine-gun nests into oblivion, while the second one pursued the fleeing terrorists across the flat, rock-strewn landscape. All but one were obliterated by the accurate, withering fire from the rotary canon.

A group of 18 had packed into a pair of Toyota Land Cruisers which sped away from the pits. The pilot of the second gunship saw them raising dust clouds, wheeled towards them in a vertical bank, and from a height of 115 feet, painted them both with the independent laser designators. As soon as the system locked on, the men were doomed.

The weapons officer was spoiled for choice but in the end chose a pair of Brimstones. The gunship carried six, three on each side. No tank could resist one hit from a

Brimstone, not even a tank with Chobham armour. A Landcruiser stood no chance. Brimstone was a fire and forget weapon. Once it locked on, the target was doomed.

He fired them simultaneously and the gunship rocked slightly as the heavy rockets shot from their cradles, leaving a trail of smoke behind them. Both crewmen watched with fascination as the two missiles sped towards the trucks. The technology never failed to impress them. It worked perfectly on the ranges every time they practiced firing at old vehicles, placed on the marshes to simulate enemy targets. It impressed them equally as they fired for real for the very first time.

The fact that they were killing people with this shot didn't bother either of them. They had seen the action unfolding on the hard ground below them and they had seen at least two men go down.

They followed the Brimstones in, ready to finish the job if, by any freak chance, the missiles didn't eliminate everyone. The cars leapt into the air in a cloud of mechanical and human debris as the missiles exploded almost simultaneously against their tailgates. The whole thing was almost perfectly synchronised. The pilot later compared it to those high-board diving events when two people perform airborne acrobatics before they hit the water at exactly the same time. The weapons officer simply said that he found the impacts more of a relief than anything else; pleased that he had hit the targets.

The 18 terrorists who perished would never be identified. It was the final act in the shooting match; the end of the event.

Charlotte Bingham-Pierce was incandescent when she learned of the failure of her Yollumba plan. It was her only failure so far in the entire, illustrious history of her terror campaigns, and someone would have to pay for it. She had the families of all the men she had used eliminated, as a matter of course; they had failed, so their loved ones would die, just as she had promised. She had over 300 people terminated – men women and children. The action went some way towards restoring her image, but she needed to do more in order to re-establish herself as the top dog.

From the ashes of Yollumba, Charlotte's plan to get back at the British began to form, and she intended to grow from the Yollumba region somehow and eventually achieve something spectacular on the British mainland.

When the fighting ended at Yollumba, Jacko was completely unmarked. He held Lachy's head up and removed his helmet, hoping for something, but there was nothing. Lachy was bleeding slowly into the sand through the three large exit wounds in his back, but there was no point stopping the bloodloss, he was already long gone.

He was already with Henrietta, walking along the causeway which brought them to the long sandy beach linking their house at Solas to the ancient village of Udal. He took off his webbing and dropped it onto the sand along with his damaged body armour and combat gloves. He stripped the scrim scarf from his neck and opened the collar of his shirt. He didn't have his helmet or goggles and he couldn't understand where he had left them. He was always meticulously careful with all his kit. He hadn't even lost a pair of sun glasses during almost 20 years of service.

They walked together, hand in hand, leaving only the trail of abandoned kit behind them. Eventually they met the long-haired man and the young woman who was by his side. He called her Freyja, and she smiled at them both with an understanding of their love for each other.

They asked about Lachy's bloodstained clothing and they talked about what he had done to gain those wounds of honour. The Warrior of Udal and his gaming girl invited Lachy to sit on the Main Seat and tell them both the full story. Freyja sat on the grass on a small mound a few feet from the large stone and stared at Lachy with rapt, unwavering attention.

Lachlan relived the whole thing, from the red-phone summons to the final acts of violence at Yollumba. He remembered every detail, and the warrior realised that this was a story which was truly worthy of the ancient place of storytelling.

He mentioned Suzanna and wondered how she was, certain that she had survived the assault on the hostage house. The warrior and Freyja knew the truth of it, but decided not to break Lachy's heart with information he didn't need to know about just yet. Time enough when he was finally aware of his new place in island history, and her spirit joined his, and the hundreds of others who roamed the hills and beaches, caring for the magic of the islands. The ancient warrior listened with genuine interest to Lachy's account of the action at Yollumba. He asked questions and he got answers.

He took the seat himself and told of his own experiences of battle. He compared his own tribe attacking Viking settlements to free the islands of marauders, with the commando raid on the Yollumba plantation to free the innocent hostages.

They discussed violence and death. They decided that they had both fought for worthy causes and were right to risk lives for them. As they talked towards sunset, Lachy began to feel more relaxed and his wounds seemed unimportant. He was expiating the demons which battle had brought to his mind, and gradually, as they all talked more easily together, Lachy felt a serenity which he had never experienced before. He felt that his new life was not going to be driven by reacting to the next challenge. Somehow, he felt that this was going to be altogether a more relaxing, spiritual existence. This was a form of counselling that only very special people, in very special places can ever receive. Lachy knew that he was going through a special process; he just didn't know why. It was a healing process denied almost all the good warriors who had fought for honour and freedom across the ages. Brave men who carried the spiritual scars of battle long after the wars had been forgotten.

Eventually, the sun went down over the Atlantic and the magic of the Far Isles moved in to protected their memories, as it had done for island people for thousands of years, and as it would continue to do until the end of time.

Haunted perhaps, and mystical to some, but magical to almost everyone, the Far Isles will always reward believers with a calm serenity which belies the real world of violence and threat. Far Isle magic is one of few forces for good in the world and it always rewards those lucky enough to receive its blessing.

Epilogue

Not even the spirits know how this will all end, and their inability to predict the final act simply proves the impossibility of even guessing what the finale might entail; and if the spirits can't do it nobody can.

There are always several competing theories, which are often considered, as discussions take place around the Main Seat, long into the night. Sometimes they result in heated arguments but the enthusiasm for particular ideas is always tempered with good humour and opponents may argue, but they always remain good friends. Sitting around a fire of peat and driftwood the spirits make their cases with complete conviction, but there is never a comprehensive agreement and even heated disagreement soon peters out in laughter and thanksgiving for the days they have enjoyed.

Some favour the idea of a barely imaginable, gigantic, ocean event pushing the Atlantic waters right over all the land, simply wiping them clean of everything that was living there, and leaving just the cold, hard, bare rock.

Others imagine a plague of pestilential proportions killing crops and livestock and decimating the human population, leaving the handful of survivors to starve to death. There is a history of plague across the archipelago and the proponents of the pestilence theory remember them well.

Then there is the invasion theory, based on the memories of past attacks, when outsiders came from the sea and pillaged the Far Isles, almost to the point of human extinction. Those who favour this ending usually imagine a new type of invader, not from this Earth at all. None of them ever entirely dismiss the notion of extraterrestrial intervention and some of the earliest stone carvings show strange craft and strange creatures, possibly from another world beyond the skies.

Some believed that the Far Isles would be one of the last places to survive if the rest of the world destroyed itself in warfare, or by polluting the human environment to the point of human extinction. This version of possibility imagines that the Far Isle survivors would form the basis for a new and better world populated by their children.

New spirits brought new ideas to the Main Seat, and a climber who died on the screes below the rock face during the great storm brought ideas which involved all the islands being slowly sucked into the Atlantic seabed by the same forces which created them from molten rock, in the first place. Everyone listened with rapt attention as the new man told his story; it was a completely new idea to them all, and they found it difficult to understand but wonderfully imaginative.

They decided that it was a fine story, worthy of repeating during a 'telling', and different versions quickly developed, but they still preferred the likelihood of other endings, even though subduction was the mighty force which was eventually to remove the islands from the face of the Earth forever.

Even around the Main Seat at Solas-Udal, the spirits of the Far Isles knew that they could only depend upon one certainty, just as everyone alive on Earth could. They all preferred it that way, confirming their belief by the very words carved into the stone of the seat itself over 6,000 years before: Nareath Anathnid: 'Uncertainty is the only certainty'.

Harry Stone

Harry does not give interviews but, if you asked him what he was, he would describe himself as an islander. He has no particular national affiliation but he could claim both Icelandic and Norwegian heritage. He has an engineering degree and served in the armed forces before working for a car manufacturer in Sweden and a racing team in Italy. He has houses on Harris and in the Lofoten Islands. He usually travels around the remote parts of the Far Isles and Scandinavia in a self-built Defender-based motorhome.

He began writing as a journalist, contributing firstly to car magazines and then to newspaper travel columns. More recently he has specialised in gaming. *Causeway* is his second foray into fiction, the first being *The Svalbard Excess*, a cult novel in the little-known Norwegian Future-Shock school of dystopian metafiction. *Excess* secured an income for him when it formed the basis for a highly successful series of science fiction computer games and he wisely took a percentage, rather than a fee, when he sold the rights to Harvard Graphics.

His work on *Causeway* began some years ago and this collection of short stories is the original version. A second, parallel work, *Causeway 2*, links all these stories together in a way which reflects his interest in both science fiction and dystopian literature.

The Causeway stories are fictional, but each is based on some aspect of real experience. Harry calls it quasi-truth: a real event leading to a work of imagination, and the enduring theme is the apparent capacity of the Far Isles to have a mystical, or perhaps magical influence upon relationships and events.

Harry is currently in Svolvaer writing *Eptitude*, and he will return to the Far Isles once the novel is finished.

CPSIA information can be obtained
at www.ICGtesting.com
Printed in the USA
LVHW090844131121
702935LV00001BA/79